TONI PARKS is the pseudonym of Tony Parkinson and this is my first attempt at writing, of any description, and at the ripe age of 61! I've had the idea going round in my head for some time but work commitments with running my own business and more recently helping with the upbringing of my grandson, Tyler, meant that it might have had to stay there, on the back burner indefinitely.

A move to the Scottish Borders after retirement enabled me to put my fingers where my mouth was and begin typing away. And this is the result. It certainly has shades of both light and dark and I'm hopeful that this contrast will make it an enjoyable read.

My background is in Advertising, although not in the creative field itself. However, having been surrounded by copywriters and creative designers I hope that I have learnt at least some of their craft by osmosis and so written a thriller, which could, dare I say it stand alongside the Scandinavian authors for whom I have the highest admiration.

I hope you enjoy reading it as much as I did when writing.

BLOOD IS THICKER

BY

TONI PARKS

PUBLISHED BY

DOUBLE
elephant
ASSOCIATES

Published by
Double Elephant Associates
Orchard Cottage, Lanton, Jedburgh
Roxburghshire TD8 6SX

Blood Is Thicker
First published 2013
Second Edition (Revised) 2016

ISBN 978 0 9926261 4 3

Love to Jean and Tyler

For allowing me to sneak off and write when I should
have been doing other things

Thanks to Sandra Robson

For inserting the idea in my head in the first place

Thanks to Peter Flannery

For his invaluable advice on self-publishing

Practical Thanks to:

Jean for her Word skills; my son, Thomas for his
formatting skills in getting the book to completion;
Sarah Thompson for MAC artwork of the cover;
Shutterstock for the cover photography

PROLOGUE

JUNE NINETEEN EIGHTY THREE

From the outside looking in, it could have been any middle class family parked up, admiring the view and perhaps enjoying a tasty picnic by the water. It could have been but then again, nothing was further from the truth. The now blazing car was a dead giveaway for a start. Surprisingly, it had still remained stationary, even allowing for the fact that the handbrake was in the 'off' position, the gear stick in neutral, and it was residing on a 1 in 6 decline.

The couple inside was no ordinary couple either. In fact, so extraordinary were they that Luigi and Laura Agosti had made a pact together, a pact, condemning them to the ultimate sacrifice of never, in this world anyway, seeing their two young children again. Children that they loved and cherished above all else; even death. Their histories, complementing talents and contacts in operating on the shadier side of business dealings had quickly moved them up through the ranks, bringing them to the attention of like-minded associates. Associates who recognised their unique, minority specialism of money laundering, and the considerable contribution that could make to future profits over, what would turn out to be, the next ten frantic years. However, like all tried and tested launderers it was never to become their personal money, but it did need cleaning and keeping safe, and they were very good at both. And for this expertise and creative housekeeping the Camorra clan in Naples were prepared to pay handsomely.

Two events disrupted this gifted financial marriage: first was the inevitable in-house friction between clan members as to how the ever increasing laundered monies should be reallocated, and second was that Laura, who presumed for some years that she was infertile, became pregnant. Now, human nature played its hand in both events and shifted the status quo and dynamics, in place for such a long period of time and that, to date, had worked amazingly well.

But the unfolding drama was always inevitable: the friction having increased even further, finally erupted into street violence, and tore the very heart out of the Camorra community; and Laura, on cue, gave birth to not just one but two babies. The twins' infancy began straight forwardly enough, and was soon running in tandem with the ever increasing disorder of their parents' employers. A problematic work schedule and changed domestic life circumstances created an insurmountable strain on the new parents. The outcome of which led Laura, in particular, to take her eye off the 'business' ball of the operation. As tension mounted and fearing the worst, she knew there was nothing more sacrosanct than preserving the safety and wellbeing of her children, especially that of their identities, which must now and always remain secret no matter what the price. Luigi concurred and agreed to the formulation of a desperate and drastic plan should the warfare escalate still further and visit UK shores.

So here we are back in the present with the need to carry out that preconceived, though finite, plan. As the net had closed in quickly, and scapegoats were being hunted, so pressure was applied more forcibly to their own reluctant hand. The journey south into England concluded with a link up of an accomplice on the North Wales coast, thus enabling the final piece of a grotesque jigsaw to be placed in position. A piece hard won, and now to crown the infamy of their drastic decision, as being irreversible.

Luigi had already doused with petrol the four wicker chocks under the wheels, strategically placed there in order to hold the vehicle in position and so prevent its forward motion down the slope. He now gingerly lit the tapers leading to those chocks, climbed back into the driver's seat, looked across at Laura and whispered, "Ready, my Love?"

Even though Laura had played this moment over and over in her mind innumerable times since the scheme had first been dreamt up, she sat impassively, only glancing once behind herself as the tears streamed freely down her face. The two, silent, young ones needed help and comfort no longer, as their ends had already occurred, and vengeance would no doubt be unleashed on the guilty for their deaths. However, Laura still momentarily grieved for their souls, as soon she would grieve for her own and that of her husband. She had prayed constantly for an alternative ending but it was not to be, this was now their fate.

She reached out, looked across at her husband, pleading for an end to the misery and yet frightened at the same time of the hereafter. Kissing Luigi passionately, she replied, "Ready, my Darling. Goodbye. God bless you and protect our sweet innocent children. Let us hope that history shows we chose the right path. Now be quick before I change my ..."

The recoil jolt and noise from the gun shocked Luigi, whereas Laura just slumped limply onto his chest. He held her close, and then gently laid her head back onto the car seat. The remaining petrol was liberally sprinkled around the interior, and as he clasped her right hand in his left he flicked the cheap cigarette lighter with the thumb of his other hand. Striking metal against flint created a small, bright, innocent looking spark, which instantly ignited the permeating fumes, and within moments the car was awash with flames. A searing fire began to lick across all surfaces in its hunger for combustible materials and the additional oxygen needed to continually refuel itself, leaving Luigi no time for composure. As a precaution he had already centrally locked all the doors to prevent any human, impulsive reaction, so thwarting his desperate search for continued life and safety, by making escape impossible. With only seconds left, before he felt the searing heat and was overcome by smoke, he looked first at his now departed wife sitting to his left, then glanced over his shoulder at the two small bodies sitting inert in their child seats, before raising the gun muzzle to his right temple. He closed his eyes, in order to both calm himself and steady his aim, and finally applied the necessary pressure to the trigger.

At the sound of this second gunshot, the until now inquisitive crows took immediate flight, not to return until the vehicle had careened downhill, only losing its momentum upon impact with the open water, and coming to rest as a partly submerged smouldering wreck. And only then, when the blackened acrid smoke-filled sky had lost its singed flesh stench and become once more azure blue in colour, did they venture back.

CHAPTER ONE

FEBRUARY TWO THOUSAND AND THIRTEEN

The bitingly cold north easterly, howling over the Cheviots was enough to chill the bones of any man. Though on this particular day it had no adverse affect on John Silwith whatsoever as he lay face down at the bottom of a forty-foot ravine, just off the A68 near Camptown. Even with his broken collarbone and punctured lung he still did not feel the chill, in fact, he did not feel anything at all. To all intents and purposes he may have been a walker out for a Sunday hike, although not an experienced walker, no definitely not that. No GPS, wrong apparel and shoes made more for dancing than hiking. And with his dark clothing aiding in the disguise of his location he was to lay in that same position for a further seven days with only the company of a crescent moon waxing and alternating with a weak insipid sun; both trying desperately to play their role of beacon in their endeavours to highlight his body, tucked away in concealment under the shadow of the ravine's sheer face. And then some unsuspecting jogger, walker or dog lover would happen by, and the body, previously only subjected to the soundscape of cawing and mocking from treetop crows, counterpointed with creaking boughs and branches, suddenly welcomed the new accompaniment of pristine police tape, placed strategically in its job of cordoning off and guarding the murder scene by constantly rustling, snapping and crackling as the fierce wind whipped it round and round endlessly.

He reached into his pocket and pulled out a damp packet of Embassy king size, and finding an almost straight one he flipped it into his mouth filter side out and started sucking. 'Don't know why I buy king size any more or any bloody size for that matter when all I do is suck on them like a dummy. Who me, or the cigarette?' he questioned of himself. 'I'm the dummy for still buying them,' his mind continued berating until he heard himself shout aloud, "Come on ladies get a move on. This might be your only chance to play at Forensics and we're going to lose the light soon, if we don't freeze our bollocks off first!" The two female colleagues looked up in surprise, not specifically at the Anglo Saxon terminology but more at the sound of the voice, breaking through their otherwise soundless concentration as they slipped on frozen mud and snagged on branches. They glanced at each other, lifted their eyebrows in a knowing manner and silently mouthed 'DI Barnham', both cognisant of the fact that his derogatory remark was targeted more so at his male colleagues.

"Sorry, 'real' ladies I'd not noticed you hiding there in the bushes but jump to it all the same, it must be down to minus five already!"

Detective Inspector Terry Barnham, a roving DI of sorts, specifically chosen to front the new police cross-border initiative. More so due to his present case in Newcastle having stalled, and with the intimidation and heated threats which followed in quick succession on both sides, the timing was right for Barnham to get out of the kitchen.

The DI had bullied the daughter of Tyneside's local gangland boss to such a degree that a contract had been placed on him, inferring a change of scenery as being the only option available in order to preserve his health. Snouts were told to spread the word that he had been posted south to Birmingham to oversee black country misdemeanours, when in fact north was his destination. Here, special dispensation allowed his

CID experience to tap into and utilise existing local police resources without the necessity and expense of a full detective structure. His remit was flexible and stretched as far north as Edinburgh, east to the coast and ran within a 30 miles corridor west of the A1. And so with the authority to operate on this side of the border, he was hoping to become as renowned for his crime busting here as in his more familiar North East. But the higher echelons were not of like mind. They saw this transfer as the final 'op': opportunity to reaffirm their faith when more recently it had been proven misplaced. There was no shadow of doubt his reputation preceded him. And at 49, with only three years left of front line service he was not prepared to change, no matter what politically correct directives were rained down from on high. So should this happen to be his swan song, at least he would sing it loud and proud. The years of practical experience for diehards such as Barnham were now being challenged and superseded by the more studious and ambitious law enforcers, those who were progressing quickly via the theoretical route. More comfortable with the power of a PhD, than a Glock or a SIG Sauer.

On a personal health level, he had a propensity to simulate smoking due to doctor's orders threatening him with death and more death if he continued in his present lifestyle. He did not quite have the same restraint when it came to his drinking but at least his daily consumption was now into single figures as far as pints of lager went, and his GP was none the wiser as to his spirits intake. Then there were the women; they proved to be another of the vices, which compounded his inability to devote adequate concentration to the pressing professional tasks around him and contributed considerably to the decline of his career. All in all, a toxic mix ushering him ever closer towards the exit door.

"Sorry George, but looks like tonight's off as far as I'm concerned. It's another night at the office or should I say, more like a night stuck down a gully with not much more than a dead man for company," concluded the pathologist. Jamie Scott had already travelled the 50 or so miles from Edinburgh and he was still no nearer to getting the body moved to his Pathology lab. He was looking rather glum as he pressed the red button on his mobile having just passed on the bad news; another cancelled poker night, yet again due to pressure of work.

Barnham moved in closer now that he had finished his call and said in a somewhat lower volume than he had previously been using, "We're just about done here and then he's all yours. Got any preliminary observations?"

"Well, he's dead! Been that way for about a week to ten days at a guess but with the weather being so cold I can't give you anything more accurate until he's back at the lab. Definitely a punctured lung and shattered collar bone from the fall, or more likely a push, but there's a good chance he was still alive even after all that, and with his hands bound behind his back and his feet trussed up like a chicken it's nailed on it wasn't an accident. Although looking at how he's dressed I have to admit that you won't see many Fred Astaire dancer types walking these fells. Can't believe there's a 'Strictly' venue anywhere near here, can you? Anyway, just make sure your 'wannabe' forensic experts don't trample over any valuable evidence," Jamie replied tongue in cheek. His sanguine view being that if he was going through the night he might as well make it entertaining and he knew that the banter with Barnham would be of a consistently high quality.

"Yes, very inconsiderate of the dog walker to spot the body on a Sunday but it's the jobs we've all chosen to do. By the way, you can now arrange for the body to be moved and I will ensure that my muppets have all clues photographed and tagged, then we can get out of this damned weather." T/DC Claire Murray, one of the other 'team Geordie' members, heard Barnham say in reply as he tried to pull up his collar even higher to keep out the arctic chill, whilst at the same time giving him the thumbs up that her evidence gathering was at an end.

Claire was in the early stages of training to become a detective constable as the letter 'T' in her rank denoted. Her aspiration led her to believe that by closely following the DI's career path she too would benefit from his experience and wisdom and so progress sooner and higher. In her recent past life as a WPC she was under no illusions that her 13stones 7lbs bulk had been of great benefit on a Saturday night after the pubs had closed but now with moving into more of a detective role it may prove more of a hindrance. No more so than when she was trying gamely to scramble up the side of the steep gully whilst the sun strove competitively to drop behind the horizon before she reached the top. She surmised that at least a stone in weight would have to go to give her 5ft 9in frame a more streamlined look and to give her personally any chance of catching DI Barnham's eye for anything other than professional reasons. And to add further insult to injury, if that was needed, she snorted at herself as she thought that he would probably need to be wearing his 'beer goggles' at the time too.

Amazingly, once the decision had been reached and the order given, the five officers on the case were sitting snugly in their squad cars and wrapping their hands around warm mugs of tea, and all within the space of ten minutes. The dead man took somewhat longer to retrieve as he needed to be manoeuvred into a body bag and then man-handled up to the top of the ridge; but he was not complaining in the slightest or even bothered anymore, neither about warmth and shelter nor about a hot drink.

8.30 the following morning saw the team congregated in the made-shift incident room at Jedburgh police station. A tight squeeze by anybody's standards but at least it had all the necessary facilities. The DI was the last to arrive and witnessed the break-up of bodies huddled over the Calor Gas heater, which surprisingly enough was adequate heating with the room being of snug size to say the least. He had already detoured through the kitchen and so strode into the room with his cliché coffee firmly in his grasp.

"Morning. Let's get down to it". He stood behind the evidence desk and looked quizzically at his audience. "Right those with a chair next to them sit down and those without have 30 seconds to find one or they're out of the game." 'Why does everyone need to be treated like a child,' he pondered? "Quickly now, it isn't bloody musical chairs."

Movement stopped and hush returned to the room. Barnham took a sip of his coffee and started speaking again. "Right, I presume you're all known to each other? So let's progress, what have we got so far? WPC Sandra Whitely, I've got the name correct, haven't I?" A nod from the WPC was sufficient to allow him to continue. "I want you to take whatever hard copy material we have and tack it to the glass screen or place it on this table. Anything verbal or digital can be written or displayed on this whiteboard behind me. Away we go, who's first?"

WPC Whitely set her own ball rolling by stating, "The witness, Jason Turner, who spotted the body, made a 999 call at 11.05am on Sunday 17th February. An ambulance crew was then despatched from Borders General, near Melrose and on arrival assessed that this was no accident and so informed the police at 12.17pm. Local officers were at the scene around 1.00pm, by which time they had been requested to await your arrival," she looked at the DI to make sure he understood. "As the witness was still at the scene and was shivering a little from either shock or cold by this time, I noted down his address and phone details, ascertained that he was purely an innocent bystander walking his dog and then made the decision to send him on his way."

"Right, who's next?" asked DI Barnham, allowing the WPC time to transfer the relevant information to the white board.

"PC Paul Tranter, Sir." PC Tranter was one of the other

two Geordies on the DI's inquiry team. Very much in the vein of Newcastle United, wherever the team went the supporters followed, and DI Barnham's disciples replicated that same unswerving allegiance. "The body I'd surmise is late twenties; about 5ft 10ins; 160 pounds. Sandy coloured neat-cropped hair, clean-shaven. Didn't see the colour of his eyes. Wearing a smart suit, that probably cost over £200, plus shirt and tie and smart black shoes. No ID on him and no missing person's alert either, at this moment."

"Never mind about the eye colour for now but make a note to give Jamie Scott or one of his colleagues a ring at the lab in Edinburgh once we're through. The eye colour should help with the ID process. Who's next? What else was the deceased carrying on his person?"

"Sorry sir, I've got that sewn up as well. He had £43.70 in cash, a bus ticket, a rail ticket from Dundee to Edinburgh that's approximately two weeks old and a hankie with what looks like a smudge of lipstick on it. Unfortunately, there's no wallet, no mobile and no driving licence or such like. It's almost as if he didn't want to be identified."

"It's more like, someone else didn't want him to be identified, or not yet anyway. We can assume he wasn't mugged or the money would have gone too. So we can deduce that the killer doesn't want his identity known yet, but is not a thief. If no one has anything else to offer I'd say we've all had an early start unnecessarily but now we're here let us follow up on what leads we do know," Barnham said in conclusion. "I'll be in the office so let me have any new information straight away."

Those who knew DI Barnham also knew that his office would be the canteen, those who did not soon found out. It was Barnham's mobile echoing around the pots and pans which brought up the next clue even before PC Tranter had chance to make a phone call of his own. "Hi Barmy, it's Jamie here. Haven't got you out of bed, have I? Thought you might want to know of any positive progress since our guesswork at the scene. Seeing as I missed my poker night, I got in at six to ascertain what we'd got. Sorry to say, it's not a lot. 6ft dead 'pardon the pun'; 170 lbs; smart short-cropped sandy coloured hair, most likely dyed as it's a bit darker at the roots; face wise he had blue eyes, quite pale blue actually; dominant eyebrows, slightly darker than hair; straight nose; strong, clean-shaven chin and I'd guess he was late twenties. Only one unusual thing. I took a punt on a toxicology test and as well as alcohol he tested positive for benzodiazepines. It could have been a very small dose but then again it may have been working its way through his system for several days before he died. There's also something else there but we can't quite isolate it yet. I'll have to come back later with that answer. I'm only telling you this, as there were no telltale needle tracks, neither on his arms nor between his toes etcetera. So if it was his first foray into drugs it looks like he picked the wrong one to start off with. I'm still working on an actual date of death too. A few more tests should firm up that one and I'll do the usual dental practice sweep to see if we can get any luck with his ID that way. Generally do a 20 miles radius of where the body was found if that's OK with you?"

"Jamie, you're ahead of me on all fronts. Had any success with the adhesive tape that bound him? Fingerprints or DNA would be good?"

"No such luck. Passed that onto Forensics but it looks a professional clean-up job. They've confirmed no traces of either. They're going to try and identify the manufacturer of the tape but personally I think it's a long shot."

"Well, keep me posted on any further progress. Bye for now." Barnham then called WPC Whitely on the internal and relayed over the revised information. "Make sure Tranter knows about the eyes. That will be useful when looking through missing persons."

CHAPTER TWO

'5ft 11ins in imperial so what's that in metric? Come on brain; convert the feet to inches and multiply by 25.4, that equals 1803mm. Heavy muscular build with a full head of pepper grey hair, blue eyes, strong chin line complete with designer stubble and a generous mouth. Semi smartly dressed; in a sombre grey suit, slightly crumpled, with white shirt and conservative stripy tie and black brogues. Oh dear, I must stop looking at my colleagues as if they are all possible suspects or victims in some murder inquiry,' she chided herself, knowing that in reality it was only one colleague in particular who underwent this fantasy. 'I'm sure if I search thoroughly enough I'll be able to dig up his fingerprints too. Help. This can't be how other girls imagine their prospective dates!'

Unlike T/DC Murray's daydream, Jessica Lambert had neither a problem with catching the eye of the likes of Terry Barnham, nor any other passing admirers for that matter, or her own weight as that was seriously in check too. Her eight stones fit snugly into her 5ft 3in frame still leaving room for a little cushioning in the right places. And with her present exercising regime she felt that she had actually lost weight with now fitting easily into a size 8, but then again she surmised that it was more likely the clothing manufacturers making garments slightly larger as opposed to her getting thinner. And anyway, it was who she was rather than how she looked that she had issues with.

Her selective childhood memories only allowed her a recollection of being brought up by her Grannie as sole carer. At a young age she had heard the story regaled several times of her parents' terrible accident but over time and even with the retelling it had somehow eventually blurred and faded in her otherwise fertile memory. Perhaps it was nature's way of saying that she should move on and live her own life without trying to delve too deeply, and so prevent the reopening of old wounds. In her childhood she had a vague recall of playing with a girl of a similar age, or so she thought, reminisces of them both being of comparable size. But even that memory had been banished to the extremities of her mind once she had been living for several years in her Grannie's house at Seahouses.

She could still look back with a fond reflection of her life by the sea on the north east coast. Seahouses, not quite of the same class as the more dramatic and romantic near neighbour, Bamburgh; with its prominent red stone castle dominating the skyline and rugged, undulating, tussock sand dunes leading seemingly endlessly down towards the sea. But at least here, the pace of life was more sedate with whitewashed bungalows, both smaller in scale and easier on the eye, queuing up and expectantly waiting for each day's sunrise over the dramatic North Sea. In her younger days the town had taken on huge proportions but on each of her returns from the University of Edinburgh she contemplated how much smaller it was becoming, bit-by-bit as the wider world opened up to turn her childhood imagination into reality. She embraced this recognition and, never being scared of change, it triggered her now formulated plans into action. Her progress through school and her continued interest in the sixth form had drawn her into psychology and the scientific study of the human mind, and five years later she had been rewarded with a first class degree. This was quickly followed by her one and only job to date, working for The Borders Agency on Buccleuch Street in Dalkeith as a counsellor of both men and women, although mainly women, who have suffered violence in the form of physical and/or sexual abuse. Generally servicing the city of Edinburgh, although at times seconded to Glasgow, Jessica had a good understanding of the corridor between both cities and an even better understanding of the predominant underclass of clients who lived within.

Her reminiscing brought her back to the present with a start as when ruthlessly deciding what to keep or throw she came across a shoebox containing documents, photos and her own copious books of crosswords, the more cryptic the better. Her two weeks holiday entitlement was being utilised in revisiting her Grannie's house but tragically not to see her Grandma, who had passed away peacefully three months previously. Grannie had counted herself fortunate that both her mental faculties and physical mobility had stayed true through her 84 years, and being a firm believer in God she had known he would take her when the time was right, and so he had. Flicking through the newly discovered shoebox Jessica transported herself back in time. To the fuzzy memory of her parents, whom she only vaguely remembered, smiling gaily out of several photos, to plenty of other snaps of her grandparents holding her as a small child too. She even found her own little album, showing her as a tiny tot pirouetting on her toes, digging and making sandcastles on a beach, and to her surprise still attached to the rings on the spine was that cherished key ring. The key ring she always kissed because it said 'love from Papa', and that always held securely and secretly one mysterious solitary key. She even came across her Grannie's birth certificate showing her maiden name as Lambert and fuelling Jessica's inquisitiveness as to why she too had that name. Her family life somewhat streamlined and her family tree no less stunted.

Of course, she had known more of her Grandad's life and death than her parents' own, it having occurred when she was still a young age but not too young for her memory to be non receptive. He had died, crushed beneath a tractor; a tractor, which overturned on an incline that he had negotiated successfully many times before. It was reported, at the time, that he may have lay there trapped for up to five hours. Soon after the tragedy and subsequent funeral her Grannie had said, "There's only you and me now Jessica, so we'll have to look after each other". But that was not to be the case as George arrived on the scene and soon became part of both their lives. At first he had been everything Grannie and Jessica dreamed he would be; but that was at first. It did not take too long before Jessica, on being tucked up for the night and thought to be sleeping, would hear her Grannie sobbing, so making her own heart ache too. Then there was a short period of time when she could not remember George at all, as if her memory had totally blocked him out. And then there he was again, the day Grannie told her that there had been a terrible accident. George's boat had capsized and he had died out at sea fishing off the Farne Islands. But to Jessica's delight instead of it making Grannie more sad and despondent it had the exact opposite effect and she seemed to blossom in her twilight years, regaining both her health and joie de vivre with only her allergies to concern her. They were happy times until God finally got in the way.

And now picking over the other photos she came across a well thumbed one with her little friend whom she vaguely recollected, and turning it over she read to herself, 'J and M catching crabs in the rock pools', written neatly in Grannie's curly writing. It had been dated too, and although that was now smudged and illegible Jessica thought they both must have looked about three or four years old. And just like a vast number of children's photos and memorabilia they vanished from time to time only to resurface at the most unexpected moments. But in Jessica's case there had been no facts given even based on the evidence found, and when she had tackled Grannie about the girl in the photograph the conversation always ended up becoming evasive and confused. Her Grannie's memory of who she was referring to or where that photo had come from and where it had gone was non existent, but Jessica knew now that at least one secret had passed away with her death.

She nonchalantly put the shoebox in the pile 'to keep' and continued sifting through the remaining personal items carefully rebuilting her Grannie's life and her own part within it. She was aggrieved that 84 years of life could boil down to such a meager amount; a few boxes with treasured possessions, sticks of old worn-out furniture and a couple of building society savings passbooks. She was not meaning it in any derogatory manner but she felt strongly that everyone had their own opportunity to leave a mark on this earth, to say this is me I was here, and so few do. But glancing around at the few spartan chattels she was still grateful to her Grannie, as without her where would she herself be; 'but now I'm getting maudlin,' she thought. 'It must be time to ring the estate agents and put the house on the market.' And so, two days later she handed over the keys to a very confident young sales executive with the world at her feet and optimism in her head with regards to a quick sale.

Jessica drove away from her childhood with, "Yes, they usually sell pretty quickly, what with their commanding positions, quirky gardens full of pebbles and hardy plants and a realistic price tag. I don't think you'll have much trouble attracting second home buyers either," endlessly replaying in her head. And now she was more determined than ever that with her aspirations set high she would leave more of a legacy than just a few battered boxes when her time came.

Tess Danvers, Jessica's case line manager left her under no illusion as to how long her job induction would be, not long at all was the answer. "You breezed through the application form and HR interview with flying colours. And you've got the qualifications to back it up, and obviously with knowing all the theory you must have a good idea as to why most people do what they do. But two things are sacred in this job," she said, taking a deep breath before continuing, "One, where children are involved that part of the case must be immediately referred to Social Services and two, never ever get personally involved or attached to any client". Jessica thought it was just common sense but it had to be said, and that was the limit of the pep talk with all the practicalities being gleaned on the job through experience.

'Well that's a first,' thought Jessica as she slowed down and just about managed to pull her phone out of her jogging bottoms before it rang off. "Hello, hello can you hear me? I'm in Lanton Woods at present," she continued, "and I didn't think there would be a signal in here, and it appears as if I might be right?" she concluded more to herself than the lost caller.

She gave a shrug of the shoulders, held her mobile tightly and set off to complete the last 7 minutes of the 45 minutes of her fartlek; a session consisting of alternate fast running with jog recoveries, one she had promised herself the day before. Continuing the exercise, she bemoaned the fact that she had brought her mobile in the first place as her mind drifted more towards questioning who had rung rather than concentrating on the effort she should have been putting into her running. And though she usually found these workouts an exhausting challenge she could still really enjoy them once in the swing. It was as if she lost herself in the magic of the narrow track, cocooned as it was with the svelte like silver birch waving their leafless arms, whilst the much taller Scots pine neighbours, interspersed with Douglas firs on either side, appeared to be cheering silently in acknowledgment of her labours. And even a total drenching from the sudden outburst was prevented, thanks in the main to the overhead canopy's protective shelter. Instead, it just allowed an occasional, invigorating and refreshing, cascade of droplets to filter their way down through limbs and branches.

This part of Jessica's routine also allowed her a chance to think. What often began as a daydream would soon be superseded with tasks, problems and even errands, as they leapt into her mind, and were compartmentalised into their correct pigeonholes. But today she struggled with even that and eventually 'threw in the towel' without completing the full session. Irritability forced her again to look at her mobile and register that it had been 'work' calling, and even more annoyingly that they had not left a message by way of consolation.

She did not need too long to satisfy her pique as, on arriving home, there were two messages blinking in the 'in box' of her Apple Book. She soon knew the culprit who had so rudely disturbed her concentration. None other than Joe Foster, the mature student who had started working at the same time as her but having joined without the psychology background, it was he who had left an email requesting that she contact him at the office asap. Jessica took a quick refreshing shower and pulled on her sloppy clothes, the ones she usually slouched about in, the ones, which acted as much as a comfort blanket but 'all over' instead of just being to hug. She fussed about preparing her lunch and then took that plus her coffee into the study, spare bedroom actually, and rang the office. As she waited for reception to trace Joe her mind wandered. Mid thirties with two failed marriages to his name was not a good indicator for Joe's staying power in making relationships work. But Jessica knew that part of his failing could be put down to the nature of his job and so her job too. This lack of emotional commitment tended to be an indicator that they were likely to be more wedded to their careers rather than any chosen spouse or partner. However, Joe's track record and busy work schedule had never stood in his way, the cup was always half full at least and could get even fuller quite quickly if the other party was willing to take a drink from it. Jessica certainly was not willing. He had hinted often enough but not pushed it any further as he already had his own list of 'possibles' to work through before returning to the desperate section, the one containing the most difficult challenges. She, in turn, had recently been through a couple of short but messy courtships and had just extricated herself from the latest one with mind intact if not body. So, the barn door was well and truly closed on that one as at present she had more pressing matters on her mind other than sex.

Not that S-E-X was not a recurring itch that needed scratching and attending to, in fact since taking up running seriously three years earlier she had noticed that her libido had risen considerably. And being a modern kind of a woman, rather than prudish and standoffish, she fervently held the view that women could have as equally a strong sex drive as men and should be able to enjoy casual sex as long as both parties were willing and the act was fulfilling. However, it did not have to mean love and to that extent she was a firm advocate of Tina Turner's song 'What's love got to do with it?' That being said, she still wanted to think her relationships would be meaningful and could lead in a positive direction, even if the majority to date had fizzled out eventually and so proved otherwise. Her brown eyes, full mouth and pale olive skin, complemented by her medium length dark hair gave her a Mediterranean sultry look, which in the past had proved to be her strongest asset and very pleasing to the male eye.

"Jessica, Jessica. Are you there? Calling Jessica?"

"Hi Joe, you've finally been tracked down! And here's me thinking that I must be in bed dreaming, with waiting so long. What did you want me for?"

"Ooh, is that an offer? Tess has had a report of a disturbance from the police on your File S42 and needs you to visit the couple, like now."

"Is it an aggressive disturbance? Are we talking, physical violence? Will I need support? And no, it isn't an offer. You've already used up your share of the female sex as far as wives go."

"No, she didn't mention assistance, so I'm presuming the aggro can't have been too violent, maybe just a 'pots and pans' type of thing. And I wasn't thinking of proposing, not straight away!"

"Right, I'll get on to it now, and stop flirting with me. It can be classed as sexual harassment, but you probably get your kicks out of that too." Ringing off with a bright cheerio Jessica began to get the relevant files together and changed into sensible clothing so as not to send out the wrong signals, and which might prove useful in case of a speedy exit. Part of the reason for keeping herself in trim was to enable her to handle all eventualities when turning up for meetings with 'clients'; the department's word not hers. Initially, she had very carefully chosen three sports to ensure that she could take care of herself and at the same time add kudos to her CV, but now they did actually complement her lifestyle too. She particularly got a buzz from the knowledge that her heart rate at rest had reduced to the high fifties beats per minute. Her regular activities included taekwondo, as it was the only martial arts class being held in her village hall, and she was conscious of being able to look after herself physically; a general gym session to improve her upper body strength and give her a six pack that she had been envious of seeing other girls sport, even pop stars; and her running, which she felt improved her stamina, gave her general fitness and kept her body in trim and well-toned. Combined together this regime furnished her with the confidence to take on most challenges that life and her job threw at her but she was circumspect in only sharing her sporting experiences with others of like mind, those who took up the same exercise courses or used the same gym equipment. On one occasion, a work colleague had accosted her by the coffee machine at the edge of the open plan area and asked about the benefits of her jogging to which she had replied rather haughtily, "I don't do jogging. With clocking out miles consistently in less than seven minutes each I class myself as a runner, not a jogger. Perhaps I jog my memory now and again but never my body." Her colleague made an apologetic grimace as if to say 'sorry for thinking that you were human and for entering into a conversation,' before moving off as quickly as she could, possibly even faster than at seven minutes mile pace.

CHAPTER THREE

Now here's a question every wrong-minded young man should ask himself at least once in his life.

What is the definitive age at which to become a murderer?

Vinny Varnish had asked himself that very same question on innumerable occasions and on each and every one his answer had always been different. He had even approached his father for advice but been swatted away with an 'If you need to ask lad, you're not old enough.' Having heard the wise man's words and still been none the wiser for hearing them he made a list of his own most probable answers, and here they are, in no particular order. But first, can you remember the question?

What is the definitive age at which to become a murderer?

One, whilst you are in your teens, as then it will give you a definite career path to follow, there can be no turning back and you will not appear a cissy. And it may become another of those tick list things achieved before you leave your teenage years, just like the losing your virginity stigma.

Two, when you are 21, the original recognised landmark of reaching manhood. Get the feel of what damage a gun or other weapon of choice can do at the same time as the key to the door.

Three, when in a rage and without giving it a second thought. Then the cops will have no motive, and so have no idea where to start looking.

Four, when someone is particularly annoying, loathsome

or disrespectful to your close family and friends.

Five, no particular time at all, a good old random shoot out just for the hell of it.

Vinny's answer of choice always changed to suit the circumstances just like the weather but in his case there were no sunny spells on the horizon anytime soon. Certain milestones on his wish list had already fallen by the wayside so he was now desperate to break his duck and win a trophy or two in the 'dying stakes', not least to show his Pops that he had 'bigged' up and could tool up, and so become man enough to hold his corner. Any concerned father knowing of these dark thoughts would take their son to one side and offer stern advice on the benefits of a chosen career path. Vinny's father was no different, excepting in his geographical approach to the problem; as rather than being sent northwards his son was directed southwards instead. Vinny himself was proud of this change of direction, not necessarily the geographical one mind, but at last he had a good feeling that his otherwise latent talents were now being appreciated for their true value. And whatever he achieved in the future would be achieved by him alone and with no outside help. This in itself was a cap feather of which he could be proud; a point proved that his constant badgering had finally paid off. Pop Varney, never to be called that to his face, acknowledged that his son's uncontrollable twitchy finger was an accident waiting to happen and decided the time was right to unleash his Vinny on the outside world. He argued that it was the playing of too many bloodthirsty computer games and the reading of too many graphic violence comic books as opposed to his son's immediate surroundings but Vinny knew otherwise, he just gave a silent nod to his genes; it was in his blood. But at the same time he also had a hankering to be the producer of that computer game or illustrator or writer of that graphic comic. And in the back of his mind he contemplated the benefit of documenting his real life experiences as putting him in good stead for any of the options should he prove a failure on the killing front.

Now sitting here, chewing his bubblegum and blowing occasional bubbles, he wanted to let the world know that it better watch out, well to let the inside of his Fiat know anyway.

This is me, Vinny, sat in my Fiat, a Fiat Punto. That's the value Pops thinks I'm worth and the level he thinks I can operate from. It's hardly the wheels of a professional now, is it? Why not at least a Subaru or Hummer or even a Beamer? I mean how is one expected to fit all the necessary hardware into a car this size? But I'll do it, I'll show him; I'll show them all. They've sent me off a boy and I'll go back home a man. The assumption is that I'll fail, and even if I do, no doubt they'll just pat me on the head, put me back in my box, and give me back my toys. But to me failure's not an option, no Sir! The deed will be done and if I take in a little practice on the way, well who is to stop me? I know Pops said to keep out of trouble, well not said, actually ordered, but surely it'll make him proud if I light up the media a little whilst I'm here.

His pep thoughts over, Vinny turned over the engine, pressed 'play' and drove off to the sound of *Born to be Wild* from his 'best music to drive to' CD compilation. Yes, his father's present disappointment would soon be replaced by pride at the realisation that his youngest son did after all possess that vital killing instinct so redolent of the family's infamous history. But no matter how grown up Vinny felt he still was not man enough to chew regular gum.

CHAPTER FOUR

Living on the Edinburgh Sighthill sink estate, just off the A71, did not exactly endow anyone with advantages that could be traded in their future lives, although a price could not be placed on the experience gained either. But to escape was always going to be a difficult ask and would pose as much a leap of faith as a leap of endurance. Sighthill, originally boasting high rise flats, with Emma Flynn's particular choice of necessity being Weir Court, was complemented by its own concrete monstrosity masquerading as a shopping centre. This edifice took on the mantel of being the breeding ground for would-be shoplifters and petty thieves, all out to make a living at someone else's expense. The whole area showcased an array of burned out cars parked up at odd angles, with their own fate of destruction being realised to protect the guilty and the evidence. Tyreless abandoned trophies and souvenirs of motor efficiency devoted to assisting and aiding carjackers, in the servicing of their self-contained and insular world of places to go and things to do.

Emma Flynn had spent 25 of her 33 years being part of this world. Work was an anathema to both her and her peers, and she knew from experience it could not be found anyway as the long gone winding queues to the docks had proved. EU money, pumped into the area to compensate for the loss of world trade, was never going to reach the underbelly that inhabited the peripheral housing estates well away from public view. The labour force came and went, leaving behind more than just a blip in socio-economic history, whilst at the same time adding significantly to the birth rate. And jobs for life turned out to be no more than a pipedream on which workers' children could be deceived. Emma never had the chance to revel in the nostalgia of following in her father's footsteps, especially as she had no idea who he was and even less idea as to where those footsteps had led. He was not dissimilar to passing ships on the Forth only his time came to an end that much sooner. However, Emma did follow in her aunt's footsteps instead and although they proved to be good grounding in the education of life, by offering a steady 'black economy' income, they also confirmed the fact, in her eyes anyway, that the term 'sink estate' had been coined to mean exactly that, 'sink'. Everyone there lived on their wit, intuition, guile and stealth, earning enough to get by from whatever underhand methods were available to them and all tax-free.

But Emma did have one regret in her life and it visited her every day, as soon as her brain logged on at whatever hour, day or night. That regret was of her never being able to revert back to that 11-year-old girl with those 11-year-old innocent thoughts and, more importantly, dreams. Not that they were always so innocent but at least they were hers and not bent and twisted by chemicals and alcohol. Similar to the other unfortunates making up the unspecified percentage of the Edinburgh population, Emma had not taken long to become hooked on heroin, and more than a little partial to alcohol too. As she put on years, the euphoria and 'grown up' effect wore off leaving her with the constant ever present drag of being totally dependent on heroin to this present day. Now at 33 years of age she had a handle on how to cope with her addiction but her dizzying life to date had been a merry go round of Social Services, foster parents, care homes, dead end jobs, pimps and drug dealers. Thanks to her aunt's chosen career path and teaching, Emma had spent as much time working horizontally as she had vertically, if only she could remember which came first. And if she had not been a quick learner at primary school, picking up the rudimentary of the three R's, she would have been illiterate too. But perhaps now things were maybe looking more optimistic as Emma had been given a vital punch to the stomach, by way of a brush with death leading to a severe wake-up call, and boy had she finally woken up.

Even with her level of literacy she knew that the difference between fate and fatal could be infinitesimal, but still she had pushed her daily limit. And that was even taking into consideration the fact that the word on the street was of a new batch being *the motherfucker of all batches*. Found unconscious from an overdose, she had been rushed to hospital where she could have died from the heroin excess or, if not that, then at least hypothermia, but she did not die from either so hence her new-found optimism. Only by chance, a police call-out had reached her in time thus giving her the last 45 minutes of her life to fight for more. The heroin was already coursing through her veins and making its final journey to her heart whilst the cold night penetrated every bone and fibre of her body, slowly offering its false embrace of comfort and warmth. Even in the emergency room it was still touch and go as to whether she could be brought out of the coma and if yes would it be as a vegetable?

A fiery character at the best of times Emma now fought to regain control of her mind. Flashbacks appeared subliminally paving the way to her past and ending with her visiting a green field blanketed in spring flowers, a bough from a tree creaking in the breeze and the constant buzzing of bees flitting about their daily work. Not the usual fairytale images of a Sighthill resident, no matter what the trip! Now a voice too seemed to be calling out to arouse her from her slumber, and a hand was giving her arm a gentle shake to stimulate and speed up the process.

"Can you hear me? You need to open your eyes now."

Emma's brain slowly responded, forcing her body to

achieve consciousness with finally her eyes opening. Confusingly, she said, "Bloody hell it's Florence Nightingale. What are you doing in my dream?" Amusing enough, but delivered in a very reedy, croaky sounding voice.

The nurse, who had no resemblance to Florence Nightingale whatsoever, raised a smile and a sigh of relief as her patient had finally awoken and seemed to be of sound mind, even if it was at her own expense. She checked that the saline drip was still functioning correctly, helped Emma to take a sip of water and then went off in search of the doctor. He arrived at Emma's bedside with another character wearing a crumpled suit, which looked like it had seen far worse times than even Emma's own skimpy clothes, which remained draped over, yet no way covering, the back of a chair.

"Glad to see you've returned to us. We were somewhat worried as to when and possibly whether you'd wake up, as with most OD's there's never any firm guarantee of timescale or of the mental state either. But as you're back with us now and only if you're feeling up to it this gentleman here needs to ask you some questions?" said the warm, soothing, bedside-manner voice that only doctors can perfect.

"Well, my mind's a bit fuzzy but I'll give it a go."

"Hello. Can we start with names? I'm DI Barnham and I'm investigating a murder in this area. I need your name and address details and an idea of what you've been doing over the last 48 hours."

Emma's facial expression erred on the quizzical as if doing a double take on the word *murder*. But she still managed to give her name, and her present address as 'Emma Flynn, Flat 61, The Towers, Burnwood, Edinburgh', even though she then stared gormlessly ahead with her mouth open.

"OK. And what are you able to remember of the last 48 hours?"

"That might be more difficult?" She paused and then continued, "Is this about BJ?" she asked, thinking that this might be all part of the surreal dream.

"BJ? Who's BJ?" questioned the DI.

"I'm not joking, my head is all fuzzy. It's like I've been eating cotton wool and it's still stuck up there. Just give me a second to recollect my thoughts, and then I'll try and start from the beginning. 48 hours you say. Well, is it Friday today?" A nod in reply prompted the following. "OK, on Wednesday morning, I got up as usual about 11.30. Don't look so shocked, I don't get to bed 'til late. Like I say, I got up about 11.30, flicked on both the TV and emersion heater and made a strong coffee. I showered, got dressed and then tarted myself up. All that must have taken me to say one o' clock, and then I went to the post office for my dole money. I know, I know it's not called that anymore, it's job seekers allowance now, but really where are you going to go seeking a job around here? Anyway, got that and like I do every Wednesday I went to The Feathers for a few drinks and some food. Just before I moved on from there my mate Melanie showed up flashing a bunch of fivers. I thought 'good girl looks like you've done with flashing your knickers for the day'. Due desserts to her, she's always generous when flush and bought in another round, and I'm not going to miss out on a free drink, would you? Should have called her 'millionaire Mel', what with her constant wheeling and dealing she's never really short of the readies"

Here Emma went quiet for a moment as she reflected on the time Melanie had been out of cash and starving into the bargain, and had offered the guy at the food-bank sex in return for something to eat. Melanie had reminisced on it later, justifying the gratuitous sex by concluding, 'Well I know which side my bread's buttered on, don't I'. That always brought a smile to her face.

After an indeterminable pause, which Barnham thought would never end, Emma chortled to herself, and then continued, "Yes, as I was saying that just about wrote off the rest of Wednesday. A few other mates came in, so by teatime we were all merry, to say the least. Then we moved on to buy some gear and by the end of the night I'd spent all my money bar £30 I'd just earned that night, but you don't need to know how I came by that, do you?"

"No, you're right, I'm not an accountant. Did you go back to Flat 61, was it?"

"No, don't think so. I was heading off that way but Melanie persuaded me to go back to hers for a nightcap. Well, it's never the normal sort of nightcap at Mel's. She'd got some extra stuff there and was feeling generous enough to share. And just like the booze, I'm was never going to refuse a free high so I went along even though I knew she would be after something else too. And sure enough we started with some hash which always makes her, how can I put it, amorous. She wanted her pound of flesh before the main course and as there weren't any blokes about, I knew I was on the menu. Not a huge shock really as it had happened before and I was quite attracted to her as it goes. Anyway we fooled about for a time and then even Melanie was getting irritated, so we prepped the heroin and shot up. She went first and I followed. I don't remember much else then until, well it must have been around 7.00am. I think it was around then as it was getting light. I felt movement in the bed and heard the whisper of a deep voice, which I knew couldn't possibly be Melanie's even with all the hash smoking we'd done. And sure enough there was BJ, Melanie's ex, already under the duvet and presumably trying to get his end away. Melanie was still off with the fairies and I wasn't much better but I had the senses about me to know that we were both underdressed and obviously vulnerable. 'Hi Em, been keeping the oven warm for me, have you?' he smirked as he rolled my way. 'Just got off the night shift and I thought I'd see how Mel's doing? Very nicely by the feel of it.'

"By this time I was panicking as Mel still hadn't woken up and I didn't really want to become the main course, and have to confront BJ in my state. I instinctively jumped out of bed and he just lay there, raised up on his elbows with his eyes bulging. Then I understood why, I hadn't got a stitch on. So I rushed into the bathroom, which unfortunately for me hadn't got a lock on the door, but it had a scruffy dressing gown hanging off a hook on the wall, so I wrapped myself in it and plonked down on the toilet seat to think. I hadn't a clue what BJ had been taking but I knew that the state Mel and I were in neither of us were safe. So whilst BJ was stumbling back into his jeans I slipped into the kitchen and made a couple of coffees and I dropped a Diazipan in his, and gave it a quick swish round. As expected, with Mel still being out of it, he came looking for me again and I just about managed to get him to sit and talk whilst we drank our drinks. You can imagine it was a bit of a monosyllabic conversation but at least it ensured that he drank as he spoke. Every sentence he uttered had a double meaning and there were more innuendoes than in a 'Carry On' film but I just kept hoping that the Diazipan would kick in and do its work. In the end he made another move for me and we both fell off the stool that I was sitting on as it toppled backwards. He banged his head on the floor and just lay there motionless, half on and half off me. I don't know which had brought him to a stop; the sleeping tablet or the crack on the head but I was grateful for either or both."

"So, what did you do then Emma? Call for an ambulance. Wake your friend? Melanie wasn't it, or what?"

"Well neither actually. To be honest I just crashed out again. I had a quick look at the cut on his head and I'd already checked that he was breathing, and made sure he was on his side like they do on telly, in case he threw up or something. And then I just went and lay back down on the bed. With so much activity, I couldn't concentrate any longer and just needed more sleep. I'd have had no chance threading a needle anyway if he'd needed stitches so I just stuck a plaster over the cut and left it at that. Must have been elevenish yesterday morning when Mel woke me; she was as bad as BJ trying to get on top of me but that all changed when I told her he was back. She checked the kitchen and sure enough he was still where I'd left him covered up with the blanket from the sofa.

She began whimpering when she saw the blood and the Elastoplast on his forehead, as if he was a little child but when he started to come round I made my excuses, threw my clothes on, and left within minutes."

"So that takes us to say Thursday noon. We've still got 12 hours to fill before you were found next to a dead body?" This statement shocked Emma to the core as she knew she had definitely chanced her arm on a number of occasions and been in close proximity to very inert torsos but never actually been in the same vicinity as that of a dead body. And more shockingly in this instance she had no knowledge of being close to any body, whether alive or dead.

"A dead body. I was found next to a dead body? Jeez. Was it a man or a woman?"

"Well actually, it was a man and we've got a picture here if you can bear to look." Emma scrutinised the dead man's photo and although she managed to keep a blank expression on her own face she did recognise the face staring back at her. The twelve hours were slowly rewinding but she needed time and space on her own before admitting to knowing a dead man and to becoming any more deeply involved in the murder of the same.

By way of distraction and in a bid to play for more time she began to make uncontrollable movements in the bed, whilst saying, "No, he's not ringing any bells, although like I say I'm a bit shaky about the last twelve hours anyway. And right now I really need the loo," she exclaimed as she fidgeted and squirmed. "Perhaps after another sleep I might start to see things more clearly."

But even in her cotton woolly head she knew time was not going to be on her side. Events were unfolding rapidly before her eyes and she was worried that her visible agitation would confirm her complicity to the crime. Now she made exaggerated jerky movements as she endeavoured to get off the bed, and on succeeding, she collapsed in a heap on the floor. Whatever had happened to her had certainly sapped all her strength and energy, and the thought crossed her mind that she would be crawling on all fours to the toilet if she did not get any form of assistance soon. A nurse hearing the commotion came and chided her for exerting herself too much and her visitor for being the cause of the exertion. In the end she rode to the toilet, reminiscent of Boudica astride her chariot as portrayed at London's Westminster Bridge, in the comfort of a wheelchair with her drip bag wafting like a pennant in the breeze. Once there, she hoped to gain at least a ten-minute cushion in order to pull herself together. On her intrepid return relief spread across her face as the immediate space surrounding her bed was devoid of any bodies, either dead or alive. So rather than flop back into it she hurriedly disconnected the drip, threw on her few clothes and then calmly staggered to the emergency exit, which she had reccied earlier whilst on her way to the bathroom. En route she gave silent thanks to all the nicotine addicts who even though they had littered the external pathway with their spent time bombs, had more importantly ensured her an easy getaway through a constantly ajar door, synonymous with smokers the world over. She still had twelve hours to recall but she was not going to be giving up that information freely, especially if it could implicate her in murder.

DI Barnham crumpled the polystyrene coffee cup, aimed, threw, and missed the bin, yet again. He had taken a fancy to the hospital reception area as his new personal emergency office where he could mull over this latest murder, his third, but at least this time with a surviving witness, who could even, at a long shot, turn out to be the murderer herself? A far more valuable piece of evidence than was be said for the other two murders. He turned to PC Blackwell, "I've got to get back to the station. Make sure that you stay here in reception and keep an eye on that corridor over there, if the patient makes a move, it will be from that direction. I'm convinced that she holds the key to this third murder. She's got a story to tell and we've got to press the right buttons to find out what happened in those last twelve hours leading up to the murder itself. Be careful though, she might try and sign herself out and we can't have her going underground at this stage of the game."

PC Blackwell gave a curt, "Yes Sir," whilst at the same time thinking that he was being asked to play nursemaid again. He had been cock-a-hoop when chosen to accompany the DI but now he was stuck in a hospital making sure that a druggie did not do a runner. But orders were orders and being the methodical kind of PC, he first picked up the DI's discarded and poorly aimed cups, popped them in the bin and then went off in search of a coffee for himself.

DI Barnham headed back to the station questioning how he could now have three murders on his patch all at the same time, and not even one solid lead, well apart from this Emma Flynn who by the way she talked sounded more like the feminine version of a 'Jack the lad'.

Although, originally working out of Jedburgh for the initial murder investigation of John Selwith, he had made the decision to move all available resources to Edinburgh now that bodies, in the plural, were being found, dotted around the Scottish Borders. He had hoped to extract more information out of Emma Flynn, there and then, but for the moment that had proved to be just another brick wall. And being a gambler, the same as Jamie Scott, he now surmised that he could be playing pontoon but in his case only using tarot cards instead, and every time he asked the banker for a twist another dead body turned up. Three with this one, and he still was not any nearer solving the first two murders neither. Three dead bodies. Last time he'd got three of anything was when he had won a tenner for three balls on the lottery. Was it just coincidence or were these murders linked? Surely, there must be a breakthrough soon; it was going to be impossible for the dead bodies to remain clueless indefinitely unless he was dealing with a professional. A professional, the thought sent a chill down his spine. 'A professional, that's all we need. One of those bastards running loose on my patch,' he muttered to himself as he collided with a newspaper vendor shouting, "Read all about it." 'They will be reading all about it if I don't get some results soon. And my boss will be reading me the riot act too,' he muttered again as he side stepped bag-laden shoppers exiting the local Coop.

He managed to find his car without any further rugby tackling incidents and headed back towards the A700, which in turn would lead him to the Lothian & Borders police station. Snow flurries charged towards the windscreen in hallucinating shapes, consciously forcing him to slow his speed so as not to collide with the charging horses or was it a 'fireless' breathing dragon or a line of school children on a pelican crossing. Sliding to a halt he heaved a sigh of relief; relief that he had managed to stop at all, as it was the latter, four miniature snowmen gaily walking across the road at what they thought was a safe spot and he thought, 'Too many late nights and too much caffeine. I'll have even more deaths to contend with if I don't change my routine'.

Once back inside the station he went to grab another coffee but thought better of it, as following the near mishap he gauged his caffeine levels were high enough already; so he called a progress meeting instead. Four of his team were present, two from Jedburgh, who had been part of the first murder inquiry and two additional colleagues from the Lothian & Borders police station; and he was hopeful that by adding this third murder to the other two he might start to see a pattern emerging even though there were not particularly any details or clues at this stage. "Right, we've now got three dead bodies on our hands and next to nothing to go on." The surprise of that startling statistic even shocked him. "It's over two weeks since twinkle toes was found, after he presumably tripped his last 'light fantastic', and according to Jamie that means a good three weeks since he died. Did we get anywhere with his ID?" Barnham threw out the question to the officers present.

He scanned the four heads as in turn they all moved side to side in a negative motion. "What nothing at all! No missing persons. No results from Pathology on the dental records! No concerned mother, wife, lover, sister, brother ....dog! Nothing from Forensics neither? Come on people ramp it up. The killer can't just drop off the face of the earth without leaving some sort of history behind him. We all agree he's human, don't we? Someone's got to know something, and if it wasn't for this bloody snow I'd have a good mind to send you all back to the crime scene to shake you out of your lethargy and waken you up. Oh, and what about the lipstick smudged hankie and the tape binding him?"

"I've got a DNA response on the lipstick but it doesn't perfect-match anything on the database and the adhesive tape is clean, Sir. So they've just been logged in under the 'dancing John Doe dead body,' at the moment." The reply came from one of the now fretful negative nodding dogs who was not looking forward at all to the prospect of a trip back to Camptown, where he had visions of replicating one of a troupe of synchronised amateur cross country skiers tramping clumsily downhill through at least a foot of snow.

"Nothing else? Well then, that's body number one as far as it goes! As for number three, this one's particularly sickening so I'll leave it alone until we are able to receive a full statement from the suspect found with the body. She's under surveillance at the hospital recovering from a drug overdose and a fantasy implant by the sounds of her. Jamie Scott's team and Forensics still have the scene completely cordoned off, and they are confident that the killer may have become sloppy and left behind something for us to go on. So we'll move on to analysing the body of victim number two. But before I do let me ask you, why does it seem that everybody wants to either kill each other or themselves in Scotland? I mean I've only been here what seems like five minutes and we've already got ourselves three murders to contend with. Perhaps you can give that some thought? Right moan over, second victim, a totally different location …," droned on Barnham.

CHAPTER FIVE

Jessica always felt her Friday afternoons became a bit of a conundrum. On the one hand it was nearly the weekend so time to relax and do her own thing but on the other she still had to go through the weekly rigmarole of 'off loading' her cases to her line manager. It was not Jessica's favourite aspect of the job, nor was the recipient of the call her favourite colleague. And Jessica, never being one to hand out smiles freely felt that the conversation today was one of those occasions when a smile would not be forthcoming. 'The only saving grace is that I get to work from home and it's on the phone so she has no idea whether she's getting a smile or not!' she thought smugly.

Just then, the line connected. "Good afternoon, Tess Danvers."

"Hi Tess. It's Jessica here. I'm just ringing in for the weekly download. Have I caught you at a bad time?" she asked in hope.

"No, I'm fine at the moment, I can give you say 40 minutes. Then I've got to prepare for a 3.30 meeting"

Disappointedly Jessica continued, "OK, I'll get right to it. I've got five cases this week, three of which are continuations of current cases plus two new ones. I'll start with the three that are carried over from before. Interrupt if you need any reminders as to what's already transpired. Firstly, 'File S47'. This one involves two women living together as a couple; both officially unemployed and living off benefits but a near certainty that one of them was soliciting for extra cash. If you recall, this attracted our attention when one of the women was admitted to Edinburgh Infirmary with a broken nose and a severe cut to the back of the head, which required 15 stitches. As I mentioned in a previous report, I suspected the partner rather than a third party had inflicted the wounds. And when I visited the victim in hospital she didn't deny this but wasn't very communicative about it either. So after I suggested that there could be 'bodily harm' charges brought against her partner she asked for some time to think it over. I've since been back to the flat and it turns out it wasn't her partner at all but one of her punters. The couple has since had a big bust up and the uninjured partner, who incidentally is now injured too with bruises to her face and arms caused by the prostitute's pimp, was in the process of packing her clothes and other possessions into a bin liner. Not, as she admitted because of the physical violence but more because of the mental anguish of knowing that a man, or more likely more than one man, had been in the 'special place' she thought was reserved for her alone. And as far as she was concerned their chosen way of living had now been violated with this embracing of men rather than deleting them."

"OK. You wonder if some people don't think to question where the money comes from. Don't bother planning in a return visit unless you find out that the other woman returns. I presume the relevant punter's and pimp's names have not been divulged?"

"No Tess. Both were too worried for their own safety to reveal any names, and now the flat's taken on the life of a nunnery, particularly with this vow of silence and men not getting as far as the threshold, let alone over it. It's as if man was never created. Moving on to 'File S32'. This one's a bit like a bad penny. I seem to have been reporting on it ad infinitum. It concerns a weak husband living with three kids and his dominant wife. Week in, week out he's out there working to keep them above the breadline and when he does get a chance to be at home she abuses him physically and either ignores him totally or when she does speak it's to threaten to leave him and take the three kids. The kids generally run around in rags looking totally neglected even though he's earning quite good money, which by the way, he does cough up. It's just that she throws it away on bingo, cigarettes, booze and drugs. On the last visit, four days ago, both parents were in and eventually he admitted that she'd attacked him with a hammer, had also thrown various items at him including a hot iron and on one recent drug addled occasion when her paranoia had set in she'd fronted up to him with her fists and a knife. I managed to get him to one side and he told me that not so long ago she'd put a plastic bag over his head when he'd fallen asleep in front of the TV and he doesn't know what would have happened if the eldest girl hadn't walked in looking for a drink. Problem is that he loves the kids and it was pathetic to see a grown man, with ugly cuts and bruises all over his face and neck, crying and almost denying that there is a problem."

"Is this man a saint or what? He seems to be giving everything to this family but his time whilst all she wants is cash to fuel her habits. Where do the children fit into this love match? You really need to make these two aware that with their present behaviour they stand a good chance of an order being placed to take the children into care."

"Tess, I've already advised the husband of the likely scenario, but his wife had already gone out before that conversation and she nearly took the door off the hinges to boot. He was gutted with the prospect and reality of his situation but feels he's in a 'Catch 22'. He needs to work to earn the money to pay for the home to house the kids in, but at the same time he needs to devote time to caring for them and ensuring that they are safe from their mother and her extremely aggressive anger and mood swings. He knows the future of the children in their present environment is in jeopardy and that Social Services will become involved if not only to monitor their welfare short term. His parting shot, which was a dig at his wife really, was that recently she'd been seen cavorting with some sort of artist on the High Street. So adultery now looks like an extra vice to add to the others and it's probably another nail in her, and possibly her family's, coffin".

"Right. We'll send our files to Social Services and you'll need to work closely with them on the children's behalf and monitor the adults at the same time. What time is it now? 3.24. I can probably squeeze another one in if you're quick."

"I'll do one of the new ones then, as there's nothing much to report. 'File S63'. This is a recently opened case of the classic domineering man versus the equally weak-willed woman. Neighbours have reported their concerns, particularly after making several unsuccessful attempts to see the woman, even to the extent of knocking at her door. They say she never answers and they don't know if it's because the TV's too loud, which some say it is, or maybe that she's ill and can't get to it. One of the neighbours found out from an acquaintance in The Rievers' Return, the local pub on the ground floor of their flats, that her partner was ill-treating her and she'd been told that he had been boasting about a list of punishments to suit her bad behaviour. It transpires that he locks her in the house everyday whilst he goes about his daily business. I'm not sure yet what that business is as he seems very vague about it, and on further investigations I've ascertained that he has had no active HMRC records for the last three years. I've made one attempt so far at visiting when he's there so that I can at least get a foot in the door, but to no avail. I'll make one further attempt before I obtain an order for a locksmith to force the door. I predict that this one will be featuring regularly for some weeks to come."

Tess hurriedly started wrapping up the conversation with, "Yes, keep that one moving along. Don't leave it too long before you try to arrange another visit, as we can't really know what's going on behind that door and the neighbours could be spot-on with their concerns. This character maybe doing her more damage than we can ever imagine. Whoops, sorry, got to dash the meeting's about to start and I've not collected my papers together. Can you call back at 5.15? Is that OK?"

Jessica answered equally as quick, "Yes, 5.15 is no problem, speak to you then," before she registered that she was talking to a disconnect tone. However, that did not bother her one bit as she now had over 90 minutes to get changed, do some warm up stretches, have a run, get showered and be back at her desk before the 5.15 deadline loomed. Life was not looking so bad after all she reflected whilst pulling on her running tights and wondering where she had left her sports bra. Ten minutes later she was cutting across the back of the park that led up through the old railway cutting and on into the woods. Her favourite training ground, where she knew especially today that her physical exercise would actually play a part in exorcising all the demons that floated round her brain when the 'off loading' of her casework took place.

The blood, gore and evil that people inflicted on each other never ceased to amaze her. She generally tried to block these images out of her mind and, if the truth be known and admitted, these phone conversations really did help with dissecting the present status of the cases. It enabled her to let go of the clutter and to 'defrag' her brain, just like a computer, ready for the next input instalments. So, as she punished herself through another 45 minutes of fast running interspersed with jogs in between she visualised the imagery of ugly stitches running across what once was a smooth cheek; a broken nose that would have made a suitable badge of honour for any up and coming boxer; and the five inch, cauterised, reddish purple wheal across a man's chest with its singed stubble running either side like a razed crop after it has been burnt off. Some injuries, she knew, had been treated at A&E but the more horrifying scars tended to be those that the recipients had botched up themselves. For an adult to see this was bad enough in itself, but for an innocent child it could leave permanent mental damage. Images only visible to those children caught up and affected by this mayhem of a life that they had never bought into but ended up in anyway. Jessica struggled to accept these humans cum animals in today's society, and so endeavoured to protect the innocent to the best of her ability and professionalism.

CHAPTER SIX

Vinny made his back ache even more as he spent the rest of the day driving around endlessly in pursuit of his elusive target. Although, there was still good sport to be had as he considered other options along the way but Pops was not going to be pleased if the prime target did not meet his maker too, and in the prescribed timescale. Easy enough for Pops to say as the directive given in their conversation, *"And that bastard Barnham, I want him dead, Vince, do you read me, dead. And I'm thinking that perhaps after all you've now grown the balls to carry it out. No prisoners, stick a bullet in him wherever you want as long as you bring him down, and then make sure you put one through that thick skull of his. You only diss this family once, and as he's going to find out that's once too often! Right Vinny?"*

Not quite the affirmation of belief Vinny wanted to hear but at least now the talking was over, he was on the road and holding the lottery ticket to the sky for that bastard Barnham's fate and lack of future. The disrespect had occurred when the DI crossed the unwritten code by hassling Vinny's younger sister. Jeez, the girl was just out of school and although already groomed for a position within the gangland hierarchy that still did not give the coppers a right to threaten her without justification. Barnham had seen the harassment as no more than an opportunity of introducing the girl to the lawful side of her new world and a way of getting to know her better. In reality he had been digging for information, and had done it on more than one occasion. Pops, Charlie Varnish, the main man, took offense and made three decisions. He would have a quiet word in a sympathetic ear to find out where this Barnham irritation was now residing, then take care of it, and get his son Vinny out of his hair at the same time. In truth, Varnish senior was happy just to have Barnham scared off, it was not a priority to put him six feet under, but if it gave his Vince a purpose and took him away from the volatile North East scene for a few weeks then all well and good.

Vinny, the departed, was proud of being given such a grave undertaking and even more proud of his ability in tracking the DI to Edinburgh, and not southwards at all.

Pops the silly old fool, had me believe this Barnham character had been shipped off to the Midlands. Said he had it on good authority, but after bumbling around there for a while I chanced upon a hard up PC who put me right. I got chatting over a couple of pints, and he let slip that they had never seen hide nor hair of him, the whole thing had all been a ruse and Barnham's real destination was actually northwards. So there you are Pops, one in the eye for you. Writing this I'm almost embarrassed to remember how the PC came to lose his life, and all for the price of two beers and a wagging tongue. But such is death. I keep thinking I might come back and rewrite this bit as I could be the hero but the truth of it is I'm actually not. I was not instrumental in his death, not really, I did buy him the beer but it was him who went to the toilet, I didn't force him to go. Although maybe when I'm back home I might be more than happy to take the plaudits, I'll have to give it serious thought in the meantime. Anyway the PC sauntered off to the outside loo, he slipped on the wet cobbles and cracked his head on a stone planter, allegedly there to make the courtyard look pretty. Certainly made PC Plod look pretty, a pretty mess! It was as simple as that. That being his last journey I gathered I better take my next one pretty sharpish too. So I did.

Whilst awaiting the PC's return and upon hearing the commotion outside, he instinctively downed the PC's bought and paid for pint, more in shock than greed or an unquenching thirst, and then seamlessly melted into the background on his way to the exit.

But the target himself was proving a far more slippery character, one who had obviously played the game before by keeping his routines irregular and making sure he was constantly in other people's company. And the recent plethora of murders had something to do with Barnham's vanishing act too but Vinny knew that patience and opportunity would be his friends. One chance had occurred in a freak blizzard as his target stopped his vehicle at a pelican crossing for some young children, but unfortunately for Vinny even he knew that stray bullets were off limits for the likes of them. So he had just carried on, taking one day at a time, living out of his holdall, and content in the knowledge that with each new day came more experience and another possible chance of Barnham letting his guard slip, and of Vinny rising up in his father's estimation.

*

The second body was a totally different kettle of fish, and had literally come out of the blue. A quiet and generally sedate spot on the banks of the River Teviot, south of Kelso, had proved far too eventful and disappointing for all concerned. The riverside path, usually the domain of dog walkers and joggers exercising both two and four legs until a fisherman struck lucky and thought it was payday when he hooked what he was sure would be a whopper. He could already imagine the tales he would be telling in his local with his arms stretched wide like aeroplane wings. Turned out his story was going nowhere as dead bodies did not get you in Angling Times nor free pints at the pub neither. The other man in the boat who had sat quite still and patient whilst holding the oars shouted that Mr Pugh would have to let the whopper go or they would both end up in the drink as well, and that definitely was not the place to be in late February. The oarsman manoeuvred the boat towards the riverbank and still the fisherman refused and held on to his catch. He started to reel it in but then with reluctance, he acknowledged that the huge fish was not fighting against him. There was tension on the line alright but that was influenced by the weight of the ensnared item and the flow of the river.

In the interview notes Geoff Finch, the boatman had said, "I thought his rod was going to snap in half, it was almost bent double, so there must have been a good few pounds of weight on the line. But when it bobbed up to the surface as this blue object I just instinctively waded in. Bloody hell, was it cold in there but I didn't want him to break his rod in two as they're not cheap and anyway it's part of my job to clear rogue debris out of the river. But when I got there I couldn't get hold, with it being so slippery so in the end I just cut the line." Barnham had to laugh when the boatman had then continued with, "Good job the ghillie wasn't here today. He hates any foreign bodies being thrown in and contaminating these sacred waters."

Quick as a flash the interviewer, T/DC Murray, had retorted, "Well it is a good job he doesn't know what this foreign body is that his precious salmon have been nibbling, or they'll all be morphing into piranhas before the day's out." The fisherman, George Pugh, had not been able to offer any further information and was left licking his wounds somewhat as to what might have been and feeling the impact on his wallet at the expense of a day's fishing with nothing to show for it. Both men confirmed the exact location of where the body was first snagged as being adjacent to Teviot Bridge. They were thanked for their assistance and asked to keep it under wraps, but like all good fishing stories the interviewer was convinced it would surface sooner rather than later.

Forensics headed to the Teviot Bridge location, laden down with stakes and 'DO NOT CROSS' red and white tape whilst Jamie Scott, the pathologist, met Barnham on the left riverbank just as the frogmen were suited up for their first dive. "I thought two would be sufficient as we've got a good idea of where the body was last seen and the current's not too strong to drag it any significant distance," said Barnham.

"I can tell you've never been inducted onto the hallowed banks of fishermen, Terry. Most rivers don't look particularly fast but it's deceptive, that body could be over 200 metres downstream, unless it's snagged on a branch or something similar. Do you fancy a little bet? A tenner says it's passed that willow on the bend," Jamie said throwing down the wager, as was his liking to mix pleasure with business.

"OK. So I've got the whole area up to the willow. Correct?" Fifteen minutes later Terry was £10 lighter. The current had indeed taken the body 50 metres beyond the other side of the bend by Brigend Park, and fortunately for the divers it had indeed snagged on an overhanging bough that over time had been buffeted by the exposed winds and now bent obligingly to offer its services in police detection.

"Well that has come out of the blue," joked Jamie. "Looks like a gift wrapped Smurf or an Egyptian mummy that's gone off. At least this one's 'to go', seeing as it's already in its body bag."

"Have a bit of reverence here, will you? I know you like joshing while you work but until we've got a handle on this victim I think we should reserve our judgment and show respect," retorted Terry, a little irritated.

"Hey you only lost £10, not like it's a fortune, is it? I think you better start smoking properly again Barnham, or is it just getting too hot for you in the kitchen? Not your kind of job after all? Murders cropping up too regularly on your patch, are they? OK let's get serious, I'll tell you what I see so far. The blue material looks to be some form of industrial shrink-wrap. The sort of thing most trades use to palletise goods. Looking at the bundle I reckon it's probably 5ft 5in or 5ft 6in and with the undulations most likely female, although there's definitely a flattened edge there too. I won't open the package until it is back in the lab, so as not to contaminate the evidence." Jamie finished with a curt nod in Barnham's direction and another nod to his own colleagues, who then placed the body on a stretcher and walked gingerly up the riverbank hoping to find better traction on the higher, firmer ground.

Meanwhile, Barnham strode back to his car troubled by his friend's barbed comments. It was not so much that there were dead bodies springing up like crocuses it was more that if he did not get a handle on it all soon he would have the powers that be breathing down his neck and no doubt be superseded by some jumped up graduate with qualifications coming out of his arse. His worst nightmare imaginable becoming reality.

A rather concerned, "Sir? Sir?" brought him back to the present.

He looked at his colleagues with a little bewilderment, changed his expression immediately and remembering that he had not eaten since last night, blurted out the first thing that came into his head, "Right a cup of sweet tea and a sausage butty. I'm buying. But no one's getting any of that namby-pamby veggie stuff!" The five officers preparing to hang onto his every astute word looked on in puzzlement, but as the case was going nowhere at present a refreshment break hit the spot for each and every one of them. "Don't think you're off the hook yet? This is just to recharge your batteries. We still need to collate any information gleaned from passers-by or homeowners near the river who might have heard some commotion over the last 24 or 48 hours, cars coming and going, that sort of thing. Then the pathology report needs chasing up and let's inform forensics to fast track theirs too." He knew the latter was wishful thinking as the body could have drifted quite a distance from where it originally started its voyage.

A precise 5.00pm beckoned but working late proved a more accurate timepiece. By now the team had swelled to six plus the DI. There was a general buzz in the inquiry room with polite social chitchat being passed backwards and forwards about each other's expectant evening activities. The 'Crazy Frog' ring tone of the DI's mobile put a stop to all that, freezing everyone's conversations in mid sentence. "Hi. Jamie here. You wanted it by close of play today, so this is what I've got. Hope I'm not encroaching on your evening by the way?"

"Jamie, you know as well as I do that I don't have evenings. To me, they are just an extension of the working day, just more often than not a bit darker and cooler. Give me 20 seconds to fathom out how to put this damn phone on speaker and then we all can listen in."

His team retained a total hush, now knowing in their hearts that the longer Jamie spoke the less chance they would have of fulfilling any of their evening's personal dreams, but they still hung on to his every word anyway. Jamie could not give a toss for convention or respect for technology and its usage, and just ploughed ahead regardless, "Right, nineteen, twenty, time's up. We unwrapped the body of victim two, as she is now known. And as suspected it's of a female, 5ft 6ins tall and probably around 35 years of age. Slim build with what I would have said was a pretty face framed with strawberry blond hair reaching to her shoulders, dyed of course, blue eyes, plump lips, and a mouth graced with slightly dodgy teeth. By that, I mean brownish in appearance, so probably a habitual smoker of some years, and they're chipped in places too. A few oldish looking bruises here and there indicate some recent physical violence. Can't believe they're sports inflicted and that might have a bearing on the chipped teeth too. We've got her hands in saline with the hope of getting a good set of prints off but that's too early too tell. I'll get X rays of said teeth and do the usual dental sweep. To complement the bruises she's sporting an intricate set of recently acquired tattoos running across her bust just below the cleavage. I say recent as there is no visual fade to the inks and at a guess the design represents three roses intertwined but if I'm being honest most kids could have done it better. I don't know if it's meant to depict a bunch of

Valentine roses or a crown of thorns? Perhaps she did it for a bet?

"Similar to that first body we found, barely dressed for this time of year. So as not to confuse, I mean she was wearing the usual gear girls tend to wear to go clubbing, in the middle of winter; and made up to the nines as if she was definitely on the pull, certainly not the usual attire for snorkelling anyway. Oh, and the flat edge across her chest turns out to be her handbag with the strap conveniently wrapped round her neck, which I'm presuming was a partial asphyxiation to prevent her from struggling too much. Again, similar to last time in that she was bound hand and foot with adhesive tape, so we definitely do seem to be getting a pattern here. And pattern being the operative word I ran a toxicology report, and sure enough there were traces of benzodiazepines in the blood. Again not a significant dose but this one was using anyway with tracks from here to Glasgow to prove it.

"But here's a surprise though, even with the telltale tracks there was no heroin evident, although there were other substances, which we're trying to identify as I speak. I'll email photos in five but I'm convinced, just like the first body, that this woman was more than likely alive when she was thrown in the Teviot. And you might be thinking why didn't she suffocate in her shroud? Well the evil bastard who dumped her had punctured several air holes around her nose and mouth to ensure she'd greedily gulp in as much air as possible. When the air turned to water she drowned; and we've got lungs full of H_2O to substantiate that." After Jamie rang off there was a cacophony of sound as if the volume control had been turned up to eleven. Everyone could see the similarities in the two cases and each team member picked out a certain aspect of Jamie's conversation.

"Barely dressed," that's an oxy whatsit, isn't it?"

"Moron".

"No need to be like that. I was just trying to educate you. It's one of them 'contradictions in terms'".

"Yes, that's what I'm telling you. It's an oxymoron."

"Oh, I see. Oxymoron. You weren't inferring that I was a moron then. Are you sure?"

"Drowning. What a way to die."

"Handbag strap round the neck. What sort of a freak, are we dealing with?"

"Remind me not to look up her tattooist."

Barnham waited until the banter died down and then said, "Let's move on. This gives us a breakthrough and nothing, all at the same time. We have got the message now that this killer is clever and thorough but we've still no motive and we're still uncertain as to whether it's one or more perpetrators. So from now on make sure your metaphorical torches are fully charged with new batteries as at present we're stumbling around completely in the dark."

The three beeps dragged Barnham back from his reverie. He stood up with a start sending his bottle of Stella into a spin and then flying off the sofa arm to crash innocently on the floor. He orientated himself, thanked the bottle for being empty and gingerly retrieved yet another TV dinner from the microwave, and all choreographed to the sound and pictures of News 24 blaring out of his 21-inch flat screen. Knowing the department's budget for what it was, his bedsit in Grosvenor Street was not exactly an example of furnishings by John Peters, and he felt sure that the room was shrinking, the walls seemed to be closing in day by day. 'I've got to get away. Newcastle looks positively idyllic compared to this 'Wendy' house, and at least I can call it home. When will I get recalled? How I miss my own modest creature comforts,' he thought. But he knew his agitation was more to do with retaining the mental comfort of being in control and staying close to the action, and both priorities were a guarantee that he would not be going anywhere soon.

He had only closed his eyes for a second but it felt like he'd been asleep for hours. 'Hours,' Barnham thought, 'Three hours assessing victim two info and surmising what could possibly link that body to victim one but still no eureka moment. And as the saying goes everything comes in three's, I've now got this third body to contend with!' He picked at his food, puffing knowingly as he gave three blows for cooling before taking every mouthful. 'How long can we continue getting nowhere before the press starts sniffing round and how long can I continue eating this junk and living this lifestyle?'

CHAPTER SEVEN

The next morning turned out to be a bright, dry and crisp day. A clear blue sky encouraged the early watery sun to shine through the slats of a bedroom-shuttered window, striping the quilt on its travels upwards in its quest to wake Barnham from his deep slumber. He did wake, felt invigorated, rose and threw open the french windows that led onto the open expanse of terracing. Here, he stood motionless, facing into the zephyr of a breeze as he embraced the new day, whilst at the same time letting the waft of the aroma of the freshly brewed finest Italian filter coffee play on his senses. Coffee, he knew that had been made almost lovingly by the housemaid, old enough to be his mother.

Then he really did wake up. Neither, in that style, nor fashion, and definitely not in that location but it did feel like some kind of epiphany anyway.

He did feel refreshed and was convinced that soon there would be a serious breakthrough. That negative feeling from the night before was now washed away with his daily lukewarm shower. Another of Barnham's regular gripes to the landlord as yet unfulfilled. 'You'd think that being in CID would pull more weight and a few more strings; and gain you a little bit of respect but it seems the exact opposite is the case. Everyone just obstructs the police at every hurdle,' he surmised as he scampered from the shower, drying himself quickly as he stumbled towards the antiquated chest of drawers that contained all his worldly goods, well his clothes anyway, and particularly his underwear at this point in time.

And within no time at all he was pulling up outside the Lothian & Borders police station, dressed and booted, ready for action. The team must have been of the same mindset as they were all present and eager to progress any clues that had arisen from the previous night's meeting. A manilla envelope, a folder containing photographs and an empty handbag had been delivered from both labs and the meagre contents of the envelope were now spilled out across the evidence table, not dissimilar to the remains of a hurried takeaway, consumed after too much booze even though it had seemed like a good idea at the point of purchase.

Thinking on his feet, Barnham greeted his audience with, "Morning everyone. Let's not beat about the bush. It looks like we've got a serial killer on our hands. He's liable to strike again at will, so time is against us. PC Gough can you do the honours and log in the items asap and check for any identification whilst WPC Whitely gets these photos up on the board. T/DC Murray, the tape and shrink-wrap, do you have any leads? What about that ghastly tattoo? PC Tranter, can you check with one of Jamie Scott's colleagues as to whether there had been any sexual activity; probably a long shot with her being in the water for so long but maybe the shrink-wrap prevented a total washout, no pun intended."

T/DC Murray was the first to reply. "Gov, as far as the tape and shrink-wrap goes I'd been thinking about that as I reckoned that the killer either has close links to some kind of despatch business or he just bought them at a DIY or hardware shop. So on the way here I called at the local one and they, surprise, surprise, they sell both items. I've brought samples in of each but you can see that the blue of the evidence shrink-wrap is slightly different, although that could be because it's been in the water, whereas the tape itself is an exact match. Taking it further, to its logical conclusion, I checked on their security procedures and it turns out that the shop has three videotapes, which get wiped every 16 hours. So had the perpetrator been doing a spot of shopping there, then his mug shot would have been long gone anyway."

"Good work T/DC Murray, glad to see that there's a brain working with initiative no matter what time of day or night. We'll make a detective of you yet," replied Barnham. "As a bonus you can also follow up on dodgy tattooists. I want to know who inked in that ghastly flourishing rose garden on her chest. It could help with her identification, if nothing else." At this point WPC Whitely had sifted through the handbag's soggy contents and concluded that her own handbag probably wasn't waterproof either. She then tacked the pictures from the Path lab onto the board, making room for them by moving over the first victim's shots.

"Sir, not much success in the handbag department. Four items of makeup, I'd say mid priced and on sale in most supermarkets: a bottle of Fendi perfume, a £20 note, a pack of very soggy tissues, gold ring and a pack of very dry durex. Looks like she was prepared," she jested, with a blush of embarrassment appearing on her face and neck as soon as she had said it. Collecting herself she continued, "Photos are up on the board now but they don't seem to reveal much more than what Jamie had told us yesterday, but at least we have a vague idea of what she looked like. And as he hoped, he did manage to get fingerprints so that's an extra bonus."

"Yes, very good," replied Barnham dryly, "nothing to identify her at all but fingerprints and a tasteless tattoo. No mobile, no address book, no driving licence, no keys," he mused.

"No Sir. Must have been taken by the killer and just as before, it wasn't some mugging as there was still that £20 note left. But I'd hazard a guess that the ring's most probably her wedding ring as there looks to be an indentation on the third finger, so there's a real chance she could have been married."

As if on cue, PC Tranter finished his telephone conversation with one of Jamie Scott's colleagues. "Right

Tranter, what have you got?"

"Couple of interesting things. The Path lab had sent the handbag direct to Forensics who, then, took out and kept a syringe still in its wrapper, and a couple of 'e's, which were just loose but with no adverse effect from the water and so were still intact. Forensics weren't hopeful of getting anything off the tablets but they're checking for prints on the syringe wrapper. They'll get back within the hour. As for any action down there, they feel that she may have had intercourse but that's only due to a slight inflammation of the vagina but otherwise clean as far as DNA goes," he said hurriedly so as to get over that last point without stuttering or stumbling over his words. In a slightly calmer tone of voice he continued, "The Path lab also asked us to look for a ring as they noticed the groove on her finger and were unsure if it had been taken off by the killer. Oh, one more thing, they also confirmed that there was no dental confirmation on the first victim. So their view is that he either had bloody good teeth or more than likely had any necessary work done abroad."

Barnham barked out his new orders, "OK. I want you all to get a copy of the woman's face and that ghastly tattoo. We'll all give T/DC Murray a hand with this one. So it looks like we've some legwork ahead of us. First off you'll need to visit pubs, clubs, shops, any local community centres, and obviously tattoo parlours, within a 15 miles radius of where the body was located. If we don't get any hits we'll have to widen the search. Hopefully we'll get some ID based on those teeth. Perhaps her mother had the sense to take her to a local dentist at some point during her childhood even if she never went back as an adult." Then he thought, 'Two down, who knows how many more to go before we catch this psycho'?

*

Emma's brush with death left her both exhausted and quizzical. Exhausted from both the endotracheal tube and subsequent stomach tube inserted into her esophagus, and then on down to the stomach. Her sore throat and croaky voice were testament to that, whilst her mouth still had the bitter dry taste of charcoal the medics used to neutralise any lingering drugs not caught by the pumping. And quizzical because even she realised that the whole premise of what she was about to embark on and what she hoped to achieve by it were purely based on a whim, a whim of recognising someone. Someone, from nothing more than a fleeting glance, that literally lasted at the most two seconds. She had a vague idea of what she needed to do but only time would tell if she was going about it in the right order.

Her first port of call meant a trip across the city and left Emma with more than a little trepidation as to whether or not it was a wild goose chase. She did not know if it was the correct location and neither did she know how to find the relevant information once she got there. In reality, the only thing she did know was that there were facts out there, which she needed to piece together and her computer illiteracy could prove her undoing, thus ending her quest before it had even started. However, in order to achieve anything her first challenge was to check out which hospital had been attending her. So wearing a nurse's tunic top and carrying her own medical notes' clipboard, she exited the open door, gingerly walked down the fire escape, and breezed back through the reception entrance to the best of her ability. Here she found a patients' public notice board and made a note of a local taxi company number, then went outside to ring on her mobile. "Hello, taxi please from Royal Infirmary of Edinburgh, located on Old Dalkeith Road, I think. I'll be waiting at the A&E entrance, name of Flynn. Emma Flynn." The taxi arrived with no problem and was directed west to a destination where 10 minutes later Emma had divested her nurse's tunic and was £10 lighter too. Fortunately for her, she had stolen a £20 note from the guy she had met the night before. So as the taxi dropped her off outside Ladywell House on Ladywell Road, she still felt £10 to the good. NRS Central Register stood out prominently on a shiny metal strip running across the centre of the double fronted glass doors.

Emma entered and once inside, a sign informed her that NRS was the acronym for National Records of Scotland. 'So far so good, looks like this is the right place then,' she thought. 'Now I've just got to find myself a nice hulk who works here and convince him that I'm a helpless dumb blond.'

This was easier said than done even though she looked exactly the part for the job. But that was where her luck ran out as physically she was still feeling very fragile from her passionless night lying in an upturned skip with far too much strong and seemingly dodgy heroin coursing through her veins. This was still one better than could be said for the man who had accompanied her and shared in her passionate fatal desire. All he paid into was a guaranteed promise but ended up in a permanent passive state instead, with no comeback whatsoever. And then to add insult to injury her stomach had been turned inside out to accomplish the drug's removal. What a waste.

Her other more immediate problem was that most of the would-be hulks turned out to be female, and even they were few in number as the majority of staff were hidden away behind screens. So Emma just did what came natural to her at this point and visited the ladies room to take stock of the situation. Once there, she leant over the sink counter and splashed water onto her face, took a long drink from the running tap, and then several deep breaths to calm herself. On exiting she came face to face with a man who stepped back just in time so as not to become embarrassingly upfront and personal.

"Whoops, sorry about that. I wasn't paying attention," said Emma to her knight in shining armour, who looked at first glance to possess all the gallantry she could possibly require.

"No. The apology's all mine. How could such a pretty thing as you be at fault," replied the knight. "Are you new here?"

"No. No, I don't work here, but thank you for thinking that

I do. I'm just here to gather some information but it all looks a bit daunting. Even these different coloured directional signs faze me, pointing where to go, and presuming I'll know what to do when I get there," she replied a little breathily which she was certainly feeling.

"Do you need assistance? I mean, if I'm not intruding? I'm going on a break now, which reminds me I need the loo. Give me two minutes and I'll take you for a coffee and, if you want, you can tell me what you're looking for and then perhaps I can point you in the right direction rather than the signs. But only if it's what you want. I've actually worked here 12 years so I should be able to find my way around most departments," he replied enthusiastically as he reversed through the door marked 'Gents'. True to his word, two minutes later he reappeared and greeted Emma with a warm smile and an outstretched arm impersonating an arrow. "OK, this way to the cafeteria. I'm John by the way but most folk call me Jonnie."

"Oh. Yes, hello. My name's Emma but most folk call me Emma," she said jokingly. She was pleasantly surprised how comfortable she felt in his company, and despite the fact of knowing him for all of five minutes she still felt a closeness unlike that of most of her other friends or acquaintances.

"Shall we take that table over there? Now are you a full caffeine hit, cappuccino, latte or decaf, kind of person?" asked Jonnie with sincerity.

Never usually having so many options, as 'instant' was her normal fayre, Emma replied, "Latte's fine thanks, and would you mind getting me a bottle of water too"?

"Still or sparkling? Say 'sparkling'."

"No, still please. But why did you want me to say 'sparkling'?"

"So I could say, to match your eyes," replied Jonnie triumphantly.

Emma groaned and thought, 'he can't be looking too closely at them or he'd be shocked at how small my pupils are at present'. She then spent the next five minutes glancing around the cafeteria, marveling at the American style banquette seating with tables to match, and she contemplated what she was going to be searching for after this little interlude had ended.

"There you go. I've brought both sugar and sweetener sachets as I didn't know if you had a sweet tooth or whether you might be watching your figure? Not that you need to watch your figure, but ..," he laughed and left the sentence hanging.

"Sugar's fine usually. But I only take it in tea, so I'll let you off."

"Phew. So Emma I was thinking back there, competing against the coffee machine and milk steamer making all sorts of weird noises, I've only got ten minutes of my break left at present, and by the time we've finished these that will be it. What I'm thinking is that I could get my boss to allow me to sign out for an hour or so, we work flexitime anyway, so it shouldn't be a problem; and then I can give you the grand tour and maybe be of assistance in your research as well."

"Jonnie. I don't want to put you to any trouble. I'm sure I'll be able to wander round and eventually stumble upon the department I'm looking for," Emma replied looking very hesitant and not just a little crestfallen.

"Wouldn't dream of it, Emma. If you're sure I'm not being too pushy I'd be glad to help."

Emma agreed knowing that her uncertainty had been executed with just the right measure of 'blond' helplessness, and anyway she did not want to cut short so soon the possibility of a future blossoming relationship. She excused herself with, "This coffee runs right through you," but in reality her intention was to nip off and apply some much-needed make-up, having not had the opportunity at the hospital. Whilst there, she also popped a couple of paracetamols into her mouth, and swallowed them down with scoopfuls of water from the tap, hoping they would keep her pounding head at bay. She gave herself a final check in the mirror, and immediately recognised and squirmed at the fact that she was both overdressed and underdressed in the previous night's skimpy outfit. Overdressed because she looked to all intents to be heading for a night out and underdressed because the material making up her skimpy outfit was under pressure to retain all the goods that needed containing therein. She then shrugged to her reflection as if to say 'what can I do?' and made her return. Fifteen minutes later they were both sitting cosily close in front of a computer screen with a visual-aid sign offering useful hints on how to get started. Jonnie robustly moved it to one side, as he knew already how to get started and proved it by attacking the keyboard with a vengeance. "Right. This is where I get to know more about you." Emma had briefly told him of her reason for being there and now as he said she was going to have to reveal more about herself, more than she might really want to do.

"OK. My name is Emma Jayne Flynn. I was born on 31st May 1980. I don't know where, but the first home I remember was a third floor flat at Weir Court in Sighthill, Edinburgh but that's now been demolished." Jonnie manipulated the keyboard and the screen responded with a choice of possible names all starting with 'Mr and Mrs'. "That's not going to be right Jonnie. I'm looking for an auntie with the name of Flynn. Unfortunately, she's dead now and it's always the case that you never ask about this kind of important stuff when you see them every day. So could it be under just Miss Flynn or even Ms Flynn, as she never married?"

Jonnie tapped on the keys again to narrow down his fields and three options came up; and when he searched all three sure enough one came up with Flat 33, Weir Court, Sighthill. Taking that information across to another two tabs should have enabled Jonnie to locate natural parents, which would have been the logical option for most dependants but in this case it informed him, *Flynn: Emma Jayne, adopted at age 3 years and 2 months.*

"If you were adopted it looks like your surname could have been changed from your birth surname, but we won't be able to access those kinds of files here," said Jonnie by way of apology. "But it's a start. Do you want me to look for anything else whilst I'm logged in?"

Emma couldn't really think clearly. She didn't know how far she wanted to take it but now she had started her inquisitiveness was quickly turning into a crusade, one that needed following through. But the more she concentrated her thoughts the more a slow nagging developed at the back of her head, complementing the physical headache which was already there; both just enough for her to acknowledge their presence. "I'm going to have to think about it Jonnie." She paused, thought for a minute and then asked, "Do you know where I can get old newspapers from?"

"What do you mean 'old newspapers'?" Jonnie asked bemusedly. "Do you want to read them or wrap up fish and chips in them?"

"Don't be daft. It's to read them, silly. And I mean really old, like years ago."

"Ah, I see. You want to carry on your research by looking through editorials or 'Births & Deaths', that sort of thing, from around the time you were born."

"I can see how you got yourself a full time job. That's exactly what I mean," replied Emma mischievously.

"Well, I'll do a deal with you. I'll tell you how to go about that, if you agree to meeting up for a drink sometime."

"Agreed," said Emma thinking that she could always renege if she wanted to but having a good feeling about Jonnie anyway, so thought a drink might be fun.

"Right. Pass me your mobile and I'll key in my number." Thirty seconds later he finished with, "Just this final tweek, now you've got to ring within a week or your phone will explode." Emma giggled at this as Jonnie went on, "Now my part of the bargain. What you need to do is go to the Central Library. It's at the junction of Cowgate and George IV Bridge.

Big building, you can't miss it. They have a very comprehensive microfiche system, which has all the newspapers going back years, and all stored on tiny reels of film. I'm sure somebody there will show you what to do. But don't let them chat you up and ask you out! Remember, I saw you first."

"Don't worry Jonnie. I don't make a habit of asking more than one computer geek out at any one time," she said teasingly. With that they had a slightly embarrassing goodbye embrace and again Emma promised to ring, and yes, before the phone was blown to smithereens.

Once outside, she greedily gulped in the fresh air as if she were stealing it from everyone else. She could have done with eating something at the cafeteria but Jonnie had not offered and she did not want to appear 'grabby'. So now as well as the gnawing at the back of her head and a normal headache, she also had a hollow ache in her stomach. 'Well another two paras will have to settle the lot for the present,' she thought. She looked up and down for a bus stop, where a bus would take her into the city but then decided on blowing some of the remaining £10 on a taxi, thinking 'easy come, easy go'.

The taxi dropped Emma outside the library and left her studying over both a maths and a health problem. Nothing to do with the taxi fare either, which had basically taken the whole £10; no this was more to do with time. She reckoned she had about three hours left before the niggle in her head would become so pronounced that it would prevent her from concentrating on absolutely anything other than accomplishing her next hit. And the health problem, running in tandem, was one of taking the risk that a shot of heroin in her present vulnerable state could prove fatal. She had always believed that her willpower would prevent a situation like this from ever occurring but the reality now was that she had probably hoodwinked herself and was therefore no better than any junkie you might happen to see staggering round, looking in bins for food or sleeping rough in doorways and on park benches. 'Still no point in beating myself up about it,' she thought, 'I've had plenty of that from other people.' She was just going to have to get back to her stomping ground and do some hustling. And as she knew from experience punters were the same as pushers, you had to recognise the signals to see whether they were buying or selling. But first, armed with only an obligatory telltale bottle of water, it was the library.

As Emma entered yet another alien environment she became a small child again. Heavy, carved wooden doors invited her through to row upon row and shelf upon shelf of books, all clambering to be touched and read in order to fulfil their raison d'etre. She had never understood the attraction of hallowed halls like these with their mute browsers, flitting around from book to book or sat studiously hunched over some tome or other, whilst breathing in the familiar musty smell of old paper and printing inks; and this business of keeping quiet had certainly passed her by. Any previous visits to any libraries had always ended with her being physically dragged out by her aunt, usually due to her aunt's embarrassment. But today, she was more confident and her positive actions led her to a bank of microfiche screens where she met up with several likeminded users. She sat in front of the only vacant terminal and was immediately lost by what confronted her. Her immediate neighbour, a young girl, who looked not long out of school, leant across and said, "New here? It can be a bit daunting the first time. Let me show you. This gives you the list of papers available and then you press this button to access the correct date. You might have to change the film a few times as you can only look at so many years at once but all the other ones are stored in chronological order in that cabinet."

"Thanks for that. It would have taken me ages to fathom it out. So if I'm wanting to find 1983 and it's not already in the machine I look over there for it."

"That's right. You've got it. If it's not there, it could be

72

that there is someone else here, who might be referencing that period in time," replied the girl.

"OK. I'll remember that," Emma replied amiably and thought to herself, 'well, she's definitely not going to be asking me out Jonnie, so you might be still in with a chance'.

Her auntie had mentioned years ago, about a car accident in the family, personal information Emma had not felt happy about divulging to Jonnie, as realistically speaking he was still technically a stranger, being as they had only just met. But now she was here her mind began slotting everything into place and she needed to trace this to its logical conclusion. Twenty minutes later she started feeling hot under the collar and could sense her face burning up. It was not the room temperature or her craving, but more so what she had stumbled across. Making the decision to research English and Scottish national newspapers published from just before her adoption date, she started from April 1983 onwards and narrowed her field down to 'car accidents'. One article that took her interest, on page 2 of the Daily Mail, June 6th 1983, read as follows:

TRAGIC CAR ACCIDENT KILLS FOUR

A burned out car was discovered at the bottom of Blagdon Lake in Somerset. Divers have recovered four bodies from the wreckage but police are unable to clearly identify any victims, due to multiple burns and the effects of the water. However, it is thought to be that of two adults and two children.

A spokesman for the police made the following statement, 'We're not 100% certain but we think that we have been searching for this missing couple for some time now and information received indicates that they could have been the victims of a revenge killing. To compound the tragedy it appears that their two small children have been caught up in the violence too. That being the case we are prepared to release the names of those alleged to have died in order to gain a reaction from next of kin or other interested parties. The couple in question is Mr Luigi Agosti and Mrs Laura Agosti, nee Flynn and their two young children.

The article continued but Emma did not. 'Flynn' jumped out at her immediately, but then she became confused as to the two dead children. Did she have siblings who were killed in the accident? So as not to jump to conclusions she flicked through to the end of 1983 and then changed to the Daily Mirror. It had also picked up on the same story but a day later than the Daily Mail where it was positioned on page 7. However, they had fleshed it out with a more sinister motive for the deaths and headed their article:

'INNOCENTS DIE IN MURDER RETRIBUTION'

Again the two young children were mentioned. Over the weeks following, neither paper had follow-up stories so all Emma could deduce was that no next of kin came forward to confirm or deny the actual tragedy. Or perhaps that maybe the police had put an embargo over the investigation? But if so, why?

'Well, for a minute it looked as if they could have been my parents,' Emma thought as she borrowed a pen and paper from her neighbour and wrote down the names in full and the dates of the newspaper articles and ordered photocopies at the counter. She handed over the £1.20 fee and gingerly walked back out through the big oak doors feeling triumphant but now extremely tired to add to her already queasiness. Once outside, she checked her financial situation by counting up the remaining loose change in her bag and decided to nip into a snack bar and buy a pasty and a soft drink. The only uninvited downside being that she would now have to endure an uncomfortable walk home in her 3" heels, but this was outweighed by the fact that she would be refreshed from a little nutrition of sorts.

Feeling exhausted, dizzy and not a little desperate, Emma went straight to her usual patch. She did not even have time to freshen up as the monkey on her shoulder was constantly chattering about getting a rush and getting it now. On her journey home she had texted four of her usual dealers and of those who were interested, none of them could make a rendezvous to meet her deadline, nor were they prepared to sell on credit, so she knew she would be calling on the last resort. Not her ideal but 'beggars can't be choosers,' she thought resignedly. She weaved unevenly across the rough ground praying that her stiletto heels would not snap at any moment on the broken brickwork and bits of masonry underfoot. She sidestepped the bent-wheeled bikes and distorted prams, detoured around the various makes of rusting stripped down cars and cautiously avoided the innumerable broken bottles whilst turning a blind eye to the discarded condoms; shuddering to think how many of those had probably been intended for her. Even if she had not known the two pushers personally she would have recognised them straight away for what they were. Both leant against a long ago burned out car that had been jacked up on bricks so that at least it was horizontally level and acted on their behalf as a makeshift storeroom.

"Hi guys," she called. "I need a gram and I've no cash. Are you interested? Usual terms?" Yes, usually they were but it depended on how brisk business had been and whether their boss had given them any grief recently. Fortunately business had been good so far and 'no' to the latter too. Not today anyway.

"Hello Ems. Always good to see a generous face. Are you up for the two of us then? Merchandise is shooting up, do you get it, shooting up. And so as not to have any mis-understanding before the deal is struck, it's a blow-job for Billy and me and I get to go first. Right?" demanded Huey.

"Yes, I'm always willing to satisfy someone else's craving if I can get a little something to satisfy my own in return," she replied untruthfully and without enthusiasm. Feeling very much under the weather, it was the last exercise Emma wanted but, forever the professional, she said, "Come on then, get a move on. I'm starting to shake a little here. And let's hope you've had a shower or a bath since the last time?"

"Well, if not, that might add a little extra spice, don't you think? Step into the office. Watch your head, or maybe that should be watch my head," joked Huey.

"Less of the humour and more of the action with that zip Mister Mouth. I hope it's ready. I haven't time today to be playing with little boys."

Six minutes later with Huey's parting shot of, "I'll pimp for you anytime Ems," Emma was tiptoeing back over the rubble, again anxious to keep her heels intact, but this time with a small cellophane packet clutched in her hand as well as a bitter taste in her mouth. She used the last of the water she had bought earlier to swill the worst of it out but was impatient to get back to the flat so that she could give her mouth a good dose of mouthwash and her bloodstream a good syringe of heroin. She had managed to put a smile on the pushers' faces and now she was hoping it would be her turn to feel that extra warm glow she only experienced with her hypodermic 'friend'.

But Emma's brain was playing devil's advocate with her being desperate to score but in a quandary as to whether she would OD again. Fortunately, on arriving closer to The Towers the decision was taken out of her hands. A police officer guarded her path. He was slouched in a police car so advertising his presence from at least 100 metres. Emma reached the end of the waste ground, did a double take, instinctively thought that they wanted to reconvene their interview, and swore profusely. She berated anybody who would listen with, "Why is my life so full of shit?" And a few other choice expletives but not even the scurrying rats cared to stop, look and listen.

Like the majority of the estate, it was expected that your respect for the police would be less than favourable, in fact it was inbred, and all Emma could assume was that they were going to try and frame her for Peter's murder. It never crossed her mind that she might be seen as a victim who needed police protection. A live victim at that, one who was quite possibly in serious danger for that very reason; and even though her life had been shit over the last 24 hours she would still never have considered the other option of aiding the police.

CHAPTER EIGHT

After a week of driving around with very little to show for his efforts, Vinny's patience had grown exceedingly thin. He was almost in need of erecting some form of warning sign saying 'danger - patience at an end, proceed with caution', with it having by now reached its critical lower limit. And to add insult to injury he fairly jumped out of his skin at the ringing of his mobile.

Pops rang, and of all the times he could have chosen. I tell you I was a bit short with him. I hope he doesn't bear a grudge like he does with some of the others. Bruiser Boris had a run in with Pops a few days before I left and it was still simmering on my departure. He did not dare look Pops in the eye. I'm sure he would have had his head bitten off, and all he did was help Harmless Andy put an end to one of our competitors. We call him Harmless because one of his arms doesn't work right, I think he had polio as a kid but Pops still took him on and so expects him to earn his crust. But it was Bruiser who did the topping, Harmless just watched mesmerised as the guy's blood shot up in the air, after Bruiser had slit his throat, just like a geyser. That's what Bruiser said anyway when Pops put a gun to his head with one bullet in, like in that Deerstalker film, I think it was. Although come to think of it that was about war, wasn't it. Where was I? Oh Yer, holding a grudge. To be honest I don't even think he noticed. He asked how it was going and actually said I'd done well finding out he was in

Scotland and not the Midlands, told me Mum missed me, and reminded me to keep moving so that no one would be able to trace my movements.

As well as impatient, Vinny now found himself lonely and not a little homesick, which surprised even him especially when he had all the toys to hand that he could ever desire, but that phone call had geed him up in a good way, and he now wanted the deed done, a hero's welcome return, and his own bed. But he knew that was not going to happen without either his gun or knife handle being carved with that know-all notch to signify that Barnham was dead and the family honour had been restored.

*

Jessica was as equally refreshed as she was relaxed when she rang back through to the office for part two with Tess, her manager. The phone rang out for longer than expected so she switched it to loudspeaker mode and replaced the handset in the cradle. Whilst she was reorganising her remaining files Joe's voice interrupted her concentration. Jessica picked up the handset and was informed that Tess' meeting had run on longer than expected but as Joe looked through the conference window he could see that it appeared to be breaking up. "I'll catch Tess as soon as possible and let her know you're available. Shall I say you'll ring back in 10 minutes?"

"Yes, Joe. Thanks for that," replied Jessica resignedly. She took out her frustration on the handset by slamming it down with force; and was just in the process of beginning a rhetorical rant, when the phone ringing tone suddenly preempted her. "Hello, Jessica speaking."

"Hi Jessica. Sorry to be messing you about like this and be encroaching on your weekend. The meeting overran somewhat, it's finished now and everyone's been accompanied off the premises, so if you've got your files together we can sign off the balance of those reports. Then you can treat yourself to a well-earned glass of wine and put your feet up."

Jessica reached over to her filing cabinet and said, "Good idea. Got the files here, so I better look sharp and we can then both toast ourselves. Right, there are two left. First one is 'File S29'. It concerns a mother living with her three children in a small two bed flat. The man of the house works away on the oilrigs and when he comes home it's usually fireworks. I've filed written statements from her and her neighbours stating that she and her three children have all suffered physical abuse. Incidentally, the couple is not married; she is in fact his common-law wife, which adds a further twist to the relationship. Anyway, on his last visit home, four weeks ago, he was particularly violent towards the eldest child, who is only eight, and no surprise but he is not her biological father. He proceeded to force himself on his partner, including the act of sexual intercourse without her consent, so now she's been in contact with the police alleging rape, which he's obviously categorically denied."

"Have you interviewed him to get his side of the story? Is he being maligned here?" asked Tess.

"Yes and no, I interviewed him when they were both together, let me see, three months ago; before this latest level of abuse arose. He came across very sane and inferred that she was the problem, so I don't know if he has some kind of hold over her which he's using as a lever to manipulate her mental and physical behaviour. I saw them both on this latest occasion mentioned earlier, but again, that was a joint interview and the woman could have felt too intimidated by him to state the true seriousness of the violence in the relationship. It was at this time that I forcefully informed them that with the children being exposed to such a volatile environment, the chances of Social Services taking decisive action would be high. Subsequent to that meeting the mother has admitted that her eldest has been attacked and I've since had an email from the police which confirms the reporting of the alleged rape and states that they haven't been able to question him further with regards to the allegation as he hasn't been seen locally for over three weeks, even though he's not yet due back in the North Sea. They have no other clues at present as to his whereabouts. Perhaps he's gone somewhere to cool off and hide below the public radar."

"Well, I'm sure she'll be happier with him away at the moment. Don't see that we can do anything else about it just now," said Tess with a little sadness in her voice.

"And finally," replied Jessica taking Tess' last comment as an indicator to move on and now somewhat more upbeat. "'File S42'. The one you earlier instructed Joe to ask me to specifically visit asap. This involves a couple just made for each other, both living together with no real commitment, and from the sounds of it, stealing off each other at every opportunity. The two of them are addicted to smack and the female has tried to commit suicide on two occasions, the last time, being within the previous six months. She's been consistently receiving reasonable money in benefits consisting of housing allowance etcetera and that's mostly thanks to her four-year old daughter, not her present partner's child by the way. DSS don't yet know that he co-habits and I'm not sure how often he's actually in the flat as their love-hate relationship means that she falls soft and takes him back then pushes him away again when their true personalities come to the fore. I think there is one playing the Jekyll and the other the Hyde.

"Anyway, Social Services are monitoring her month on month to make sure the little girl is being treated well. You did request that I make an urgent visit due to a report that there had been 'shouting, 'f'ing and blinding' and the banging of anything that could make a noise', which incidentally had been going on at all hours of the night too, according to neighbours. It culminated with the man dislocating her jaw and hitting her in the face so hard that she needed seven stitches. Luckily for her, a friend across the landing took in her daughter whilst she went in an ambulance to get patched up.

After these flare ups his usual tendency is to storm out, but that's not before he's nicked all her benefits' money. He then either lives rough or looks up one of his other floozies. Very much a 'fly by night' character: here today and gone tomorrow. The woman is distraught at the prospect of having her daughter taken away so I'm working with the DSS to hopefully come up with a positive strategy and plan of action. And that wraps it up really".

"Yes, Jessica I'm sure it does. Please ensure that all of the detailed reports are filed in the archives by late Monday with any contact mobile numbers and email addresses, if they have such a thing. These cases sound like they could run and run, so the more ammunition we have the better. And thanks for your patience. I can understand that you won't have wanted to split the job in two but I couldn't move that meeting for 'love nor money'. Have a good weekend."

"Yes, have a good weekend yourself. I hope it's relaxing. Glass of wine here I come," replied Jessica with more cheer in her voice than she felt in her heart.

*

DI Barnham had no cheer in his heart either; in fact he had been absolutely livid with PC Blackwell. So much so that he literally threw the book at him and the waste bin too. Emma Flynn, their only suspect or witness, depending on which way you looked at the case, had done a runner; right under PC Blackwell's nose. Within 20 minutes the PC had followed the DI back to the office with somewhat of a hang-dog look about him, but he did manage to avoid knocking over any newspaper vendors or laden shoppers en route; so that was at least a plus in his favour. He had arrived back just as the next update meeting had got underway. "Right Blackwell as a penance you can pin up all the pics from the third murder case," photographs which had been emailed over whilst Barnham and Blackwell were trying not to lose Emma.

"Now as we've no witness to speak of, the rest of us will have to use our own intuition and foresight as to what went on at this specific crime scene. WPC Whitely, can I trust you to put out an APB for Emma Flynn. And I particularly want 24 hours surveillance on her flat, and I mean 24 hours, every day until we track her down. PC Blackwell once we've finished here, you're doing the surveilling, if there is such a word? So you better nip off to Boots for a toothbrush. I'll send PC Tranter to relieve you when I think you've made up for your slackness. Right, the dead body in the skip; some of us were at the scene but for the benefit of those here present who were not, who is going to present the information," asked the DI?

"Sir, I've checked over my notes – so I could do that."

"T/DC Murray that would be a delight. Away you go."

"Right, at 4am on Friday morning, that's this morning. A 999 call came through stating that two bodies had been spotted in an up-turned rubbish skip just off Queen Street Gardens on Gloucester Lane. The instigator of the call is a postal worker at St James Post Office on James Craig Walk, the one near Leith Street. The caller was cycling to work for his early shift when he came across the victims. There was a squad car and ambulance on the scene within 20 minutes and with me being allocated for the emergency night shift I was one of those called out to attend the incident, which is why, if you remember, Sir, I was the one who woke you. I was also the officer who interviewed the still shocked cyclist but he couldn't supply any further information other than being responsible for finding the bodies. So after taking his name, address and other contact details I advised him to go back home, ring in sick and have a stiff drink, even though it was still not yet 5am! And if his employers needed confirmation as to why he'd not turned in I told him we would verify his excuse.

"The bodies were both found in a horizontal position with the man on his back and the woman, who we now know to be Emma Flynn ..," she gave a slight turn of her head in the direction of PC Blackwell, "... on her stomach. At first we presumed that both were dead but on closer examination it became apparent that the woman, Emma Flynn, was still breathing, although very shallowly. Forensics had a team on site within 30 minutes and the crime scene was sealed off and photographs quickly taken as the paramedics strongly advised that the woman should be rushed to hospital because she was in serious danger of losing her life. Apart from anything else she could have died of hypothermia due to her lack of suitable clothing for this time of year. My observations of the male body were that he was probably late thirties, casually dressed, hands and feet bound with adhesive tape, as our previous victims, and for whatever reason he also had a drip hanging off the top of the up-turned skip that led down directly into his arm."

"What exactly do you mean by a drip?" asked PC Tranter. "Is it one you'd find being used in a hospital?"

"Yes, exactly that. The ones that usually contain saline to replenish your body fluids or the blood bag type. Forensics was scouring the ground for any vital clues whilst Jamie Scott and his team stood around scratching their heads over this drip, feeding directly into the dead man's vein. Jamie was his usual ebullient self even though it was so early. I've written his comment down somewhere," she said fumbling through her notebook. "Ah yes, here it is. 'It must have been a right party for these two to have knocked themselves out in this way. Looks like this one overcooked it with his 'Heath Robinson device', don't you think?' I mean, really, you can't make it up! Jamie Scott told me to remind you that now we have a total of three murder cases on our hands so he's rushing through the results, hopefully before close of play today. He also said he was mindful of the fact that it was Friday and he's not going to miss another poker night for anybody, particularly Barmy Barnham. That's what he said, Sir."

"Good, if it speeds up the results I don't care if he's playing strip poker with the whole of the England women's football team!" replied DI Barnham with a grin, and then returned his attention to the skip photos. "So what do we all think? It was certainly an unusual and gruesome sight. Not in the least your cosy love-nest, and now as with no Emma Flynn to assist us I'll set out my own view of the scenario." Here he paused, took out one of his dummies and flipped it into his mouth, giving the 'silent seconds' a chance to build the dramatic effect. Then he began, "Imagine if you will: 'Girl meets guy either casually or planned; both attracted to each other, more so the guy, especially as we know Emma was scantily clad in her glad rags. Let's say they have a few drinks and do a bit of recreational drugs, to be confirmed; things get a bit heated and your, as yet not dead man suggests that they go outside in order to get to know each other a little better. She's up for it and knows just the spot where they can be alone, without any prying eyes; she takes him to the skip that she's previously reccied, and once there she doesn't give him what he's expecting but instead knocks him out and then sets to with the 'nursey' bit by applying the drip. We can assume that there is something powerful in that drip that killed him. Everybody buy that or has anybody got a different take?"

PC Blackwell responded, "Gov, I'm with you up to a point but you've met Emma," he said her name with a slight blush, "and you know what state she was in. I mean would you practically kill yourself at the crime scene to prove your complicity? Doesn't it really prove the exact opposite, her innocence?"

"Good point, PC Blackwell. Perhaps you might not be doing the full 24 hours after all. So what you're saying is that Emma may have been, unfortunately for her, in the wrong place at the wrong time and that there is a third person involved, the killer."

"Yes Gov. That's exactly what I'm saying."

"Well, we'll still keep tabs on her anyway. She wouldn't have done a runner if she didn't have something to hide," replied Barnham. "If nobody else has any views or opinions we'll wait for Forensics and the Path lab to get back with their findings."

As Forensics and the Path lab had been on the case since the early hours both had reports available by 3.00pm and 4.00pm respectively. Forensics was in written form sent via email whilst the Path lab was a Jamie Scott verbose, verbal statement with written confirmation to follow. DI Barnham was holding a meeting with several of the team chewing over the Forensics offering when Jamie rang. PC George Gough had been left with the task of manning the phones; and so, he ended up with his first introduction to Jamie Scott's wit and wisdom.

"Hello, Jamie Scott here. Is Barmy about?"

"Sorry Mr Scott, Barmy's … DI Barnham's in a meeting, but I'm in charge of the phones at present so if you'd like to leave a message?" replied PC Gough.

"No. I haven't got time to be hanging about waiting until he's free. I'll miss the game again and that would never do! Have you got a pen and paper, laddie? Good. I presume he received the email containing the photos, quite a big file really; but hopefully it turned up OK? Right, let's have a look at this fella. I'd say the time of death was around 2.00am but with what was going through him via that drip, he'd have had no idea what hit him and, no doubt, he'd have been well out of it within seconds of the needle puncturing his vein. His physical characteristics are: 5ft 10ins in height; 12st 4lb in weight; muscular body, so could be an active member of a gym; dark brown hair; blue eyes; 2 or 3 days stubble. Age wise, I'd say probably between mid to late 30's.

"Needle marks are there although not in great numbers, but his toxicology report does show cocaine amongst other things, which I will now expound on. The drip consisted of pure ketanest, which is a derivative of ketamine; but we also found benzodiazepines in his body and by taking both drugs together it increases the latter's effects. This concoction puts a whole new spin on 'speedballing'. You are getting all this down, aren't you? Do you want me to spell anything? Well, it will all be in the report anyway. Tell Barnham that this ketamine came to prominence with the dance culture in Hong

Kong in the late 1990's and it's been with us ever since. Apart from vivid dreams and hallucinations this stuff could 'knock a horse out and send it to cloud nine for a little R & R'.

"Where was I? Ah, yes. Now that I've had a fresh 'recently deceased' body to test, without the ravages of time or effects of water I'm confident that all three victims have been at least sedated with this form of cocktail but the first two were not exposed to the full drip volume! That leads me to surmise that we have a pathological pharmacist on the loose, who has more than likely turned into a ruthless murderer to boot. That's one and the same person, if you get my drift. Someone with the knowledge to combine fairly intricate drugs that aren't necessarily readily available. The other point of note is that this victim had a slightly unusual mark on his thigh which I can only conclude is made from an auto injector pen. This leads me on to think that he was either prone to anaphylaxis or this was indeed the method used to inject the initial dose in order to make the victim submissive. This fact has been proved by the presence of epinephrine in the 'toxi' tests. And as epinephrine is an adrenalin hormone used to counteract allergic reactions I rest my case. If I was in the assailant's shoes I would take out a quantity of epinephrine already supplied in the injector and replace it with my concoction of choice. So based on this theory I've backtracked on the previous two bodies and sure enough there is a slight mark on the first victim's thigh but some bruising, which must have been inflicted several days earlier, had masked the second victim's. Neither victim particularly showed up for these extra drugs but that is more than likely because one could have remained alive for several days or several hours, in the case of victim two, after the injector application. And one last thing, I've still no positive results yet from the dental screening on the teeth of victims one and two; the search area keeps getting wider so it will then take longer to achieve a hit. Have you got all that? … Gough, was it?"

"It was, Mr Scott and yes I have. I'm fairly adept at my

version of shorthand, you know 'old school', and I'll look up the drugs you've talked about on the Internet to make sure I spell them correctly for Barmy, sorry DI Barnham," replied PC Gough, relieved that the verbal report had at last come to an end.

"Good lad. Tell him I'm here until 4.30pm but not much later as it has been a very long day already."

After he'd done a little research PC Gough, knowing that the rest of the inquiry team was over-stretched, transferred as much of the new material as possible on to the whiteboard in the incident room; where it would sit adjacent to victim three's photos. It was not long before the DI's meeting wound up and everyone converged on him.

"Looks like you've been busy Gough. Are these your thoughts or have you had some divine inspiration?" asked DI Barnham.

"You could call it divine intervention, but actually if the truth be known it came from the mouth of the oracle himself, Jamie Scott. As you can see, I've written up all the salient points ensuring that I'm on the right tracks with the drugs that he mentioned. I can run through it whenever you're free, Gov."

"No time like the present. Anyone needing a loo stop and refreshment fill? Better do it now and I'll have a white coffee with sugar while you're at it; but none of the airy-fairy decaff stuff," answered the Governor.

Ten minutes later PC Gough was presenting the findings of Jamie Scott in his best professional manner. DI Barnham nodded at various points during the process but no one interrupted PC Gough's flow. For his rhetorical finale he gesticulated what he felt was Jamie Scott's best line. "The mixture of drugs in the drip could 'knock a horse out and send it to cloud nine for a little R & R'. Those are Jamie Scott's words not mine."

"Thank you PC Gough for that very informative

presentation, even to the inclusion of the humour of our good friend, Jamie. Now, if we add what Forensics came up with, we see quite a strong picture starting to build of what we can only presume is a very dangerous serial killer, and where that killer does and does not draw the line. Two bodies lying helpless and prone, ready to be despatched but only one is given the lethal drip. Two bodies with personal items, which would help with their identification but only one body is stripped of all identity. That tells us one of two things, that either, the killer targeted one person only and the second one just happened to be there accidentally or, that the killer was interrupted during the pre-planned operation. If it's the latter then the perpetrator must have been disguised in some way so that Emma would not be able to identify him and then he, in turn, neutralised her so she wouldn't get in the way of his task. Forensics drew a blank on fingerprints; they were hopeful the drip might reveal something but it's totally clean, so no clues there. We must set about making enquiries as to how all these medical supplies are being obtained and whether the killer is from a pharmaceutical background. In view of Emma running out of the hospital, what do we know about her, if anything? Do we have her on file? Has she got a record of any description? If she has, that means we'll have a photo of her and one of victim three, so we can show the two photographs together as a item around bars, restaurants and clubs. Someone's bound to have served them, or at least, seen them together."

"Sorry to butt in Gov, but after Jamie rang off and I'd sorted the whiteboard in the incident room I did a bit of research on our Ms Flynn and sure enough she's got form. It does appear Emma has various convictions and cautions for misdemeanours relating to, wait for it: theft, affray, drug abuse and possession, soliciting, in fact, the full bag of tricks, so to speak, but she's been off the records for at least six months."

"Good work, Gough. Thought I recognised her," replied the DI tongue in cheek, to smirks all round and continued, "no

I wasn't a client of hers. I'd have definitely remembered her then! Anyway don't start getting too giddy just because it's Friday. By the way, is her DNA profile listed in any of those files?"

"Yes, Gov," replied PC Gough, "in all her encrypted numbers' sequences and strands."

"Bloody hell, Gough. If I'd wanted a lecture on DNA I'd have called in Professor Stephen Hawking or someone! Where was I? Oh yes, I want you all to think about one thing over the weekend and that's 'MOTIVE'. Is it a turf war between incumbent drugs' syndicates thinning out the opposition or do we have some more of our Eastern European friends muscling in on the existing drug pushers' patches? I wouldn't be surprised if drugs aren't at the centre of these three murders, and if we find the link we can prevent any further escalation. We've been building a pattern of how the murderer operates but with this 'drip' thing he was obviously not confident that the body would remain undiscovered for a number of days. So we deduce that he is able to adapt, and no doubt did so in advance of this hit.

"And finally, I lied with regards to there being only one thing to think about; there are in fact three other points to mull over too. One - we still need an identification from the photo of victim two; at the same time consider whether all the victims are being transported some distance from their own stomping ground, making it more difficult to identify them but giving us a small chance of catching a body in transit. Two - we all continually think that the perpetrator is a man but turn your mindset on its head and think the improbable, that it just as easily could be a woman. And three - Emma Flynn, remember her? She must be found. She is the only person still alive linking us to the murderer and it is very likely that she's seen him or her. That being the case, with hindsight, her life must now be in danger.

"Whoops sorry, there is a four, I lied again – at present I don't envisage calling you in over the weekend but if there is an escalation in the case then all leave will be cancelled. Understood? As a team I really think we are now making progress, but we must continue to pull together. So go home, relax and refresh yourselves, and let's achieve some results on Monday."

CHAPTER NINE

Early one morning an opportunity had arisen as his target exited from his bedsit but Vinny had not quite plucked up the nerve or pulled out his gun in time, and so both the moment and Barnham had passed. He subsequently followed him to what can only be described as an outdoors makeshift field hospital site with bodies and drips lying around. He thought about completing his task there, but recognised that there were more vertical bodies wandering around than horizontal ones on the ground, and he would have required a much bigger weapon to which he could apply all the additional notches. So he reasoned it was for that reason alone he would drop back into the shadows.

Taking his job more seriously and now feeling somewhat of a pussy for his earlier failing on Barnham's doorstep, Vinny set off in the middle of the following night with the intention of a little target practise. Perhaps the odd bird in flight or maybe the felling of a four-legged rodent on the run might help to 'home in' his eye, and prove to be good starting points for the bigger picture.

What could be better than a little night-time driving? Well, not driving through a dodgy looking housing estate for starters. I mean I know the North East dock area of Newcastle is no oil painting but that estate did take the biscuit. Eventually I arrived at what looked like deserted wasteland. An area that must have seen better times but all I could see was just a series of broken down fences, snagging barbed wire, dangerously strange looking patches of overgrown vegetables and tumbled down weather-beaten shacks. Well that's what I saw, courtesy of the moon's luminosity, and there's no way you can argue any differently. It wasn't everyone's cup of tea but I'd say it was just the location I was after to while away a few hours without disturbing anyone from their slumber.

Art and the artist were at one as he loaded, took aim and fired at anything and everything, animated or not. Vinny's mind conjured up every figment of the imagination he possessed and he was getting a far greater buzz from the feel of the real thing in his hands than boring computers or comics had ever achieved. The only downsides being that more often than not he missed his intended targets whilst they never fired back, and as the shots rang out so too a chorus of dogs' howls began as they woke, turned their muzzles to the moon and expressed their annoyance. And unsurprising to Vinny that little thought in the back of his head saying it was wrong to take a life was not visiting him at present either. But tinkering around the edges was never going to achieve those elusive stripes to set him apart as a winner rather than a loser but at least it gave him focus as well as making him feel alive.

*

Emma took yet another two paracetamol chasers to follow the others she had been popping, like clockwork, every two hours. She cupped her hand into the overflowing barrel and gulped greedily of the water to help the tablets go down. She was certain she would regret this repetitive cycle of drinking from an unhygienic source but, with the external tap having been disconnected long ago, her options were limited. And in the scheme of things to come, she anticipated that a little extra stomach pain now would not go amiss.

She had holed herself up in an old shack, like a latter day Ned Kelly, on the run down waste ground posing as a euphemism for an allotment. She had made her way there circuitously after scarpering from the hospital, and her subsequent visits to the NRS and the library. Hunkered down with her back leaning against an uncomfortable wall and taking the regular stabs of pain in her stride she thought fondly of Jonnie. She resolved only to call him as a last resort, not because she did not find him attractive but more so, as she did not want to drag him into her nightmare life. One in this nightmare was already one too many. But her first priority was still to drink plenty of fluids if only to relieve her unquenchable thirst and then to find some way of easing her increasing anxiety and clammy sensation brought about by the unbelievable, almost animal, desire to inject more smack, and so take away that never relenting craving and angst.

From previous experiences she recognised these as the first symptoms of withdrawal and knew that they would be quickly followed by stomach cramps and nausea, soon spiraling her downwards into a very dangerous situation. At that point her mind would not be lucid enough to care for her own needs; and the hideaway she had chosen was as described, a hideaway, and therefore not easily found and far removed from sanitised too. She looked at and fingered the wrap longingly in her shaky hands, whilst at the same time glancing at herself in the cracked mirror hanging crookedly from a nail on the rough wooden planked wall. The reflective glass, one of the few spartan possessions that the old shack could boast of as paying homage to the 20th century. In her cursory glance she saw a face still wearing make-up, albeit now smeared across it rather than applied, reminding her of how she had earned her hit and, with fondness as well as disgust, of her negotiation and subsequent transaction with Huey and Billy. 'They both had certainly been satisfied with their part of the bargain,' she recalled. With an unknown willpower she clung onto her wealth without making any serious effort to prepare or inject it. Even in her present desperation she knew that additional unhygienic dangers would occur, due to the lack of sterile tools of the trade being at hand, and so add to her mounting problems.

The shack, which was definitely no 'Priory' as easily confirmed by the evident short supply of celebrities, had in its past life been rented by her uncle or one of her aunt's fancy men, she could not remember which. But that had been back in the days when healthy living meant 'growing your own', whereas now no one rented allotments because no one really cared enough about their own lives let alone how the planet was going to continue feeding them in the future. And should anyone have had the willpower to eat their quota, it was found to be far easier to steal the vegetables than grow them. But even in her pain and misery, with just a blister pack of paracetamols for company, she was continually wracking her brain in order to recall the remaining six hours of Thursday night, or at least she thought it was six and then the early hours of Friday morning. Unsuccessfully I might add, as her mind finally closed down and she drifted off into a fitful sleep. An uneasy sleep, which would be broken by its intermittent alarm clock interruptions: when her guts and bowels made their presence felt, and once when she was convinced that fireworks were exploding around her ears and dogs were barking at close quarters.

Again, she drifted but this time found herself mining the recesses of her mind for the remaining period, the one before she had come face to face with death. She recalled that her leaving of Melanie's had been uneventful and she had then arrived back home without any further inappropriate propositions. She had spent the afternoon chilling with a little help from BJ's stash, purloined as recompense for his presumption that she was always up for sex without reward. She had needed sleep badly and could not now knock BJ's gift because it certainly helped in that department. Early evening, found her drifting back to consciousness whilst subconsciously being serenaded by a cacophony of profanities, couched in the Edinburgh twang. All were emanating from what she presumed to be 'innocent' mouths as young as eight years old, maybe even younger; groups of children in three's and four's scattered across the landscape of desolation that in better days would have been once termed open parkland. And no doubt each of them were learning their craft and jostling for position in the pecking order of life.

She could stay in this ethereal reverie of the post high, courtesy of BJ, which by now had lost its altitude, and slowly starve to death, or more practically she could shake her bones and look for food. She had a desperate urge to eat, drink and search for her next hit, having had the taste for it. Dozily she arose to find herself still dressed in clothes from Wednesday, the day she had collected her benefits, and so unsurprisingly was now in desperate need of a shower.

The searing spray lashed her skin as it cleansed the rank smell and grime of her 'working day', refreshingly coating her in a new vitality for life. She patted herself dry and liberally applied deodorant whilst surveying her copious possessions, and eventually decided on one of her skimpiest outfits, nothing too tarty mind, just a little number which would both complement her figure as well as her eyes. She then raised those same eyes in thanks to Superdrug for their generosity in allowing her to paint a beautiful mask onto her tired face using their 'free' cosmetics, ones she had stolen over the previous three-week period. From start to finish the whole 'wonder woman spin around' experience took just thirty minutes with the result being that she had transformed herself into a different woman. A broken woman maybe but now she was revitalised and looking the part, to hustle for some food, a few drinks and who knew what else. She presumed that she would have to go through the rigmarole of identifying and targeting a punter, perhaps then letting him score to enable her to score too. And her body's alertness and anticipation was already concurring and inferring the sooner the better.

Dropping the latch and banging the door behind her, she stepped out for what she expected to be an evening of fun, and with that she thought philosophically, 'and so the world goes round and nothing ever changes'.

Experience had shown her that the bistros and wine bars in the centre of Edinburgh tended to offer the best opportunities. Businessmen, sportsmen, academic men and lonely men frequented these the most, but with most being innocent in their desire to just enjoy a drink, maybe a meal, and to embrace their friends' company. Although some probably had other ulterior motives. And it was these 'some' that Emma was gambling on attracting. However, Thursday night seemed particularly slow. She had already visited three of the bars and not had a drink in any. Her usual ploy was to walk in holding her head high and purposefully scanning the whole bar area as if searching for an acquaintance at a pre-planned rendezvous; and if unsuccessful she would then stroll into the ladies to give the illusion of already being part of that scene before moving on to the next bar. Tonight, the fourth bar on George Street brought her first result. As soon as Emma walked through the door she clocked a 'nailed-on' punter. He was close to the bar itself, nursing a pint of Stella and more encouragingly, already cultivating a slight glaze over his eyes as he himself scanned the room trying to make eye contact with any willing filly. Emma pressed play to gamble and took her chance. She approached the bar and ordered a glass of Pinot Grigio, and at the same time slightly nudged her target's arm.

"Sorry, did I spill your drink? Let me get you another," she speculated, followed by an open smile at the unsuspecting potential customer.

"No, no. It was nothing. Here let me get you one. What was it you ordered?" replied the said potential customer smiling in return as he discreetly but slyly focused on Emma's assets to the best of his ability, and she in turn began to reel him in.

"Are you sure? I've just ordered a Pinot Grigio. Thank you very much, you're too kind," replied Emma as, with the bar being crowded, she intentionally manoeuvred herself closer to her new found catch on the pretence that she could hear him better and vice versa. But the real reason was so that her breasts could lightly brush against his arm, as he remained half turned towards the bartender and half towards her. They introduced themselves. His name was Peter and he lived on the outskirts of Edinburgh and was having a night out as a way of treating himself after working hard for several weeks. Emma nodded positively but took whatever he said with a pinch of salt. And as the evening wore on so did he. His continual pints of Stella and frequent trips to the gents started to have their marked effect. Emma's hunger meant that she constantly grazed on the olives, breadsticks and peanuts scattered along the bar even though she was still confident that at the very least a good meal would be fleeced off her target before he became too comatose. She continually revealed a surprised look, as on each return from the loo he appeared reinvigorated and much more alive and upbeat. Being in the know she presumed he was taking something, most probably cocaine. On one of such trips he carelessly left his wallet on the bar, so Emma picked it up for safe keeping and 'borrowed' £20 from the wad for her trouble. 'At least the night won't be a complete wash out even if he does go AWOL or crash out on me,' she surmised.

On his return she handed the wallet back, leaving her hand on his for a few seconds longer than necessary, and scolding him for not being more careful in potentially throwing his hard-earned money about. By this time it was getting late and Emma was feeling tired, twitchy and concerned that he was possibly a time waster. The option of a romantic candlelit dinner had long since been snuffed out. Also she was becoming annoyed that he was liberally satisfying his urges but not offering her anything in return. Feeling that she had played by the book up to this point and possibly been a little reserved in her affection with only offering a few light touches to various parts of his body plus a little flirtatious necking, she recognised the time was right to move up a gear.

"Peter, what are your plans for the rest of the evening?" she asked casually.

"Erh, what do you mean, are you leaving me now. I thought we were getting on so well?"

"No. I don't intend going anywhere. In fact, I'm enjoying your company too but I'm thinking that maybe we need to be somewhere a little more private and secluded. It's a bit exposed here for playing lovebirds. But first I've got to say that I've noticed there might be something which you're not sharing with me."

"What do you know about my partner?" he blurted. "That bitch! What's she been saying?"

"No, calm down Peter, I'm not interested in your partner or anybody else for that matter. I'm referring to your trips to the loo. I mean we've all got our needs and secrets."

"What's it worth?" he retorted by way of negotiation.

"Well, I don't know what you're on but I'd hazard a guess at cocaine, looking at your alternating snowy nose, clean nose. My poison takes a little longer to prepare so we'd definitely need somewhere more quiet and intimate. The only problem is that I'm a bit short of the readies but if you're interested in helping I'm sure I could make it worth your while," she whispered amorously.

Peter's head jerked upwards as he desperately tried to hear her soft voice and follow the conversation that was now unscrambling through eight pints of lager and not many less lines of coke. Once the offer had been computed in his brain he took out his wallet, placed his hand on it as if a bible, and said just the one word, "Deal".

Emma stood up, offered her hand and helped Peter to his feet too, guiding him swaying and stumbling out of the bar and into the street. Whilst exiting she caught a fleeting glance of another customer staring at both of them. Emma presumed it was due to her pickup's condition, or perhaps a recognition of the trade that she was dealing in and perhaps the fact that she was intruding on this other girl's patch; whichever, she shrugged it off with the thought, 'well, we've all got to make a living!'

Once outside Peter informed her apologetically that they could not go back to his place, because of his partner and all that entailed, and Emma reciprocated the same, which was not true at all. But now being in a bit of a rush herself she said, "Before we get that far I need first of all to track down one of my usual dealers. I'll be no use to anybody if I don't have the comfort of my other 'friend' beside me."

Peter had not a clue as to what she was talking about but was happy to be guided in whatever direction the situation took him, twosome, threesome, what the hell, who cared what gender this friend was! They made an odd couple weaving around the edge of Queen Street Gardens towards Jamaica Street with Peter shuffling his feet and Emma tugging him onwards faster and faster as she became physically more agitated by the minute. Suddenly she stopped and turned to him saying, "When we find the dealer, I don't want you to say a word. I'll look after the negotiation side and you just hand over whatever cash is involved. It will be around forty quid. You have got that on you, haven't you?"

"And what am I getting out of it?" slurred Peter.

"Don't worry. I'll give you what you want but first of all I've got to get this angst laid to rest. So here's the deal, I'll buy a small dose of methadone just to tide me over the next half hour or so and also buy a wrap for later, you know, for when the methadone starts to wear off. That way we both come out winners," she replied in quite a businesslike and democratic manner.

As they neared their destination Peter handed over his wallet and made a detour behind a row of dustbins with a mumble, "You're on your own. I think I'm going to throw up". Emma acknowledged his intention and carried on until she came upon the white Mercedes with its engine running and Ace Hood's 'Double Cup' blaring out of the pimped up audio system. The bass woofers rocked the car far more than it would have been rocked driving at speed over The Meadows parkland. Emma approached it, accompanied by the orchestration of her friend Peter throwing up his hard bought beer, hoping in her mind that sex with him would be limited to a hand job. She could not contemplate going anywhere near his bile-riddled mouth especially as now her appetite was only for her even closer friend 'heroin'. And being in charge of the cash, she greedily considered increasing the dose this time round, even allowing for the effect of BJ's stash still in her system. She rapped twice on the blacked out driver's window and it soundlessly slid open to the deafening release of white noise emanating from the interior. Shaking her head from the eardrum violation she said by way of greeting, "What ya, Zlatko. How's it hanging?"

"What's you's after, bitch?" replied Zlatko graciously.

"How much will 2g of heroin and 20mg of liquid methadone knock me back?"

"Which H is you's after? There's a more pure version just arrived if you're interested."

"What price are we talking about for that and the methadone?"

"Forty euros to you."

"What's that in Scottish notes Zlatko, and why the euros? You're not even in the EU yet, are you?" retorted Emma huffily.

"OK. OK. Thirty-five smackers in your money and it's the boss, init? He says we've got to practice for the change over, so that's what we're doing."

"I've only got £30 tops. But I still want the good stuff. Are you interested?"

"You drive a hard bargain, bitch, but as long as you promise to come back for more I'll do it at £30 but be careful with the H. I've got to tell ya that it's powerful and already has a dodgy street cred with some of my customers, if you know what I mean. Do po-kasno."

Peter wandered onto the scene just as Emma knocked back

the methadone. She caught sight of him, held up her hand and shouted, "I'll come to you." As she approached she linked up with him and continued, "They don't like strangers getting too close. I think their ID's a bit suspect, not to mention the fact that they're dealing in illicit drugs. As she handed him back his wallet she jokingly said, "You should be happy anyway. I've just saved you a fiver on the deal. I'd buy some lottery tickets with that; you never know your luck. Are you feeling better, by the way?"

Peter, knowing that he had already parted with £30, nodded in the affirmative and in all honesty he did look to have a slightly healthier pallor. "Good. Let's find somewhere secluded and see what we can do for you now," replied Emma who was already feeling more generous due to the afterglow effect of the methadone on her mind and body. They wandered back towards the Gardens hand-in-hand almost like two young lovers in search of a quiet spot for an intimate moment. As they approached, they unexpectedly found the gate locked but spotted an empty upturned skip on one of the side streets, outside a partly renovated terraced house. Emma said, "This looks as good a place as any if you're going to be chivalrous and put your jacket down." Peter was too eager and in too much of a hurry to worry about a laundry bill and so agreed instantly. They made a comfortable, as possible, bed area on which to transact his £30 investment as Peter added in jest, "Mm. 'Skip sweet skip.' A bed for my Lady. Just need a quick pee now, won't be a mo, don't start without me."

He only went 25 metres to find a secluded spot at which to relieve himself but that turned out to be the last 25 metres' walk of his life. As he approached his chosen comfort stop a dark figure emerged replete in black ski mask and wielding what he thought was a felt tip pen, not dissimilar to some kind of crazy midnight graffiti artist. In an instant, the 'artist' aimed the pen at Peter's thigh and it instantly hit home. Peter fell as if shot by a hunting rifle and lay totally prostrate 25 metres away from his last possible fuck. Emma became impatient as she waited; more so because she was becoming desperate for her hit rather than the prospect of Peter's amorous advances. Totally oblivious of the recent attack she blindly followed in the direction of Peter's footsteps and stumbled across him lying on the ground, lifeless. She had no idea as to what had occurred but her immediate panic-thought was to run and quickly, before the police arrived. In the near pitch-black night she surveyed the scene to orientate herself as to which side of the Gardens she was presently on, but her sight had been diminished by the drowsy effect of the methadone.

Whilst she deliberated the black figure walked silently towards her 'face on' and came to within two metres before Emma even knew that anyone was there. Emma looked into the eyes of the as yet mystery person but her brain was whirring and computing that no ordinary decent person would wear a ski mask in Edinburgh, not well after midnight anyway; unless they were up to no good. Before her brain's computation had completed its findings Emma saw that the figure in black was looking directly at her too. Both pairs of eyes confronted each other and revealed recognition. The black figure now lunged unexpectedly, without the eyes giving any advance indication of such a movement, then threw its right arm out and grabbed Emma in a headlock. Emma struggled but weakly due to tiredness, alcohol, and the various remnants of her earlier heroin hit still in her bloodstream and the dose of methadone that she had eagerly swallowed, what seemed to her like a lifetime ago. The ski mask's voice said coolly, "Sorry sweetie. Unfortunately for you, you're going to have to go the same way as 'him' but I can be generous and offer you the choice of how."

Emma's face took on the look of puzzlement as she tried to comprehend the meaning of this option with her only immediate thought being, 'I'm too young to die. I've still too much to do!' But seeing the silhouette of a helpless Peter lying prone at her feet convinced her that it was pointless to be concerned about either of their futures.

"Come on sweetie I'll have to hurry you. I know you've had a drug pick up as I've been tracking this guy all night. If you've still got it I can let you fly that way as long as I'm guaranteed that there's enough for an OD. At least it might be a more 'business class' type of experience for your last trip; or you can go the way the sleaze ball's going," said the 'man in black' quite matter of fact. Emma reluctantly yet meekly chose the former and slowly revealed her cherished wrap tucked away in her bra front. As she handed it over she too felt the auto injector suddenly jag her thigh.

The killer now knew that both victims were unconscious but to be on the safe side still bound Peter's hands and feet with tape as was becoming of the serial killer's ritual trademark. Emma herself was not bound, it only being her misfortune to be an accessory, for having hit on the guy in the first place rather than being a specific target. Both bodies were half carried and dragged back to the skip and laid next to each other. The murderer worked quickly, conscious that other innocent couples might stumble upon them in their quest for a love nest of their own or perhaps a prostitute in search of the last trick of the night. The drip was out of the rucksack and connected to the chain bucket fitting at the top of the skip within 30 seconds and inserted into Peter's arm within another 30. As the float on the drip began to flutter the black figure then directed attention to Emma. She lay serenely where she had been placed so allowing the killer to take a syringe from the rucksack and set about preparing the highest high of all. Once completed, a suitable vein was sought and found in Emma's slender yet pockmarked arm, and 20 seconds later the 2g of heroin was on its rampage around her physiology. Emma, still out for the count from the auto injector pen drug, would be in no position to report back to Zlatko as to whether this batch of heroin was more pure or not, but he was right in forewarning her of its dangerous properties, although not necessarily for the right reason.

'Two bodies, both dead, to all intents and purposes.

Perhaps one needlessly,' contemplated the grim reaper. But, even though leaving the slightest clue could turn out to be a dangerous oversight, the killer could not help feeling a little remorse for the totally wasteful and unnecessary death of the girl. No such emotion for the man but the girl was different. So different, in fact, that the murderer, completely out of character, could not resist planting a small kiss on the female victim's forehead before quietly leaving the scene.

CHAPTER TEN

Saturday morning saw DI Terry Barnham arise early and make a few positive decisions. The first was to charge his body with his early morning caffeine boost, no change there then. The second was to take a brisk walk, which would see him circling around Grosvenor Crescent and ending up at the newsagents located at the top end of Palmerston Place, once there he could carry out his third and fourth decisions. He had patronised the shop on many occasions to buy his 'dummies', the cigarettes that he never lit but which needed replacing regularly as they tended to become soggy when sucked continuously; but those visits were usually on his way to or from work, occasions when he used another form of transport other than his legs. Today, however his order was different, a pack of dummies was indeed required but in order to increase newspaper circulation figures and give the local economy a boost at the same time he also picked up a few of the national dailies. Well, the Red Tops in reality. 'There's a limit as to what a DI's salary can stretch to,' he thought defensively. As he joined the already busy queue leading up to the counter he glanced at the front-page headlines. Shock hit him like an unexpected sonic boom on a tranquil summer's day, and as if in a trance he retraced his steps to the newspaper racks to check out the local dailies too. A fellow shopper stepped aside giving him an inquisitive look as if questioning his unusual movements. Glumly, he then rejoined the back of the now even longer queue, on its slow shuffling journey to the counter.

Eventually, Phil the shopkeeper said, "Hi Terry. It's a big shop today then. Wondered if I'd be seeing you, what with all this going on in the papers? It does seem like you're being picked out as the scapegoat for not getting the results. But keep your chin up; the murderer is bound to make a mistake sooner or later. They always do, well on telly anyway. That's £13.20 with the cigs."

Terry looked at Phil sheepishly as he pulled a £20 note out of his wallet before replying, "Unfortunately, the telly's usually all fiction; they can make it up as they go along, so they have a bit of an advantage there. But you're right, I'm going to have to dash back home, take all this in and pray for a breakthrough," he replied guardedly, with his thinking being on far more serious lines than his conversation. 'This doesn't reflect well on me. I've got to assimilate all this negativity, formulate a plan and try to identify the mysterious source who has been blabbing to the press; and do it all at the same time. If it's one of mine, there's going to be some shit flying. Probably will be flying anyway, so I better make sure I'm proactive and deflect it before it sticks on me,' he concluded.

Phil handed him the change with a cheery, "Yeh, well remember Terry, 'while there's life, there's hope'."

"Yes, thanks for that encouragement, I will mate. But I didn't have you down as a budding philosopher Phil, or is that one of your own quotes?"

"Not unless I'm related to Cicero. It's his actually, but it still holds true today, don't you think?"

Terry left the shop carrying his bundle, which made him look like an overgrown paperboy, and at that particular moment in time that did seem like the far better career prospect. He also felt just a little pang of concern that Phil might have missed his way in the university of life too.

He got to within 400 metres of the flat when his mobile chirped. Of the two choices available to him he chose the one of answering the call. Wrong decision as it was his boss, Chief

Inspector Brogan. Barnham pressed receive, "Barnham here."

"Hello, DI Barnham. It's Chief Inspector Brogan. Have you seen today's papers? The murder inquiry is all over them. I thought we'd agreed to keep it under wraps for the moment? And who's this source they keep banging on about, must be someone in your department? Have you got a plan of action in place?" asked the Chief Inspector with a sound somewhat of annoyance in his voice.

Barnham thought that if the governor carried on at this rate he would not be able to remember any of the questions even if he was ever going to be given an opportunity to answer them. "Yes Sir, I've got the papers right here. I'll be reading them front to back, well excluding the sport."

"Barnham. This is too serious a situation to be flippant!"

"Sorry Sir, I honestly don't think it's one of my team leaking information but I'll get them together and read them the riot act just in case. Although, thinking about it, it could just as easily be someone out of the Pathology lab or Forensics," he answered defensively to deflect the attack on his department and himself.

"Could be right? Could be right? But whatever the case we need some ID's on your dead victims, which hopefully then, should lead to tracking down this mad murderer. Give me an update on Monday on how you propose to move forward. Meanwhile, I'll talk to the PR department and try to get the press off your back."

"Thanks Sir. That would be helpful. I will report back on Monday with the plan of action as instructed. Is that all, Sir?"

"No, there is just one more thing. I'm going to give you Tess Danvers' phone number. She runs a division of The Borders Agency out in Dalkeith, generally involved in looking into attacks of physical and sexual abuse in adults. But that's not the reason I'm telling you this, it's more about one of her caseworkers who happens to be into psychology too. And I've had it on good authority that this particular caseworker can plot a good 'profiling' pattern, which should at the least, help us understand more fully how the killer's mind works. I've already spoken to Tess, Ms Danvers, so I want you to give her a ring and get hold of this colleague. Have you got a pen?" He then began dictating both her office and home numbers.

Barnham did have a pen, and so with not a little gymnastic skill he spent the next minute hopping on one leg, like some amateur actor auditioning for the part of Long John Silver in the local pantomime, whilst writing down the numbers on the edge of a newspaper, and with his own phone glued to his ear, thinking 'don't try this at home folks'! He then said, "But Gov, I not convinced about this looking in people's heads thing. It's ..."

He did not get a chance to finish as the Chief Inspector retorted, "It's not a request Barnham. It's an order. We've not heard the last of this press onslaught and when TV and radio pick it up we'll be pushing against the tide on all fronts. So you'll take whatever help is offered from whatever quarter with no questions asked. Now get out there and find that killer. I'm not going to take the rap if you fail. I've already got pressure from above, as apparently, a small percentage drop in tourism will see a serious shrinking in the Scottish GDP. And as I have overall responsibility for this case rather than a travel agency or the Government's Ministry for Tourism, I've only got one boat to burn, if you get my drift!" And as a final sign off to add his grammatical full point, he said, "Enjoy the rest of your weekend".

"I fully understand where you're coming from, and you too, Sir," Barnham replied meekly. The rest of the journey back to the flat was in no way as enjoyable as the one out, not least with the amount of commuters driving past laughing and tooting at his Karate Kid pose. Barnham, already shaken with the newspaper headlines was now absolutely beside himself with the content matter of his mobile conversation. He rushed back home and, without even considering another coffee, began feverishly scanning through the papers for all articles referring to the murders. Page after page of bad press opened up before him in an array of typefaces with all the headlines in large and powerful font sizes so as not to be missed, and to add insult to injury, all were bold, very bold. He scanned them all feverishly, so as to get over the total dismay of what lay in front of him as quickly as possible. Then he made a decision. 'I'll now have that coffee, get out one of my 'dummies', and re-read everything again.' The Red Tops and local dailies were certainly not holding anything back.

3 bodies In the Borders- Tourism board crying out for action

The tourism industry has begun a campaign whereby hotels, B&B and self-catering facilities' owners are all lobbying their local MPs in the hope of preventing any further cancellation of future bookings to the area. One distraught owner commented, 'Bookings have dropped through the floor since the murder psycho started with these killings. People don't want to come on holiday and not feel safe. So I can't see them coming to Scotland until he's behind bars'. DI Barnham, the inspector in charge of the case was unavailable for comment. This paper will endeavour to champion the tourist industry's cause and help keep Scotland at the centre of the UK tourist trade.

AND THEN THERE WERE THREE!

Is it safe in the Scottish Borders? Are you all still there? We're asking you the public if you know of any missing person(s) near you. If yes, ring the police or the hotline number below. We're hoping to follow up with descriptions shortly. We have it on good authority that the dead body count is now three. What's going on - is it a vendetta? Do we have a serial killer on our hands or is it just a coincidence that three murderers strike at once?

Ring 0800 888 999 now if you know of anyone unaccounted for. Or if you prefer confidentiality get in touch with the paper's own editorial staff.

THREE IS THREE TOO MANY

Today we ask whether there is a 'breakfast serial killer' in our midst in the Scottish Borders? Every morning we seem to be waking up to more dead bodies. Sources say that three bodies have been found, generally in the mornings, over a three week period and the police are no nearer solving any of the crimes. We asked the spokesperson representing DI Barnham, the DI in charge of the case, for confirmation, but the only printable answer was 'no comment'.

THREE MURDERS - NO ID-MORE LIKE NO IDEA!

Reliable sources tell us that the police now have three murders in the Scottish Borders. Can it be so coincidental that three killers all struck at a similar time or do we deduce that it is one killer, making that person a serial killer! We tried to put that question to DI Barnham, who our source tells us is in charge of the investigation, but to no avail, except to say that they were looking into a number of leads which our source denies exist. So let me tell you, DI Barnham, on behalf of the law-abiding citizens of Southern Scotland you better have some answers soon. As no leads are leading you nowhere and we might have to campaign to a higher authority to get the positive action this area needs and deserves to feel safe in our homes.

'CAN THERE REALLY BE A SCOTTISH SERIAL KILLER AMONGST US?

What to do? Barnham's wavering suggested the need for a checklist but he picked his phone up instead and began frantically pressing buttons. T/DC Murray was the first to open the text message and she groaned in dismay. 'Another Sunday screwed up. My mother won't believe that I've got to cancel again,' she thought whilst loading the weekly shop into the back of her 10 year old Micra. 'Small car for small shopping.' Still that's buying for one, for you!' she continued muttering to herself. But at least she would be able to postpone her trip to visit relatives in Yorkshire and would also have an excuse for not going to the gym, which she had been attending irregularly in the hope of shedding a few ounces in her never ending quest of winning her future beau's heart.

The totally unknowing future beau then punched in the home number of Tess Danvers, waited for the ringing tone to expire, listened to the answer phone message, delivered in a sexy husky voice that came as an intriguing surprise to Barnham, who cleared his throat quietly during its delivery before leaving a message. Thinking he had time on his hands he then squeezed into his cramped bathroom, showered and shaved. Well part shaved anyway until Crazy Frog interrupted the blade on its upward stroke on his left cheek. Grabbing a towel he went in search of his mobile whilst at the same time counting the length of the tune in his head. He pressed the green button just before the point at which he knew it would annoyingly drop the call. "Hello, Barnham."

There was a few seconds silence at the other end, which led him to believe that the frog had croaked and he had, indeed, missed the call. Just before his thumb descended onto the red button, a seductive voice said, "Yes, hello. Mr Barnham".

"Ms Danvers, hello. Thank you for getting back to me so quickly. I'm presuming you know why I called you?"

"Well yes I do. Chief Inspector Brogan said that you would be in touch, but I thought it would probably be in office hours, not this soon anyway. Incidentally, I'm intrigued as to how you knew it was me ringing you back?"

After a pregnant pause and a slight smirk from Barnham, he replied jokingly, "Well, you know, I haven't been in the police force this long without knowing who is ringing my bell, sorry phone. And has nobody ever told you that you've got a distinct sounding voice?" For 'distinct sounding' the DI was still reading 'sexy husky'!

Tess was enjoying this mild flirting, it was not something that happened every Saturday morning but her professional brain kicked in and she certainly did not want to appear too forward. "How may I be of help, Mr Barnham?"

"Call me Terry," he said invitingly. "I understand that the Chief Inspector has talked to you about the three murders that have recently been carried out on my patch. And, now, no doubt you'll have seen at least some of the bad press that came out today. Well, the Chief reckons that you may be able to help."

Tess' professional brain was now fully in focus, "Yes, the 'Chief' did brief me and yes, I've seen the Daily Record and the Scottish Sun. So I've a good idea as to why you have concerns about the three cases and yes, you can call me Tess, before you ask," she replied feeling a little tingly at the sound of his Geordie lilt.

"OK....Tess. Here's the situation. One of your colleagues is into psychology and my Gov reckons there could be a possibility of help with profiling the killer or killers. I don't believe in this nonsense myself, I think it's a load of gobbledegook but I am not going to start ignoring orders at this stage of my career. Wouldn't be good for the pension!"

"Good idea not to," replied Tess jokingly. "Your career could certainly take a nosedive if you did. And as for gobbledegook, I'll let my colleague defend that one. So if you don't believe in it personally, why the call? Why do you think it will help?"

"Erh, well, yes. Orders are orders, so obviously I do need to meet up with this colleague; I've not been given an option in the matter. Hopefully then I'll gain an understanding as to how it works. I've read a little about it in the past and been to the odd seminar but it's always been clouded by my ..," and here Terry stumbled over his words, "… my prejudice."

"There you've said it Terry. It's all uphill from here."

And as if a great sun visor had been lifted from in front of his eyes Terry reluctantly agreed. "Yes, yes, maybe it is? How quick can we meet? In view of the pressure Brogan's …… Chief Inspector Brogan's putting me under, any chance of tomorrow. I know it's Sunday and all that but 10am would be good for me."

"Must you always have your pound of flesh, so quickly?" Tess asked teasingly. "I'll have to get in touch with my colleague and check if there's a window available. Your number's already registered on my phone so I'll text you back when I've got an answer. Do you know where we are based?"
"Yes. It's The Borders Agency on Buccleuch Street in Dalkeith, isn't it? I'll wait for your message. Oh and by the way, your colleague, can you check on availability for after the meeting so that introductions can be made with the rest of my team? Bye for now then, I hope to see you tomorrow?" Terry sat looking at the phone and thinking, 'Well that went well. Don't know whose window she's after but hopefully she'll get what she wants. Could be that there's more to this gobbledegook than I first thought'. Whilst brewing yet another coffee he multi-tasked by proceeding to map out in his mind how to present the idea at the team meeting called for the next day, Sunday; at the same time being of the firm conviction that all his team had now received the text alert and would drop any prior commitments so as to be free for the 11am meeting with the 'so called' guru profiler.
His text from Tess came through mid afternoon, just as he had settled down to a homemade BLT, a hand-spooned cup of instant coffee and his latest in a long line of PlayStation 3 purchases, 'Mass Effect'; a game set 200 years into the future, which seemed to have a certain poignancy to Barnham at that

moment, as with bodies mounting up in the here and now, 200 years hence looked a rather inviting prospect. The text was short but not as sweet as the three sugars he had dumped in his coffee. 'Meeting arranged 4 9.45. c U thN. lol T.' Not being a great texter himself he just about had enough confidence to decipher what it meant, apart from 'lol'. The dreaded treble meaning: either denoting 'lots of love' or 'lots of luck' or 'laugh out loud'? "Well, the jury's out on that one, I'll have to wait and find out tomorrow, won't I,' he thought hopefully.

Understanding the vagaries of operating a 'Sat Nav' proved equally as challenging as the practicalities of texting for Barnham with him only exercising both experiences sparingly. His general concern with the Sat Nav was of it directing him up a blind alley only for a huge articulated lorry to follow behind and unknowingly crush him into dust. So admitting his navigational skills were at a lowly level on his list of capabilities and likely to be tested, and to prevent a belatedly late arrival for the meeting he set off on the Sunday morning at an exceptionally early hour. In actuality, his car would have been caught three times on the same speed trap through the centre of Dalkeith, had he not been obeying the speed limit. He did not need a fourth pass as Buccleuch Street, where The Borders Agency resided, was a left turning just off the High Street, immediately before King's Park, exactly where it had been on the previous three passes. 'Simples really,' he thought, 'perhaps the Sat Nav would have helped after all'. Still, being prepared paid off; even after his various circuits of the town he was still ten minutes early for the meeting, and so could arrive, calm, stress-free and in control. 'Who needs all this mumbo jumbo psycho whatnot to compose oneself,' he mused.

No sooner had he rung the bell than the door was opened by an attractive middle aged woman who carried herself very confidently, almost regally. 'Probably mid forties at a guess,' considered Barnham a little excited, 'and structurally sound with a wonderful facade'. As she introduced herself, and he instantly recalled that voice he thought, 'what am I thinking, she a very attractive woman, not a bloody building!'

"Hi, Terry. I'm Tess. I presume you found us OK, seeing as you're spot on time?" she said looking at her watch for effect. "Come this way. I've arranged coffee, sorry it's only instant, we're on a do-it-yourself job with it being Sunday. It's good to put a face to a name," she said smiling, by way of concluding her introduction.

"Yes Tess. I found it fine," he lied smiling back and then continuing, "and instant's never a problem as long as there's sugar." He followed close behind, catching the faintest waft of her recently applied perfume and thinking, 'Mm, when are you free for a night out?'

"I'm not going to say, 'not sweet enough then'? Oh bugger I've said it," replied Tess with her thought and speaking modes juxtaposed, so divulging the slight slip of her mask of perfection. Collecting herself she continued quickly, "My colleague's not yet here, so we'll go through to my office with the coffee and have a chat first, just so we can set down the ground rules."

Terry could see through her plan. At this point in time, she was no more interested in the ground rules than he was, and as they exchanged chitchat interspersed with ground rules rhetoric he could read her motive. His long service in the force enabled him to recognise a motive when he saw one and here was Tess' in plain sight; she was equally as interested in him as he in her. On finishing coffee the phone on Tess' desk beeped. She picked up, placed her hand over the mouthpiece whilst mouthing to Terry, 'my colleague,' then silence apart from, "Yes, in the conference room, in ten minutes. Is that OK?" Thirty seconds later she replaced the receiver and confirmed the conversation, "As I'm sure you gathered that's my colleague. Five minutes away." Inwardly, she then had a mild panic knowing that her first one-to-one opportunity with this possibly fascinating man was soon to be at an end but outwardly, she placed an almost imperceptible smile on her lips as she intriguingly thought, 'I can always request a debrief once the subsequent meeting's over'.

The ten minutes were up all too soon. Tess busied herself with putting the coffee cups, milk and sugar back on the tray. 'Not sweet enough,' did I really say that out loud, she thought embarrassingly? Terry, in order to appear busy too, rifled through his shoulder bag on the pretext of checking that he had all the necessary paper work as well as the newspapers. Both then walked in duck fashion along the narrow corridors, making their way to the conference room. Not being cognisant of having taken longer than ten minutes, Tess was surprised to see Jessica already sat there waiting with percolated coffee and pain au chocolat. Terry entered the room breathing in the wonderful inviting aroma whilst his sense of smell played tricks in its confusion at the detection of yet another perfume. He was put out of his misery by the pleasant surprise that Tess' colleague was also a woman, and a young beautiful woman at that. 'No building analogies required for this one,' thought Terry. By the fayre spread across the table he also deduced that she was sophisticated, practical, competent, generous and forward thinking; not to mention what other talents still hidden away.

Tess opened the introductions by way of, "DI Barnham this is my caseworker, Jessica Lambert. As your Chief Inspector mentioned she has a keen interest in profiling, specifically the workings of the minds of murderers, serial killers in particular. It's a talent she's studied and cultivated, although it's not usually required day to day in our jobs. You know it loosely as 'gobbledegook'."

"That's unfair! Pleased to meet you Jessica. Please call me Terry. I reserve DI Barnham for Sundays. Oh, it is Sunday. Sorry, only joking,' he said and thought 'Yes, I can see that there may be several hidden talents there, worth exploring.'

"Good morning, DI Barn... erh Terry. Hope this isn't a bit over the top. I usually enjoy a little taste of France on a

Sunday morning after my run, and even though I've missed the latter this morning, I still thought why not, anyway."

"Why not indeed," said Tess tartly, not being too good a sportsperson where 'one-upwomanship' was concerned. "Shall we make a start?"

As Terry felt the frisson between these two women, and began to enjoy yet another cup of coffee albeit this time filtered and complemented with a little French delicacy, he could not help but feel a touch of déjà vu too. Tess was busy wrapping up the preliminaries whilst he chanced a sly glance at Jessica thinking, 'I know you from somewhere? Where have we met before?' He was about to dismiss it due to the constant death of too many brain cells, thus making his recall less sharp than in years gone by, when Jessica put him out of his misery.

"I'm excited to think I can be of help to the police and that my gobbledegook may play even a small part in catching this madman, whom I've just been presumably reading about in the papers? As you may be aware I have always had a fascination with the science of reading people's minds and subsequently trying to predict their future moves. And ever since the conference we attended it became my ambition to put the theory into practice. You do remember that conference, Terry?"

"Indeed I do. Wasn't it Birmingham, a couple of years ago now?" he asked with an uncomfortable vagueness at both his uncertainty and also the fact that he had been found out ridiculing Jessica's newly acquired expertise. He did in fact remember the occasion well but for all the wrong reasons as in all honesty he had spent longer in the bars than in the conference hall. Even so, Jessica's beauty had made an impression then, and now here she was in the flesh once more, and admitting that she had noticed him there too.

"Last summer actually, but you're correct it was Birmingham. NEC if I have my facts right. And as you were informed at the time, if you had paid as much attention to the speakers as to the barmen, 72 per cent of cases where profiling had been called upon had proven successful in convicting the criminals responsible; with academic papers galore, both here and abroad, supporting these findings. So now we've verified that little statistic, shouldn't we be moving on?" said Jessica who now appeared to be wrestling the very control of the meeting from under her boss' nose.

Before Tess had chance to press the metaphorical green light to signify that the meeting should begin, Barnham chirped up, "Good idea, I'll start," and with a flourish he pulled out a selection of tabloids from his pseudo newspaper bag and walloped them down on the top of the desk. "In a nutshell, this is what we're up against! We've got a mole somewhere down the line and I'm being earmarked as the present scapegoat. By the way, I wouldn't bother wasting any more of your time reading these as all they tell you is that three people have been murdered, which is correct, but everything else is pure conjecture and speculation. And I've been given a whole 24 hours, starting from now to formulate a plan and report back to my Chief. That being the case, I've got a team meeting organised for 11am back at the incident room in Edinburgh and I'm hoping that you, Jessica, will be able to attend so I can introduce you as our newest team member. I trust that Tess informed you of that being the case? But even so, I've still got to say I'm not one hundred per cent sold on the idea of 'profiling' yet; although I'm not too old to be swayed into accepting a little change here and there."

Jessica opened her mouth to speak but the words floating through the atmosphere belonged solely to Tess. And what an atmosphere, as she almost spit them out, still smarting from being upstaged by both Jessica and Terry. "I understand your concerns and quite right too as although Jessica has had some success in this field it has only been in a limited practical capacity with the rest being purely theoretical. So, I'll be as interested as you in seeing how this particular project plays out. And yes, obviously she is aware of the onward meeting."

Jessica reciprocated sarcastically with, "I have studied

profiling for five years, largely in my own time, and as a supplement to my present career. My PhD thesis was based on that specific subject and just because there is a degree of apathy and scepticism surrounding the subject in general, and so too my own success rate, that in no way negates the reason for carrying it out in the first place. Nor is it a reflection on the success achieved in other countries, particularly, the United States; a country that believes in its use as a vital tool in aiding investigators rather than hindering them." Her words spewed out as from the barrel of a kalashnikov, without pauses for breath. "Oh and yes, I was advised of the meeting with the 'team', but that was this morning at 8.30am!"

Tess remained seated with the uncomfortable feeling that all the beanie points she had previously gained were now being stripped away or neutralised at best, and that Jessica's tantrum only made her look even more attractive in Barnham's eyes, if that was possible. She conceded defeat by saying, "Sorry Jessica it must have slipped my mind when we spoke on Saturday. But let's hope that the facts live up to the fictions, if you'll pardon my distortion of a good metaphor. You're right, the UK population in general is still a little disbelieving of these new fangled mind trips but if anyone can pull it off, I'm sure you can. Just please ensure that you find time over the next day or so to send in the completed written versions of the files we discussed on the phone on Friday. I want to ensure this department is up to date with its work before you're seconded for whatever period of time we're going to lose you." Without giving Jessica chance to reply she went on, "Gosh is that the time. You two better get a move on or you'll never make Edinburgh by 11.00am, what with all this Sunday traffic."

Terry Barnham began tidying his newspapers and notepad away whilst thinking, 'I can't believe I've just witnessed that, and they work like this every day? What fun to be a fly on the wall, how deceptive looks can be with our meek Jessica turning out to be a lioness in disguise. I'll add that to her other attributes. Oh, the dilemma of whom to target first, and whether or not they were both performing all that just for my benefit?'

"Hurry up Mr Barnham. I've got to follow you. You better have a few short cuts up your sleeve to avoid any jams?" Jessica snapped briskly, shaking him back to the present.

'Perhaps not,' thought Terry realistically.

Ending on a more positive note, Tess said warmly, "Bye for now Terry. I do hope our Jessica can turn the tide. But if there's any other assistance needed you know where to find me," whilst shaking his hand just a little embarrassingly too long.

"And thank you for your hospitality Tess. I might hold you to that," replied Terry thinking, 'perhaps all is not lost. There is always plan B'.

The journey back into Edinburgh proved uneventful for both cars. Jessica was able to follow nose to tail just like a funeral procession but without the leading hearse. And it gave her time to collect her thoughts. She had indeed met the DI, Terry Barnham, at a psychology conference in the previous summer where admittedly he had not given her any specific positive signs, leading her to presume he was either married, in a committed relationship or just not interested, and so she left it at that. At that time, he and she were paired together along with six others, forming one of a series of delegates' groups. As the morning approached midday the particular group reduced to seven, never to be favoured by his presence again.

Nevertheless she had been intrigued somewhat by his laddish behaviour and physically attracted to his rugged good lucks. And subsequently on occasion she had surreptitiously sniffed around the Internet chancing on Barnham hits whilst living in fear that her own cyber footprint might be tracked and traced back to her door. This could prove even more of a problem now that she was operating in the same orbit. She had followed his professional progress, usually played out by his bullish attitude in almost single handedly taking down the local protection racketeers, only to end up with egg on his face, and leaving plenty more to cover his colleagues' faces too. Having studied the mind and how it operates Jessica was able to identify his human flaws and failings, and recognise them for what they were as defense mechanisms activated at intervals to overcome his apparent lack of success. And whilst she baulked at weak men who whined about their lot, this particular self-destruct no hoper kept managing to turn up just like a bad penny.

This train of thought led her to wonder whether anything, other than work related, could happen now Terry Barnham had crossed her path again. And driving behind him as a captive audience of one, her girly weakness held court to her daydreaming that with a bit of fate, some hope and probably a little less chastity on her behalf, a relationship of sorts may indeed have possibilities.

The recession and spiralling cost of petrol had ensured a clear route with Sunday shoppers and drivers now being more scarce, compared to pre 2008. And upon Terry and Jessica arriving at and entering the inquiry room his team looked up over the rims of their drinks, to be greeted with, "Good morning. Thank you all for being so prompt. I hope I haven't dragged you away from anything too pressing, and that no one is suffering too much from the after effects of a Saturday night on the lash?"

Barnham then remembered the person at his side, the one who everyone opposite were already regarding with curiosity and expectancy; everyone except for T/DC Murray, who was also displaying a hint of jealousy in her look as well as a soupçon of anger too, as she registered competition in the form of this interloper. "Sorry, everyone. Let me introduce Jessica Lambert. I've known her for, erm, let me see, probably just under an hour but the Chief and I think she's going to become an invaluable member of the inquiry team. Her expertise is in the field of profiling and with the lack of leads to date, not to mention the bad press we have at the moment, I felt, well actually the Chief felt that a little science might go a long way, proving both positive and worthwhile." And then getting a little carried away he said, "So please raise your coffee mugs to Jessica Lambert.

"On a more serious note and talking of bad press I'll issue one warning now about leaks, past, present or future ones. Don't do it or I'll be down on you like a ton of bricks. We've got to keep things tight and close to our chests, as I'm not having the murderer gleaning any knowledge from the clues that we have not yet found. Erh, double negative there but you know what I mean. *I don't want anything further leaking to the media*," he emphasised. "Right, let's make a start. Jessica's got a huge learning curve coming up and I don't see it doing the rest of you any harm having a refresher on each of the three murders. T/DC Murray, can you do the honours and take us over the first murder again?"

Three hours, three coffees and three murders later, Jessica had a good grasp of the situation and gruesome sight, for the first time, of the three dead victims as supplied by the Pathology lab. Then studying in more detail it dawned on her as to why the papers only mentioned three murders with the files now confirming the same. 'I can understand why they don't want the public to know that the victims were left bound and still alive but why did the leak not release the fact that a fourth body was found at the skip site?' she questioned herself. 'Why are they keeping that one under wraps?' Reading on through the files it became apparent that the paramedics had reached Emma Flynn in time, and rushed her to hospital.

'I see. So now we have a possible eyewitness who should be able to identify the killer,' Jessica fathomed as she was in the process of trying to leave the building, laden with folders containing photocopy details of all three murders. But before her departure, she ignited the briefing meeting and floored the DI into the bargain, with her parting request.

Rather than keeping the press at bay, Jessica championed

their cause saying that accurate descriptions of all three bodies would stimulate discussion and prise out information from the public, not only on the three victims but also on the one that got away, Emma Flynn. Her reasoning being that the killer obviously already knew who had been murdered, and so would have nothing to gain by way of clues, past or present, although she did concede that future clues might be a different matter. The shock of the girl in the skip still being alive could quite easily panic the killer into making mistakes. This concept blew the DI's view of 'no more press disclosure' out of the water, but in the end he himself had to concede that it made sense to offer some specific details of the three murdered victims but held his ground in his adamancy that there should be nothing about Emma Flynn, as at this moment in time she was not in police custody and therefore her present status could not be classified as safe. Jessica nodded agreement to Barnham's thought process as she exited the door juggling with her bedtime reading, concerned that if she did not reach her car immediately with this highly sensitive material then the chances were high that it would tip, spill and scatter across the car park, thus revealing its secrets to the nosy but non-existent paparazzi.

A press conference was called for 10.00am Monday morning. In attendance were DI Barnham, Jessica Lambert and Laura Davies, the latter specialising in and coordinating the PR across all the Borders police forces. As it turned out, no journalist asked any particularly embarrassing questions of Barnham as they were more interested in the profiling angle. Neither did anyone ask the PR guru for her views as they expected that any tricky questions would be parried with the usual bland bias treatment or 'No Comment' approach. So, Jessica was left to educate the journalists on how profiling would be of benefit to what everyone now believed to be a serial killer hunt. She achieved this with confidence and without releasing any new details of the murders, knowing that her swotting up of the facts had been well worth the effort.

Once over, Barnham left Jessica to wrestle through the throng of reporters as they shouted out that one last question, the one that had not occurred to them during the press briefing. This time, Jessica chose to take a leaf out of the PR executive's book and just continuously repeated, 'No Comment'. She drove home, re-stored her now familiar highly sensitive material neatly in the second bedroom turned office, and then went for a run.

Barnham and his original team, excluding Jessica reviewed their checklist whilst he extolled on the importance of continuing their legwork around tattoo parlours, gyms and pubs; chasing up on dental records and DNA possibilities plus at the same time constantly searching for Emma Flynn. Without a doubt, opening up to the media had breathed new life into both the cases and the team. This was clearly shown by the invigoration of their endeavours in arming themselves with more facts and photos of the victims, as well as photos of Emma, the only surviving one. In reality, they knew that they were waiting for this first wave of interest to be generated once the media began to do its job, but in the meantime they would have to be content with any other positive hits, no matter how minor; and no doubt they could expect the odd nutter to raise his head above the parapets and reveal himself. Just, as they were up and running Jessica had finished hers, showered, eaten a late lunch and was on her second glass of carrot, apple and celery juice.

*

Meanwhile, Vinny's homesickness and dangerously poor diet made him mourn for his creature comforts and Mama's cooking all the more. But Pop's directive had been crystal clear, discretion was key, so he should move digs every three days to prevent detection, but what a chore. Almost as bad as his personal Holy Grail search, for that perfect location in which to find a clean shot.

I even followed Barnham into the local newsagents. There I was with my head bowed pretending to browse the 'better homes' magazines whilst discreetly checking out my options. I reckon I could have plugged him there and then or perhaps drawn a knife across his throat but I kept getting interrupted and annoyed by the constant stream of shoppers coming and going with their cries of 'excuse me mate' as they barged around me and through me. I'm telling you it was just like Piccadilly Circus. Had it happened in there the whole shebang would have ended up a bloodbath with a far greater death rate than intended, and possibly my own death into the bargain? As I surveyed the scene from my mag there were a couple of observations I had which made me cautious: a) my lack of knowledge of who might be out back, and b) whether or not the shopkeeper had a little trouble calmer hiding under the counter for just such an emergency as this.

And as an aside, and this is purely my personal view, I also thought that he should consider a supermarket style barcode checkout thing to speed up his service.

That being the state of play as seen by Vinny, he took the initiative to follow Barnham back to his home as the safer alternative but even then, and with it being a Saturday, the volume of traffic shielding Barnham from clear sight, prevented that all important shot. And by the end, seeing the guy bouncing up and down on one leg as if playing hopscotch, he was laughing so much that he would not have been able to shoot straight anyway. Next, he spent a fruitless day following the moron around Dalkeith. Now that journey made him proper dizzy, what with the number of times he drove around the High Street, he could not get to grips with the need for that! Did Barnham notice the tail and need to shake it off? So again, Vinny found no chance to put a stop to his prey as much as he wanted to. And leaving Dalkeith was no better either as there was now a convoy of cars, well at least two instead of the one; Barnham driving one and a dolly bird the other, and both taking the route back to Edinburgh and the police station.

So another day wasted with no clear opportunities. He was beginning to think this Barnham character had got nine lives! His last resort was to spend what remained of the day reading up on his mark, so hoping to gauge Barnham's future movements.

CHAPTER ELEVEN

As midnight approached Emma knew that she was in trouble. Not from the police search or even from the possibility that the killer had found out that she was still alive and her location; more from her cold turkey symptoms and the additional severe stomach gripes due to her intake of the bug-laden water. Her hands clutched a mobile in one and the heroin wrap in the other. Her craving was now so bad that had she felt competent enough and in control of her erratic movements she would have tried to prepare and inject the heroin come what may, but her mind thankfully convinced her that she was not prepared, not in the least. She berated herself over the number of lost opportunities to buy or steal the items needed since leaving the hospital, when instead her only foolish thought had been that they would be retrievable on her evening return to the flat. "Bastarding pig, why did he have to be there...then!" she said aloud and angrily. But the anger did not resolve her plight; in fact, it just brought on another wave of nausea and dizziness. She opened a hand to release the wrap, which then enabled her to make the call that she did not want to make. When it was answered at the other end she said in a very weak voice, "Hi Jonnie, remember me? You helped me at your work earlier today, the NRS computer thing?"

"Oh. Hi Emma. I didn't recognise your voice for a second. Have you just picked up a cold or something?"

"It's more like I've picked up the something. I'm in big trouble Jonnie and I can't think of anyone else to turn to. But I do need help, real bad."

Jonnie, not expecting his first-date conversation to be heading in this direction, was now becoming anxious and a little worried too as to the definition of the word *trouble* and the extent of the *help* required. "What do you want me to do Emma? Do you want picking up from somewhere?"

"Oh Jonnie, that would be great. In fact, could you invite me to stay at yours for a few days, that's if there's no one else there, I mean; I didn't get the vibe that you were seeing anyone. And I need somewhere private to crash, just until I get my head straight and feel better in myself? I won't be any trouble, promise," she lied.

"Of course you can Emma." Jonnie said feeling a little elated with the fact that his newfound 'NRS girlfriend' was already in need of his assistance, triggering a reminder of his knight in shining armour analogy. "When do you want picking up?"

"Now would be good," she croaked. "Oh and Jonnie if I tell you something you might not like will you still come?"

"Of course I will. But do you really mean right away? Is it a serious something? I mean like a dangerous something; do I need to inform the police?" he replied teasingly.

"No, it's not as bad as all that, you're not going to be put in danger and definitely don't get the police involved, whatever you do. It's just well, I better tell you now so you don't think I'm hiding anything." She took in a gulp of stale shack air combined with the pungency of her bowel movements, and gasped, "I'm a drug addict. I need you to pick me up and take me back to your place but only after making a detour to my flat. I desperately need a change of clothes and you'll need to pick up however many syringes and whatever drug paraphernalia you can find? That bit shouldn't be too difficult, as I've usually got it all stashed away at the back of my wardrobe in a Manolo Blahnik shoebox. Don't gasp. I didn't buy them! I nicked them right off the counter, after trying them on as well. I had to forego the gift-wrapping though. Shame really," she reminisced. "Anyway, sorry. So can you come now?" she pleaded.

"Well I can, but it won't be in my own car as I've been watching football and had a few lagers, so I'm probably way over the limit. But I can get a taxi. What's the address?"

"Well, that's another problem. It's a place my uncle had on an old allotment. It doesn't actually have an address but I can give you directions," she said with optimism in her voice as if Jonnie would be automatically conversant with the Burnwood area of Edinburgh. He was given directions and warned to keep north of the river and west of Burnwood, and that Emma would walk northwards to Calder Grove and be looking out for a taxi, any taxi.

Jonnie said, "OK, I think I've got that. How long will you need to get to Calder Grove?"

"You should be OK if you allow me ten minutes."

"Right, I'll text you when the taxi guy tells me we're about 15 minutes from our destination. Then, when we hit the Grove we'll 'cruise'." Emma heard the silence and presumed the connection had dropped out. "I've always wanted to say that word, we'll cruise up and down 'til we find you," came back Jonnie after his short interlude.

"It's no laughing matter Jonnie, I could be dying here for all you know but you're right, 'cruise', it is a good word isn't it. Be quick."

45 minutes later, the taxi was cruising as specified. It took two passes due to the Grove being busy to say the least and although Jonnie was riding shotgun his view was obstructed on numerous occasions. But it was Emma's own cruising that brought the taxi screeching to a halt. In her delirium or excitement she approached the car 'front on,' because it had a 'TAXI' light on the roof advertising its wares. She threw herself across the face of the bonnet a split second before it became stationary. The vehicle stopped and both occupants jumped out to make sure she had not been hit or died from the

impact or shock. Emma mumbled as she was bundled in the back to lie down, accompanied by the aroma of her 'eau de toilette', which was ripening by the second and would definitely not be destined to become a best seller. Jonnie managed to get a garbled address from Emma for The Towers in Burnwood, and was informed by the driver that thankfully it was only five minutes away. He was in the process of frisking her in his endeavour to find a door key to the flat but she just muttered, " Floor 3, Flat 61, code 1320". The taxi driver made short work of the drive round to The Towers and Jonnie, forever the competitor, was equally as quick at locating and bringing out the box containing the requisite paraphernalia.

He then requested that the taxi driver head back to his apartment on Caroline Terrace, just off Clermiston Road. The quickest way was due north through the Broomhouse Estate, which at any other time the driver may have deliberated over but tonight was an emergency. He needed to get the passengers out as quickly as possible to prevent the necessity of a total fumigation of the car interior and any other likely mishap. The exercise was undertaken and accomplished without any further problems, and Jonnie managed to manhandle the walking wounded up the flight of stairs and into his flat. He immediately marched Emma to the bathroom and, whilst waiting for the shower to run warm, he stripped her down to bra and panties.

She managed to stumble over the lip of the shower tray and shrunk away from the stinging jet of water droplets exploding on her head and body. Jonnie watched, as she slowly slid down the tiled wall, when it dawned on him that she really did need help. He stripped down to his T-shirt and pants, and half in, half out of the single cubicle, pulled her back to an upright position and supported her with one hand whilst he began to expunge her skin of the tell-tale signs of the cold turkey beginnings with the other. The warm spray eased Emma's mind as well as cleansing her body, and putting modesty aside, if she had ever known the meaning of that virtue, she unhooked her sodden bra and stripped off her panties and stood totally naked, oblivious to the fact that there was an almost total stranger staring back at her. Her look caught his and for that fraction of a second he was convinced she knew exactly what she was doing. Even in this condition she was offering herself by way of payment for his help.

Jonnie was pulled in two opposing directions; he mentally registered the view whilst physically turning off the shower, and gently guiding Emma out and wrapping her in a soft bath towel. Slumped on the toilet seat, she gargled a mouthwash and managed the task of patting herself dry as she watched Jonnie slip out of his wet clothes, dry himself and then casually redress in another T-shirt and denims. Five minutes later they were both in the lounge area, each nursing a mug of coffee, Emma with a tumbler of water chaser too, plus a slight shake she had no control over. She was wearing an elegant not, dressing gown and nibbling on a biscuit; the first thing she had eaten since the pasty earlier in the day. Jonnie was tense and felt that he could not put off the inevitable any longer. He was moving quickly into an area he had never been exposed to before and an area he did not comprehend. He coughed as a signal that he was now going to begin an important speech. Emma placed her mug on the small table, leaned across towards him and placed a light kiss on his lips. She said quietly as if worried that someone else might hear, "Thank you for what you've done already; you've been very kind. I honestly don't know whom I could have turned to. I'm a little better now if you want me to go. I'll understand, honestly."

"Emma, don't be silly. I don't want you to go anywhere. I wasn't going to say that, it hadn't even crossed my mind," he said indignantly. "If anything, I'm used to the shower scenario, as a couple of my roommates at Uni used to be constantly smashed and I had to play nursemaid by 'shower dunking' them on several occasions," he innocently replied, shocked that she might feel that he was asking her to leave.

She, in turn, was shocked as she exclaimed, "What? Are you

telling me you're gay?"

"No, no. I'm not gay. It's just what buddies do. A little encouragement was needed to get them to lectures; it could have been curtains, otherwise. No, It's the other stuff with the syringes and all that, which worries me more," he said shocked again that she thought he could be gay particularly as he had thought that there had been a sexual spark between them when they had first met.

"Look, Jonnie. At the moment I'm feeling a little better but it won't last. I'm dependent on drugs. And the truth is I'm dependent on heroin, the mother of all drugs. I've never been so frank about it with anyone before, well anyone that isn't doing it too. I suppose there hasn't been a need to tell before. Anyway, that cellophane wrap that I was clenching tightly in my hand when the taxi nearly ran me down," she smirked, "that did happen didn't it? Well, that's heroin, and I need it oh so badly at the moment. Where is it by the way? Where's my handbag? I hope I popped the wrap in there. I'm sure I put it inside the notes from the library," she said panicking.

Jonnie brought the bag for Emma and sure enough it was still safe, harmlessly tucked away in the bottom. Safe and harmlessly wrapped in cellophane as opposed to dangerous and addictive when resting on a spoon, primed for injection, waiting innocently to be drawn up through the point of a syringe.

"Can you help or do you not want to be a part of it?"

He thought sadly for a second but knowing that he was not going to change the world in a blink, he said, "I'm fine. Tell me what you need." Emma did not actually need anything except her Manolo Blahnik's treasure box. Jonnie brought that to the table and she professionally arranged the tools of the trade, in the same manner as a surgeon preparing for an operation.

She looked at him and he gave a quizzical, slightly frightened look in response. "Do you want me to talk you through it?" she asked. His imperceptive nod indicated that the process could begin. "OK. I clean my spoon with one of these alcohol swabs and take a clean syringe. I'm sure you know about Aids and all that from dirty needles?"

Again, the slight nod.

"Next, I've got to pull up some water into the syringe," she lucidly narrated as she dipped the needlepoint into her tumbler of water. "Then, place that onto the spoon along with an amount of heroin. This is the tricky bit as you've got to judge, from past experience, how much heroin you can handle without OD'ing. There, that should hit the spot. Now, with the lighter underneath I can dissolve both together. Right, we're getting to the business end of it now so I just want to say I'm really grateful for what you've done for me. You're been very kind and gentle, unlike most guys I know. But when this goes in I'm going to feel so much better although I won't be very communicative. And to be honest it's most likely I'll be out 'til morning. So I'll say goodnight now," and with that, she held the instruments in both hands as confirmation of her completing the operation, and again leaned over and kissed him lightly on the lips. "Would you be a love and cover me with a blanket when I crash out. I'll be fine here on the sofa."

By the time he returned with the blankets she had dropped another swab onto the spoon through which she was drawing up the yellowish liquid. He watched her expertly place the needle tip into a vein in her arm and as she applied pressure to the plunger her mouth broke into a broad smile and her face relaxed. He watched her eyes lose focus and a serenity ripple out to all parts of her body as if reflecting a state of transcendental meditation. He questioned whether he would ever see that same expression should they make love? But that prospect seemed a long way away as she was now lost to him, and in no position to answer. He covered her gently with the two blankets, kissed her forehead and walked off disconsolately to his bedroom thinking, 'Perhaps I can help her change'.

The weekend proved disastrous. Emma's high descended and

her stomach pains and waves of nausea increased, eventually turning into a cycle of sink, toilet, shower, sink, toilet, shower, although not necessarily always in that order. Jonnie stuck to his role as nursemaid and felt a whole new gratitude for all those nurses and their colleagues who constantly undertook this level of care with vigour, dedication, passion and good grace. He regularly replenished her tumbler with aired water and force-fed her dry toast whenever the mood took him to offer it or her to take it. The only occasion he became elated and annoyed at the same time was when she brightened up slightly but it was only in order to prep her syringe and give herself the remaining dose of her 'friendly' medicine; but at least it then meant she would be comfortable and restful, so enabling him to rest too. Sunday was very much a repeat of Saturday except that she was out of gear and so needed Jonnie to help with the purchase of some more.

In one of her more lucid moments with her craving soaring she grabbed her phone angrily and punched a text message. Three minutes later a reply pinged back. "What road are we on Jonnie?" she demanded, without an ounce of warmth. Jonnie told her and another text was despatched. One minute later the reply returned. One of her dealers would be at the end of the road in ten minutes. "Jonnie can you lend me £25? I really need some more stuff, just to get me through today. He'll be in a black BMW." Jonnie went with £25 in hand like a child shopping for his mother and bought Emma's gear. Already the novelty of this life was beginning to wear off and crumble at the edges but he felt that he could really like Emma as herself when she was Emma.

She repeated the performance he had been a party to in the early hours of Saturday morning, likening it to 'the sorcerer's apprentice', but this time his eyes refused to watch the needle entering the vein; nor did he stay for the euphoria that followed. Instead he busied himself with cleaning, as bachelors must do, paying particular attention to the bathroom. Emma's stomach gripes had eased as if all the contaminated liquid she had drunk on the allotment was now flushed through and Jonnie again looked at her now serene face, pulled the duvet higher, kissed her on the forehead and went off to bed thinking, 'some girlfriend'. And as he started to doze off another thought struck him, 'bloody hell, work tomorrow'.

Early the next morning he checked on Emma with mixed emotions. Thinking about her short time in his flat he found it amusing that he could be looking after a patient who, to all intents and purposes brought in or, bought in her own drugs; but they obviously did the trick as there certainly was an improvement. He was still struggling to block out of his mind the sight of her beautiful naked body and her look of resignation and failure after she had offered it to him in the early hours of Saturday. But if a relationship was going to blossom he wanted it to be meaningful, not just a one-night stand type of thing. Now his clumsiness in the kitchen aroused her from her sleep, and she walked in to see his token empty lager can from the previous evening disappearing into the waste bin, and mugs, plates and glasses submerging beneath the suds in the sink bowl. The noise from his iPod camouflaged her entrance, and as she came up behind him she wrapped her arms around his waist, nuzzling her face into the back of yet another T-shirt. Plucking out one of the ear buds she whispered into the same ear, "Thank you for being so understanding. I'll make it up to you. Promise."

"Don't mention it," joked Jonnie with a smile. "I'm always helping damsels in distress."

"But you've never managed to keep them in your tower, have you? In fact, I already live in a Tower, don't I?" she joked back playfully.

"No, I haven't, but that's a story for another day. And talking about distress, are you over the worst?"

"Yes, I am for the present and now I've got more of my story to tell too, if you've time to hear it?" She replied running her fingers under his T-shirt and across his chest suggestively.

Jonnie looked at his watch, stared into space, squirmed as her fingers reached a more erogenous zone, and finally with an unbeknownst willpower he engaged his brain into thinking mode and said, "Fuck. I can't miss work today, much as I'd love too. It's my six monthly review. Fuccck."

"Or not fuck," she replied as she rubbed her breasts across his back in a tantalising manner, "That is the question. Not to worry I'll still be here when you get home so I'll try to show you my appreciation then."

"OK. Deal. Now stop that; I've got to think straight. Let's have a bit of breakfast and a coffee and you can tell me about these notes you made in the library and whatever other errands you want me to sort. Oh and by the way, as I forgot your additional clothes when I collected your druggie box, I threw the ones you'd been wearing into the washer last night, so they'll be at least clean even if maybe a little crumpled. But I won't be complaining as seeing you in those skimpy things is the next best thing, if I can't see you naked instead," he joked, remembering the shower episode.

Jonnie left the apartment just before 8.15am armed with the flat keys but not his car keys as the weather looked promising and he needed the exercise. It also gave him time to check over the shopping list, in his head, 'Things to do today for Emma'. Well, at least there was hopefully one thing at the top of the list as he visualised her moving the front of her dressing gown to one side to reveal an erect nipple. How had she phrased it? 'Sure about work? I'm good at giving reviews. What time do you want pencilling in for? And where do you want me to start, big boy?' he hotly reminisced; but then moved his thinking to the much cooler other half of his brain. 'Research the family name Agosti; withdraw £100 cash from the wall; and at some point, call at the flat to pick up more of her clothes. Right that's the checklist done. Oh bugger, I did need the car after all, for the trip to the flat.'

With the review not being until 2.00pm he was able to utilise his morning break to check out Emma's old family name. He revisited the department they had been in on the Friday before and logged into one of the available pc terminals. LUIGI AGOSTI he input under male name and also the date of death as 06/06/1983. The computer innocently recalled the man's date of birth; his place of birth; nationality; last known address; occupation and next of kin. This was followed with the same information for his wife Laura, indicating that she had also died on 06/06/1983. It informed Jonnie that the couple had two children, twins in fact, born on 31/05/1980.

Bingo. He was sure Emma had said that was her birthday because she had joked with him that it was the end of May just before the 'white rabbits', signifying the first of each month, would have caught her. As he continued scrolling, the pc make its own kind of far-reaching background noises in tandem, with its fan whirring in unison, collating and retrieving all the requested information, and putting it together as a presentation. 'Ah here it is. Two children, twin girls, born 23.20pm, 31/05/1980 and they died in the same accident as their parents. Disappointment and frustration for Emma welled over him at his recognition that one of the girls was not going to be her. With the coincidence of the date of birth being the same he even questioned whether or not the data was fake. Little did he know but the computer itself was not being totally honest either. As with Jonnie innocently spending time in coaxing additional information off the screen, the computer was at the same time relaying information to a previously input program placed on numerous search engines. This program confirmed when a third party expressed interest in Mr Agosti. Jonnie, oblivious to the secretive software now tracking his every move, spent another 10 minutes searching for other Agostis, but to no avail.

*

The interest in Agosti, flagged up in Scotland Yard's cold case unit. Agosti was one of many names programmed to trigger an immediate investigation response through search engines' links to servers connected to pc's across the world. Within a nanosecond a positive hit was recorded and a location given, a location in Edinburgh, Scotland. Within a further minute Lothian & Borders cold case unit were advised of the subject matter, the location of the pc and the time code, and all without human assistance. Within a further 15 minutes, two human members of the cold case unit were asking for the senior IT technical support engineer at the reception desk of the NRS Central Register at Ladywell House on Ladywell Road. When the engineer arrived and introduced himself as David Farron, the officers showed their credentials and asked to speak to him privately; and preferably in an office where he could access the master slave terminal.

Once all three were seated around a monitor and keyboard he was informed of the task ahead. He instigated three searches into NRS' own localised intranet and commanded all terminals to solely search within the NRS building. "Name, date of the twins' birth and Agosti's date of death should be sufficient to triangulate and pinpoint a specific pc accurately," said one of the officers. Once accessed the officers requested the time code for the final input as they then presumed that they would have to trawl through CCTV footage to earmark likely candidates. The IT engineer glanced at the results on screen and said, "I can go one better than that. The person looking for the information on this character logged in using his ID card; it speeds up the access time and bypasses various safety measures. He actually works here; in fact, he's a friend of mine. Has he done something wrong?"

"Could we just have his name, Sir? I'm sure it's going to be an innocent mistake on his part but we've got to carry out a check and eliminate the person from our inquiries, you understand?"

"Yes, right. He's called Jonnie, Jonnie Raey. He works on the second floor in the logistical input department."

The officers persuaded Mr Farron to accompany them to the Human Resourses Department under the pretext of asking him for directions but in reality it was to ensure that he did not demonstrate any cavalier allegiance to his colleague Mr Raey, before his apprehension. The task was completed without drama, except to say that when approached Jonnie appeared both nonplussed and a little white about the gills. His immediate thought was that something had happened to Emma until one of the officers said, "Mr Raey, we're officers working with the Lothian & Borders cold case unit. We appear to have the same interest in a certain foreign gentleman by the name of Agosti, Luigi Agosti. Is there anything you'd like to tell us?"

"Are you actual police? What is this really about? This Agosti chap is dead, how am I going to know anything about him?" spit out Jonnie in rapid succession.

"Yes we are a form of police and we have official powers to arrest you, if needs be. And it is about Mr Agosti who was burned to death in a car accident in 1983 on 6th June, so as you say he's obviously dead. And yes, we understand that you might not have known him personally, I mean you'd have probably only been about two when he died. But you must be researching him for a reason; you were looking at specific details relating to him for 14 minutes 22 seconds! Do you want to co-operate here or would you prefer a trip to the station? Could take all day with the workload we've got on."

"I'll co-operate here and I was actually four years old but I still never met the guy!" Jonnie replied as if to get one over.

"OK, less of the flippancy, let's be serious for a moment. And no messing us around, if we think you're spinning us a yarn, it will be straight down to the station and a little sleepover with Edinburgh's finest party poopers. How do you know of Mr Agosti. And if as you say, you don't know him, then who else is involved in this Internet search?"

Jonnie did his staring into space thing, took a deep breath, apologised silently to Emma, and said, "The only reason I know about Agosti is because I helped a woman on Friday who was trying to trace someone. She didn't know her way around the computer software so I did it for her. She found some information and then went off to the library to do more research using microfiche. You know, the old newspaper files gizmo. She's now given me these notes and asked if I could take it a stage further. She was of the opinion he might be her dad but I 'm not so sure now as when I checked there definitely were two children in the family about her age but both died on the same day as their father and mother."

"And who is this person asking all the questions and did she happen to give you her address?"

"Her name's Emma Flynn and she said she lives at ...The Towers, I think it was, yes, The Towers over at Burnwood. Sorry I don't know the flat number," Jonnie answered, two thirds truthfully.

"OK, Mr Raey. We'll check that out. Are you sure that there's nothing else you can tell us?"

"No. I don't think there is. She just said she was researching the name as a family tree type of thing," he replied with a sense of relief that they were making positive signs of believing him and leaving. Jonnie stayed at work for his review but could not really concentrate either before, during or afterwards. He clocked out on flexitime and recalled Emma's checklist in his mind, 'still need her clothes and to get some cash,' his brain computed. He then jogged back to his flat, sneaked in expecting to find Emma asleep, which she was, collected the car keys, jumped in the car and motored over to The Towers, swinging by the ATM on the way. Arriving at Emma's tower block, he scanned the frontage for the two officers who had interviewed him but all looked quiet. He entered the flat and like a whirling dervish scooped up clothes, underwear and shoes; all of his choice, very much like the proverbial kid in the sweet shop who goes for the brightest, most flavoursome looking candies. He then threw them into a bag that he found on top of the wardrobe. Mission accomplished and once back at his flat Jonnie was welcomed by a kiss on the cheek from a wide-awake Emma, even though sported a confused and concerned look as if to say 'it isn't home time already'. By way of reward for her concern Jonnie enlightened her as to the events of the morning.

She was disappointed that the two children found dead in the car were exactly her age. That meant her search for her true identity would need to continue down a different route. She was shocked that these special police had been so quick in finding out about her research and even more so that they came looking personally for the instigator the instant that the Agosti name had been input. And she could see from Jonnie's face that he was not comfortable either with the new turning that his life had taken. So, feeling much stronger and by way of distraction, she began rifling through the bundle of clothes he brought and giving Jonnie his own personal fashion show with a little lap dancing thrown in for good measure; only now grasping that her appetite was returning somewhat for other delights, as well as food and drugs. And by way of fulfilling her promise of the morning, she would leave nothing to his previous daydreaming of what might have been.

Events took a turn for the better as both had yet another shower together but this one was preplanned and so purposely with their clothes off. They dried off touching each other playfully yet intimately too. Moving into the bedroom Jonnie could not believe his luck at realising his dream, and was relishing the thought of what the immediate future held. Emma was nowhere near as aroused although her professionalism and amateur acting skills easily covered that fact; unfortunately for her the sexual act did not really hold the same hidden ecstasy as it would appear to for Jonnie; she put that down to her primarily nocturnal work schedule over past years. But with her vast experience of pleasuring men through a varied career as stripper, lap dancer, escort and, heaven forbid, prostitute, she could certainly put on a good show. She would not have stayed in the profession long had she not learnt a number of tricks whilst actually performing tricks. And today was no exception. She kissed him hungrily on the mouth, pushed him down onto the bed and whispered, "Wait for me". Grabbing and wrapping herself in a towel, as defence against any would be Peeping Tom, she went into the kitchen, and hunted through the cupboards looking, in particular, for props, whilst shouting out little encouragements as she searched. Finding a likely item she quickly opened it and poured the contents into a dish; looked around for her handbag too and rooted through for another necessity, then moved back towards the bedroom.

As she approached and nudged open the door with her hip, she asked, "How are we doing in here?" performing a sexually exaggerated dance over to the bed and slowly letting the towel reveal more and more in the process, on its journey to the floor. Jonnie was doing fine, real fine and that was just feasting on the beautiful body now displayed in front of him. And, not having the benefit of a towel, his fineness was there for all to see, well at least Emma to see anyway.

"Right. Young man. Today I want to explain the phrase, 'fruit of my loins', and like all good girl guides my motto is 'be prepared' too. So I've brought to the table …erh bed actually, a little bowl of mandarins and our two bodies." She moved to straddle him whilst also discreetly placing a condom in an accessible location on the bedside table, for when the time was right. "Let the game begin…"

Jonnie lay there expectantly, grinning from ear to ear, 'God, what a wonderful gift imagination is,' and continued thinking, mischievously, 'And guess what? It's even part of my five a day!'

CHAPTER TWELVE

Results from the press conference were sluggish to say the very least. The PR executive had promised that both TV and radio would transmit the content and hotline number as soon as possible after the press conference. This in turn would begin the process of generating a series of names relating to, one and or all of the three victims; but the daily papers not being as instant as broadcast media would not be able to publish their editorials until the following day and the weeklies tended to 'go to press' on Thursday for Friday publication. This meant that Barnham's select team was still left in limbo as they waited for that first big break. Even though there were not yet any positive results, the Chief Inspector had seemed happy with the positive aspect of the chosen strategy. Support from senior personnel within Government, for the force's encouraging actions, was high; and the Chief himself even forgave Barnham for his 'Road to Damascus' priceless moment, where the DI had been allegedly overheard saying, "It suddenly occurred to me that a profiler could be the key to cracking these murders, such a person would enable us to delve inside this maniac's head. Thus allowing the force greater impetus in capturing the killer by perceiving his next move, possibly even before he did himself." Various media quoted it verbatim, so giving Barnham no chance of disputing it or indeed nowhere to hide as it continued, "It then follows that the more information we can furnish to the press the better our chances of the public identifying the victims too." But when challenged, he denied categorically that he had done any form of U turn.

Late afternoon began to look more promising. At one point, Forensics thought they had a DNA match to the saliva taken from the lipstick relating to the case of victim one. But even though it was close, once again it was not an exact match. However, the Path lab was notified of a positive match on the dental records of a victim, from a practice in Galashiels. The records proved it to be that of victim two. And most interestingly, the wearing out of shoe leather and knocking on doors finally paid off when PC Tranter tracked down the tattooist who had, what can only be said as, violated victim two's body. As it turned out he had been visited twice before but on both occasions had not admitted to any recognition of the victim. However in PC Tranter's particular spot check he was found to be residing in a totally different location. He had originally given his home address as living above the shop in Melrose but PC Tranter had now come across him at a flat in Earlston, so seven miles away by road.

When questioned about this change of address and after having been shown the latest photographs, and pressed further regarding the 'roses' tattoo, his behaviour led the PC to believe that he knew more about the murdered female than he was letting on. Initially, it was his silence but then he became flustered and aggravated, and when pressed on his demeanour he tried to do a deal, which led PC Tranter to inform him that he would be taken to the station for further questioning. At the interview there, under caution by DI Barnham, the tattooist Bernard Goldthrop, trading under the name 'Bernie G, Intricate quality tattoos of the Stars', and working out of a shop on the High Street in Melrose, finally broke down; but not to admit to the murder of victim two, whom he gave the name of Mairie Dawson, generally answering to Mary.

PC Tranter had accompanied DI Barnham during the interview and had found it hilarious to say the least. He regaled parts of it to T/DC Murray saying; "I can't remember it word for word but if you get a chance then you should give it a play. Being there certainly brightened up my day," he said, still chortling from the thought as he replayed parts of it in his head. "It made me contemplate that Barmy might be good with kids after all, the way he handled that guy in there."

After finishing her shift T/DC Murray did just that. She sat down in one of the playback booths, set the time code given by Tranter, put on the headphones and relaxed. First, she heard an unknown voice, which she presumed must be that of the tattooist, "You can't accuse me of that, I never touched her. Well I did touch her but only when she wanted me to. But I swear I never killed her. I never killed nobody. I just panicked when that officer, him there, was asking me all those questions and trying to catch me out. So then I thought I might be able to trade some information."

"So that's why you said to my colleague PC Tranter that you knew one of the victims but would only reveal the name if we could sort out your tax problem with HMRC. Am I correct?" T/DC Murray became a little hot as she recognised the resonance of her immediate boss' husky voice, even with hearing it as a distorted recording through headphones, and in the confines of the tiny booth.

"Yes, that's what I was hoping for. Like a you scratch my back and I'll scratch yours, sort of thing."

"Well let me tell you Mr G … Mr Goldthrop, we don't do any back scratching here or any other sort of scratching, either. The police and HMRC are two totally different bodies, both serving the crown and the public and both with a remit to catch criminals but generally for totally different reasons. If you persist in your stubbornness I'll have no alternative but to charge you with the victim's murder, and if that doesn't stick then how about withholding information and obstructing the police?"

"You can't do that. I've told you I didn't murder anybody and I'm going to give you the information now, aren't I? Anyway, it was worth a try, perhaps I'll be able to sell my story to the papers?"

"Perhaps you will. I'm not here to guide you on how to make your future living, but by the looks of that tattoo plastered across that poor girl's chest I'd say you may be due a career change. In fact, humour me for just a mo. It says 'of the Stars' on your trading name? Which stars would they be?"

"Hey, you can't be saying that about my professionalism. That's slander or libel or even both. I thought you said you worked for the public, not insulted them. And, just so we're straight I always tell my customers which stars I've worked on. And I'll tell you the same. I've done: Cassiopeia, Cepheus and Orion's Belt!"

"Yes, very clever. A slight twist on the word 'stars', don't you think, Mr Goldthrop? Albeit, these have been around somewhat longer! Anyway, now can we please get back to the matter in hand? Three people have died and we're trying to catch the killer, before it becomes four! Just tell me the name before I really slander you? "

"Oh threats, is it now? I'll be needing a solicitor then, will I? And it better be a woman, they're always more sympathetic to their poor victimised clients. And I'm not paying anything, I want Legal Aid."

"Right Mr Goldthrop, your final chance. If I don't get a coherent answer out of you this time, I'll put you in a cell for wasting police time. Do you understand?"

"I understand you want her name but I don't understand what sort of an answer you want. That word 'co hear ant'. Is it a foreign language or what?'

"No, Mr Goldthrop, by definition, it just means, give me a straightforward bloody answer now! Give me an answer that I'll understand! It's not rocket science. There are no cards up my sleeve or anything. Do you need brain cells removed to be a tattooist?"

"Ah. I was never much good at science at school and there's no need to swear. And don't be getting personal with me, either."

"Right. PC Tranter, take him away and lock him up, preferably on his own. Any other inmate unlucky enough to spend a night in his cell would be climbing the wall by morning."

"No, no. Don't do that. She was called Mairie Dawson but everybody called her Mary. She lived three hundred yards from me, up the High Street in a maisonette."

"Hallelujah. He finally cracks and gives us the name. Was that difficult for you?" DI Barnham asked sarcastically. "Now have you anything further that you want to elucidate on?"

"There you go, talking that foreign language stuff again. Or is it one of your fancy swear words? Do I get my deal? I've heard about plea-bargaining you know. It was on the Internet."

"I'll give you foreign language. I'll get you five years and you can do all the foreign language studying you want then, and it won't be with the aid of the Internet either," said Barnham mischievously.

"Hey. Don't be threatening me. I've told you all I know."

"What. Like the obvious fact that you were running away from something? That you may be actively involved in these murders? And if you are not involved, why had you changed address and gone into hiding?"

"I just panicked. I saw the papers, put two and two together and thought I was going to be made the patsy for this."

"Tell you what Mr Goldthrop. I can see why you might not have paid your HMRC bill, if you keep getting confused with simple addition. But I will do a deal with you. If we catch the killer thanks to you supplying the name of victim two, then I'll let you go. If we don't, I'll pin all three murders on you. At least that way I'll keep my cases neat and tidy," Barnham said playfully. Mr Goldthrop did not take it that way as reflected by his blood-drained face. Barnham continued, "Only joking, Bernie." And then turning to PC Tranter he said quietly, "Transcribe this interview but ignore that last bit. Get Bernie here to read it over, sign it and then you can let him go." He then turned back to the interviewee and said, "Bernie, several words of advice. Don't try and do deals with us. Don't run away from problems and make sure you pay that HMRC bill because if you think I'm bad, you've not seen the half of it."

Then T/DC Murray jumped as she heard Barnham bang the palm of his hands loudly on the table, saying, "Interview terminated at 3.16 pm." Through the tears running down her face she pressed the stop button and thought, 'You're right Tranter that has made my day. Let's hope it never finds its way into the media. I'm sure it would be a candidate for, 'You've Been Framed'.

*

An hour covered the length of the next breakthrough for the police and a minute covered Jonnie's. He climaxed and Emma pretended to! It left him spent but exhilarated, whilst Emma's mind drifted onto her more usual trick of a different kind. At the point of postcoital bliss, the Lothian & Borders cold case unit was coincidentally filing a standard report on the Luigi Agosti episode. The name Jonnie Raey did not figure in setting alight any bonfires but the name that followed almost raised beacons across the Borders. Emma Flynn had surfaced, and right under their noses. WPC Whitely was cross-referring and updating information received constantly through the Scottish police forces' intranet server. With her involvement on the murders she was well aware of Emma Flynn's name and importance to the case, and proceeded with a printout. Knowing the find was gold dust she was itching to relay the information to DI Barnham, and so was found hovering outside Interview Room 3, where he eventually exited in the company of PC Tranter and Bernie Goldthrop. She accosted the DI, stuck the paperwork in his hands and waited until the other two had walked further along the corridor, before gushing, "Sir, we've just had a report in on the net. Totally unrelated to our case but it gives us a lead on Emma Flynn's whereabouts."

"Emma Flynn." The DI's face passed through several

expressions; from annoyance and frustration after the recent interview, to recognition of the name and finally to one of elation that the one witness still alive to tell the tale had resurfaced. "Brilliant. That's great work Whitely. Get me a print out of that report." He then interrupted himself and shouted along the corridor, "PC Tranter, after you've done the necessary with Mr Goldthrop. He's free to go but make sure he understands that he's not allowed any overseas trips for the moment. And that includes any of our islands too!" All the while, WPC Whitely looked from Barnham's face to his hands and back, several times over. Barnham, having too much information to impart and ingest, mimicked the looks but this time from Whitely's face to his hands and back. The penny dropped and he made an apologetic shrug, which said, 'I can't help it, I'm a man and I'm human,' whilst his lips were sealed with a big grin.

PC Tranter watched the pantomime unfold but did not need to inform Mr Goldthrop of what he could and could not do, excepting in a formal capacity, as he was stood right next to him anyway, and so obviously within the same hearing distance. WPC Whitely's own slight buzz of elation began to fade and she returned to her desk proud in the knowledge that her prompt action had left her boss lost for words.

The DI hungrily devoured the report from the cold case unit. At first, he had been confused as to how Emma slotted in, but as he read on, it became apparent. He was desperate to get to the part, which revealed Emma's whereabouts but of course it was not there. The only new information, apart from a 30-year-old history lesson on a tragic event, was that a Jonnie Raey had been apprehended whilst looking up details of a suspect who had been red flagged. This Mr Raey had given Emma's address as The Towers but the DI's team already knew that anyway. He called PC Gough over, briefed him on this latest development and set him the task of locating Jonnie Raey's own address from NRS records. His gut feeling had told him that this was the road to follow and so he did, along with PC Gough when at late afternoon, they pulled up into the parking area behind 23/25 Caroline Terrace. They sat stationary, busily cleaning and peering through the misted car windscreen with dusk hindering their vision; looking for Flat 3B on the various small plaques dotted around the two entrances. Barnham was studying one door, when annoyingly a couple obscured his view as they playfully exited the building hand-in-hand and pecking at each other's faces just like two lovebirds would.

He did a double take and then exclaimed, "Bloody hell. That's her there. That's Emma Flynn. The guy with her...., he must be this Jonnie Raey, I presume."

Barnham coughed out the words, flabbergasted that it had been so easy. Tranter made for the car door handle as if to apprehend them there and then but Barnham pulled him back before he gave away their position. Not that the lovebirds would have noticed anyway as their world and vision stretched to no greater circumference than the width of their two bodies. "Let's follow. See where it takes us and what they get up to." He knew this could be a bad call as they could so easily lose them in traffic, but Barnham was convinced that neither of the two lovers had any idea that they were being observed, let alone followed, particularly by two officers of the law. The tail took them east. They picked up Corstophine Road, passing by Murrayfield Golf Course heading towards the city centre. As the A8 swept to the right, the car in front turned left, into a series of small side roads. "We'll have to be careful here as we can't get too close or they'll see us tailing them, but at the same time I don't want to lose them in this maze of roads and side streets," said Barnham concentrating on his driving.

"Only saving grace, Sir, is that they've now slowed too. Must be looking out for something?" replied Gough.

Pulling to a stop, he replied, "Or someone. In fact, both something and someone, is my guess. Clock the white Mercedes at the other end of India Street; look suspicious to you? Yes, they're pulling up now, half way up the street. I'll bet one of them is going to do a deal. Pass the binoculars Gough. Take this down. 'Kilo 1 Charlie Kilo Sierra'. Bloody hell, why do these pushers treat us like idiots and make it so obvious? White flashy Mercedes, blacked out windows and a registration plate saying, 'look at me, catch me if you can'." He then saw Emma approach the car. He took in the scene but it did not register. What he saw instead from his POV was a very attractive woman with a full figure, very nicely proportioned, and in his personal opinion carrying just the right amount of weight. He could not imagine that it was the same woman he had seen on her near deathbed in the hospital, not more than a few days ago. But it was her face that made him catch his breath. His Luger '10 times multiplication' binoculars focused on the lived-in face where each and every line held its own beauty and story, and even seeing her again for only the second time he still had a nagging feeling that they had met before. Before, any of this had even begun.

"Boss. Can you see what's happening? Is she handing something over and receiving?"

On this urgent prompt from Gough he immediately dropped his binocular eye level down to her hands and sure enough she had just handed over what he presumed was cash. She, in return received a small packet almost by sleight of hand but the power of the 10x binoculars did not lie. Barnham said, "Yes, I think they've just done the deal, so now we've got a solid enough reason to arrest both of them. At least that should keep Emma off the streets and back into safe hands until we catch the killer. But Gough when we finally apprehend them, don't write up what we've witnessed, I'd rather not have the drug handover getting in the way of our murder investigation. Just pass on the Merc's details for surveillance purposes." Rather than just thinking this he said it aloud as he was not convinced that a charge could be made to stick with him only realistically seeing the end of the transaction anyway. He had been more engrossed in studying her face, and if he was being honest, her body too that the handover had slipped his mind entirely.

PC Gough relayed the details of the dealer's vehicle and his location back to the station so that the drugs squad could follow it up; whilst they continued to track Jonnie and Emma back towards the A8 and then west, presumably completing a return run to his flat. Sensing the direction they were taking, Barnham told Gough to radio in for a back-up car to be despatched immediately to Caroline Terrace but without blaring sirens and flashing lights. Subtlety being the word, they were warned to keep out of sight too. When he recognised it was Blackwell's voice on the other end he shouted through the mike, "You'll be pleased to know that you might be sleeping in a bed tonight that is unless you forget to brief the back up team on being prepared to block the exit to the Caroline Terrace car park. Tell them to wait for our car as the signal to act, and then just follow our lead."

Barnham's car continued following at a discreet distance and once Jonnie's car turned into the parking area, Barnham swept in behind him and so blocked off any chance of an escape, by way of reversing. The other police car appeared from nowhere and moved across the exit, right on cue. Emma in particular was shocked by this action as she thought that once more her life was being threatened. And it was only on seeing DI Barnham that the concern left her pale face to be replaced by relief.

"Good evening Emma. Our paths have crossed again and this time rest assured you won't be giving me the slip or the run around. Ah, you must be Jonnie. Well Jonnie, you can count yourself lucky that I'm personally not interested in you aiding and abetting the purchase of, undoubtedly, class A drugs, and it's unlikely if I'm questioned that I will have seen you transport Emma for the purpose of her purchasing the same, either. I'm much more interested in your passenger here, she could be a suspect for a murder although probably more likely a witness to it, and she's definitely been a victim of attempted murder. So how do I square that one, perhaps I'll give you the benefit of the doubt Emma and just ask you nicely to come for a ride with us."

Jonnie was shell-shocked. He looked accusingly at Emma and pleaded, "Tell me it's not true? How can you be involved in a murder? You never told me that." He then turned his attention to the DI, now taking on a protective role, "And how do I know you're the police," he asked aggressively. "Emma said she was worried about some trouble that had occurred, but she definitely didn't tell me it was murder and that the police would become involved. In fact she made a point of saying that she didn't want the police involved."

"Oh, we're definitely police, sonny and we're definitely involved, like it or not," said DI Barnham, as he took out his warrant card. "You won't get many criminals talking like us now, will you? Just ask your girlfriend here."

"It's alright Jonnie, they are police. Look, I'll go with you if you promise that Jonnie isn't going to get into any trouble. But if I do go I'm going to need medication, either above or below board, as you've obviously witnessed already with that little transaction. I'm a heroin addict and I'm going to have to score at some point today. So what are the plans for that happening?"

"Jonnie is OK to go with no charge and I'll ring through to get advice on your addiction. We do act as a gateway to healthcare so we'll try and fast-track you in order that you can be treated before your craving becomes too severe. But I'm going to have to ask you a few questions before that," Barnham said with unexpected consideration and diplomacy.

On the drive to the station Emma bemoaned the fact that she seemed to be once more caught out without a change of clothes. More particularly, a change of knickers; neither could she get over the fact that she always seemed to be underdressed with nothing sensible to keep her warm, especially now that she might be locked up in a draughty cell with cold stonewalls. Barnham replied, "You going to be held

155

as much for your own protection as for any punishment, so you'll have an opportunity to text Jonnie, or someone else if you prefer, and he or she can bring some warm clothing and toiletries to the front counter, which will be passed on to you. But, whoever does come, make sure they don't try and smuggle anything in that they shouldn't, because we frown on that kind of behaviour." He continued informatively, although with slight annoyance, "Anyway, a detention cell is quite comfortable and cosy these days. I can only assume that you've been having too much 'Porridge' on TV for breakfast!"

At the station she was signed in, searched, photographed and fingerprinted, all at a speed unusual to the profession. As she was a drug addict she was placed in a cell with another user knowing both had similar needs and so could most likely be dealt with at the same time. The other girl in the cell, Paula, turned out to be very helpful and amiable. She assured Emma that the medics did turn up and although she would not be receiving street heroin but methadone instead, at least it would keep the nightmares at bay.

And so Emma's world began the process of rebalancing itself, as her present reality matched the experiences she had become familiar with, on the few occasions when the police had come knocking previously.

She did a 360 degrees circle in the centre of the cell and said to Paula jokingly, "Curtains at the window, pot plant in the corner and a few 'home' magazines lying out on the non existent coffee table and it would almost have the appearance of home". Paula had not much chance of getting to know her new roomie as the DI arranged a medical check to ensure that Emma was comfortable enough to undergo an informal interview. He was pushing for the interview before she received her dose of methadone, as he did not want the records to show that it had been subsequently undertaken whilst she was under the influence of drugs. A drug fuelled state, which could have been formally classified as of the force's own making. Both the medic and Emma were as one that there should be no adverse change to her condition for at least another 90 minutes. That being the case, Barnham arranged for the interview to commence within 10.

As it was not a formal interview and due to time constraints, plus the fact that no charges had yet been brought, Emma had voluntarily agreed to undertake this dialogue without legal representation but only on the proviso that a female officer was also present. So at 8.15pm, DI Terry Barnham and T/DC Murray met in Interview Room 2 with a large flask of coffee, a plate of ginger biscuits and, of course, Emma Flynn. Barnham set the ball rolling with, "Right Emma, are you comfortable? Is there anything else you need at the moment?" She answered that everything was fine, so he continued. "I want you to recall everything that happened on the night that you met the person we will refer to as 'victim number three'. If, at any point you feel dizzy or thirsty or hungry or even in need of something stronger, please let me know. The medic on call tonight will be here up until 10.00pm. I'll ensure that we are finished well before then so as not to put you in too much discomfort. And just so T/DC Murray here doesn't get too much discomfort either from writing cramp I also want to record the interview. Is that clear and understood?" Again Emma nodded in the affirmative and the DI went on, "T/DC Murray could you set up the audio recorder? It's bad enough messing about with CD's at home without continually unwrapping audio-cassettes for outdated technology," he muttered almost to himself.

T/DC Murray set it up and looking across at the DI was given the signal to press 'record'. Barnham introduced himself and stated the location, date and time, T/DC Murray and Emma stated their names, and the DI ended with, "So please tell us what you recall of the night in question?" Emma looked to the ceiling, closed her eyes and recollected the scenario. She had played it over in her mind in various splintered pieces ever since she had awoken in hospital. And now had the advantage of being economical with certain aspects of the attempted murder perpetrated on her. The killer and Emma were the only two people alive who knew those intimate details, and Barnham would never be any the wiser of the truth until he actually caught the murderer in question and that person confessed. The end of her marathon recollection took them to 9.40pm including only a coffee replenishment and one toilet break of five minutes for Emma. That being the case Barnham decided to reconvene for the conclusion of the interview on the following morning. The only clear fact that he could glean from the case so far was of the victim's first name being Peter and he had lived on the outskirts of Edinburgh. This had led him to ask, "When I spoke to you at the hospital, why didn't you say you recognised the murdered victim from the photograph? You knew his name, well his first name anyway. We could have moved forward with the case more quickly had we had a name then."

Emma had replied, "Did you ask me for a name in the hospital? I don't recall that. At the time I still thought I was dreaming and so nothing was clear or sharp. The only thing that sticks in my mind is that you mentioned a dead body. That's when I started panicking because I thought you were going to try and pin a murder on me, and I still have that concern, a little. Anyway, you know now for what it's worth."

Barnham thought, 'Yes, for what it's worth. Three murders, possibly three killers but with the binding tape leading to the likelihood of it being just the one. Let's hope that the tattooist's not been leading us a merry dance too?'

The next morning saw Emma awake, up and dressed bright and early. No room service and her shoes had not been cleaned either but at least the company was still friendly if not a tad inquisitive. "Are you going today? Bit of a flying visit, isn't it? The cops seem to be giving you an easy ride. Are you a nark or what? What are you in for anyway, and why did they take you off for all that time last night?"

'She asks as if she should be wearing a black gown and

white wig,' thought Emma. So she replied with, "Me lord. I don't know which answer to give my learned friend first. Perhaps I'll take them in the order that they were given. One. I haven't a clue if I'm going home today or not. Two. Who knows how long my visit is until I'm released. Three. Your guess is as good as mine as to why they're giving me an easy time. Four. Me lord, I must object. I do believe the prosecutor tagged that question to the one I previously answered and rolled them together. But in answer to question Three, part two. No I am definitely not a nark. I know the value of the code and I respect it and adhere to it," she giggled holding her right hand over her heart. "Four. We must be on four by now. I've been incarcerated against my wishes, as I am to be presented as a material witness to a murder. You know one of the three murders that there's been all that speculation about in the papers." At this point our learned friend had reverted back to her more familiar vernacular but as she got more into the swing of it herself she took on a third party character. Her pathos then continued with, "At first my client thought she was a suspect in the case but now I'm convinced that she's here more for her own protection. So, I put it to you your honour that the public body that has incarcerated my client will have to decide what action to take; and today at the latest."

As this rhetoric continued pouring from Emma's mouth she waved her arms about, grabbed her invisible lapels and gesticulated at Paula by pointing her finger directly at her on a number of occasions. "And Fifth and finally, Me lord. Again, I fear a two-part question combined together, solely with the purpose of actively confusing my client. Fifthly. My client undeniably was dragged from the comforts of her cell, to a place of dread and submitted to the most heinous tortures imaginable. She was withheld food and drink, whilst undergoing 'Guantanamo' style torture in order to gain her admission that she had, in fact, murdered the person hereby known only as victim three."

By this time Paula was beside herself. She was rolling about her bed with tears streaming down her cheeks, shouting, "Stop it. Stop it. I can't take anymore. I'm going to wet myself if you don't." Emma was laughing too, and suddenly felt an affinity of closeness to this stranger, almost like two sisters playacting in their childhood years.

They both reached for tissues to dry off their tears of fun and Emma said, still with a laugh in her throat, "It's not so bad in here after all". What she thought to herself was more on the lines of, 'Well I didn't get all that off Porridge, did I?' Talking of porridge, as if on cue the key turned in their lock and both women were ushered to the canteen for their breakfast, in tandem with the rest of the inmates. DI Barnham turned up as they were still eating and informed Emma he needed to recommence the interview within 30 minutes. Emma agreed that she would have enough time between now and then to finish her breakfast and take care of her toiletry requirements. This being the case the DI grabbed a coffee to go; to go to his office, and walked off whistling, 'I went to a party at the county jail'.

In order to have a sense of continuity and taking the somewhat philosophical view that two heads were better than one, Barnham decided again to bring in T/DC Murray. Last night's interview had proceeded exceptionally well, which could have been partly due to her female calming presence and he was pleased at the success of gleaning a considerable amount of information, some of which he had already surmised anyway but other elements of which he had known nothing about. However, he was still struggling to come to terms with how the final moments had played out. Emma had said last night that the killer had incapacitated her first and then Peter second but the Forensics' evidence and subsequent photographs had indicated otherwise. Barnham now asked her to revisit that part of her statement again, hoping to catch her out, and so he could more understand why she may have been economical with the truth in the first place. He had already spent the morning thus far, replaying the previous night's interview and now knew most of the salient points by heart. Emma reiterated the facts, as she saw them, by saying, "The last thing I remembered was Peter getting excited about the offer I'd put on the table, well the skip side actually if I'm being literal, and he went off very jovially to relieve his bladder. And that's basically about it, I can't really add anymore. A dark shape rushed up and bowled me over and then everything went even darker, if that was possible. Next thing I know I'm being woken up in a hospital bed."

"So in your mind you're convinced that you were attacked before Peter."

"Oh yes, definitely. I remember, because I could hear him. He was still, like peeing for Niagara Falls and I thought, 'I hope he gives that a good shake and a wipe before putting it anywhere near me'."

Barnham cringing somewhat, continued, "It's just that the Forensics' results prove that it was more than likely to be the other way round, which we think may have given you more of an opportunity to see and or possibly hear the killer. Perhaps your mind has it confused?"

Emma still trying valiantly to stick to her preconceived story replied, "No I don't think so. It is hard to remember I'll grant you that as so much has gone on since."

"Well, let me tell you what we know, how it most likely played out and why we think it's different to what you are remembering," replied Barnham in a slightly bullish business-like tone. "Forensics has positive proof that Peter went down first. And they know this for three reasons. One, your left foot was found to be overlapping Peter's right shin, and two, neither body was attacked at the skip, both were in fact dragged to it. Both your weights left scuffmarks on the ground from your heels and your own less defined markings definitely run over the top of Peter's. And three, our 'coup de gras', so to speak; there was a crumpled up ball of adhesive tape under your body which the murderer could only have thrown there after binding victim three's hands and feet, confirming that you were placed there second and not first as you state," he pronounced triumphantly.

Emma replied, "Well, from what you've just said it sounds like I was placed there after Peter but it's not proof that I wasn't attacked first, is it? I just could have been left longer in my original position than Peter. And anyway, whichever way it was, it doesn't prove that I did or didn't see the killer or hear anything for that matter. My mind's a total blank on the whole issue so it's pointless me making something up just to appease you!"

"OK. I won't push it any further. I was just hopeful that you might have been able to give us some steer as to the murderer's identity. But even so I'm still going to keep you in for a few days, if that's all right with you. With all the media interest about three murders and not four, the murderer is going to be aware that we're holding back sensitive information for a reason, and that could put you in a dangerous position. He may put two and two together and realise that only three have died and not four. That's still three people too many, and with all due respect to Jonnie, I don't think he's going to be that knight in shining armour if the killer comes a calling." Emma played a slight smirk across her lips, which did not go unnoticed. "I don't know what you've got to smile about as you've two choices, and neither include freedom. You can either stay in the detention cell with your newfound friend, whom I understand you're getting along with swimmingly; or I can arrange for a transfer to a safe house."

"Sorry, DI Barnham. It's just that I've already used up your analogy of a knight in shining armour for Jonnie. He really must be a selfless little helper if both of us have come to that same conclusion. Anyway, I'm quite happy staying here for the present. As long as you will give me an assurance that I am at liberty to leave at any time, should I so wish?"

Barnham thought but could not really argue against the

request. "Yes, that is your prerogative but I will advise against it, if and when the situation arises."

Emma nodded her agreement of understanding and was escorted back to her cell. As she meandered through the labyrinth of corridors she approached an officer, or so she presumed, who was heading in the opposite direction clutching a tray, full of steaming mugs. Their eyes met fleetingly and Jessica, who was the subject of Emma's presumption, edged towards the wall to ensure a bottleneck was avoided. This allowed more space to pass and so made an accident with hot coffee less likely. As Emma and her escort continued down the short flights of stairs, the would-be captive cum witness smugly mused, 'Who's the gaoler now? I'm withholding vital information that could help in the capture of this murderer, so that makes you Mr Barnham, DI, the main man, more of a prisoner than me! And if and when I decide to reveal it, it will be on my terms and not yours.'

Frustrated, the DI moved on. He called a meeting of the team for 11.00am with the intention of furnishing a transcript of Emma's interview and then verbally giving his own take on the final moments. He still held the view that Emma was holding back and that forensics had the stronger case in proving that she was the second one to be placed in the position she was found in and not the first, as she continually argued. He expressed interest in hearing what Jessica's comments would be if this revised development was fed to the media in order to flush out the murderer; and questioned as to whether she would then wish to champion this version of events. He also wanted to tie in the name, Peter, to victim three, in the hope that future media coverage would run with it and so jog someone's memory, the next of kin at least. But by far the most important break through had been victim two's name, and he was now desperate for an update from his team as to how that was progressing.

With the release of the name, several leads had been forthcoming but the most pre-eminent, by far, had been from a caller alleging to be a close friend of hers, who then went on to verify the address at which she generally resided. PC Blackwell now relayed the following information to the team meeting, having just returned from visiting that address.

"I was in the vicinity of Melrose anyway, canvassing all the households along the High Street but the photographs of the bloated face were not really making recognition of the victim very easy. In fact, most of the locals expressed revulsion at the sight of them. Of those who could look, one or two had suggested it was a woman who went missing on a regular basis. A woman known to have had several affairs with husbands after they had taken too much drink. Only this one generally turned up after two or three weeks; just like a bad penny but with a guilty conscience instead. Others thought it looked like a woman who had inferred that she was moving to Hawick. And others again who were sure they had seen her working in a supermarket at Kelso. So all in all the photographs were not doing their job and confusion reigned. The heavens rained too but as we know that's all part and parcel of door-to-door police work.

"Anyway, as I was saying I was still in Melrose, now canvassing one of the quieter residential areas when I received WPC Whitely's communication. She informed me of the call she'd received about the address on Abbey Street, which is just off the High Street. When I knocked on the relevant door a man opened it looking both resigned and apologetic at the same time; he also had the last tinges of bruising on his face as if he'd been in the ring and come off second best. I ascertained that he was Mr Dawson and before I could say the reason for the visit he butted in and said to me," here PC Blackwell opened his notebook and read: " 'I'm sorry if the kids have been causing problems with the neighbours but I'm trying to do my best, but you see the wife's left me, I'm working all hours and then I've got to sort the kids out the rest of the time. I don't think I've slept more than three hours a night what with making meals, washing and cleaning. Not that you'd notice the cleaning with the state of the place!'

"He invited me in and I could see what he meant about cleaning. I then proceeded to inform Mr Dawson that I was investigating the disappearance of his wife. 'But haven't I just told you that?' he interrupted again. 'That she has disappeared already, buggered off and left me.' I replied that I would explain further if he would refrain from interrupting. I proceeded to show him the photographs and he eventually confirmed that it was, indeed, his Mairie. But the reason he deliberated was that he didn't recognise the gaudy tattoo on her chest. His actual comment was, 'That wasn't there the last time I saw them.' He then broke down realising what this meant. I asked him if he had not seen the press or TV lately, or even heard the radio. He looked at me sorrowfully and said, 'What do you think? If I got chance to do any of those things I'd fall asleep within seconds.' So I then asked if he was oblivious to what had been going on around him with the three murders and he just simply answered, 'What murders?' The upshot is that he definitely confirms victim two as his wife and he last saw her four days prior to her death; which I'd given him approximately, based on the pathologist's estimation."

"Thank you for your diligence. I'm presuming that you didn't feel it necessary to bring in Mr Dawson for further questioning, as a possible suspect?" asked Barnham.

"Well, no Sir with respect. I suspected that he was more likely to have enough on his plate already and I honestly didn't feel in his predicament that he would have time to go around murdering two people plus his wayward wife, what with his hands full with the kids and working."

"You're probably correct in that assumption. Right, WPC Whitely, update the whiteboard. It's only a shame that all the clues have related to victim two and not to one or both of the other victims but at least we are now moving in the right direction. Let's hope the press still has a few surprises between its pages, a little excitement to generate some heat into those phones! And surely now Jessica, it will give you plenty of additional material to help expand your profiler's web and trap this killer before we have any more deaths on our hands. Come on team let's give it all we've got and find this bastard."

CHAPTER THIRTEEN

Since the day Jessica was seconded to the murder inquiry team, Joe Foster, her colleague at The Borders Agency, had mixed feelings of both total dejection and deflation. His main perception of the situation and concern for himself was of Jessica leaving the department to commence an exciting and challenging new position. One, taking her on an ever-upward trajectory and propelling her into the limelight, far and away, eclipsing his own very ambitious dreams of career advancement. To counteract this feeling of negativity he made a decision to hone and enhance his personal skills and bring them to the fore. He never professed to be a profiler in the way Jessica purported to be, having had no experience in that field; but having watched a lot of TV dramas he did question of himself as to how difficult it could be to imagine being inside someone else's head and guessing their next move. And, his other more personal motive, if he was being totally honest, was that he missed seeing her attractive face and lithe body; a body he had to admit, to himself at least that he lusted after, although one that had eluded him so far, except in his fantasies.

His theoretical forte at university had been behavioural sciences, which in the main studied and observed the activities and interactions of humans. And with psychology and cognitive science playing their individual parts in that mix, so he ventured that they could work now. His excitement at this prospect found him working far longer hours than previous, and to all intents and purposes he now had two jobs: his usual job at The Borders Agency, which in itself was far busier anyway due to Jessica's absence and his other job as a freelance detective. The latter being undertaken at home and in his free time, so that he could keep these extra-curricular activities under wraps, and out of sight from his boss, Tess Danvers.

He was actually enjoying the reality of living this double life as it filled a gap in his otherwise leisure timetable which previously had been taken up by one of his two former wives and in a strange way to his thinking it moved him inexorably closer to the sphere that Jessica herself now orbited. He christened these two functions simply as 'day job' and 'night job'.

With the press awareness of the murders well into its second week, that's including their first week's weak offerings whereby they included as much fiction as fact, Joe was feverishly cutting out articles and photos and tacking them to both his living room and hall walls; in fact any wall that did not rebel against the intrusion. He applied lengths of different coloured wool to cross-reference what he perceived to be direct links between each victim and stared continuously at the intersections of these lengths of yarn in the hope and expectation that they would reveal the murderer's identity.

He became obsessed and so was prone to chant silently, 'who are you, what are you, where are you, you can't hide forever'? It was on one such occasion that Mairie Dawson's name jumped right off the wall. He'd heard of it, read it or seen it somewhere before, but where? 'Of course you have, stupid. It's been plastered over all the papers, TV and radio and now all over your walls. How could you not have subconsciously noticed it?' he thought berating himself. But as he showered, and then shaved, and then ate breakfast, and then left for work, all in the automaton fashion which he had adopted due to his tiredness at the elongation of the working day; it had struck him, 'under my nose, yet out of sight'. He'd heard that phrase in a nursery rhyme or as a riddle in a book, or maybe on TV; but it was now so obvious.

He arrived at work, put to one side the 'day job' files that were cluttering his desk from previous, and searched the database for Mairie Dawson or Mary Dawson. Why he had not come up with the name before he had no idea but there was a 50/50 chance that she could have crossed the Agency's path and that being the case, it may shed some light on the other company she had kept. The computer confirmed positively that Mairie Dawson had indeed been brought to The Borders Agency's attention. Next, he methodically checked against the database to confirm that it was one and the same person. But agonisingly, he did not have the press cutting at work; the one, which had published the street and town where Mairie Dawson had resided; and so he broke the local government's employees' rule of 'no personal use of the Internet'. He wracked his brain trying to remember the paper in question which published the details but the more he thought, the more it eluded him; so in the end he 'Googled' her name to see what links the search engine would display. After two clicks he had confirmation of the address he needed as, 'Abbey Street, Melrose'. His internal search cross-referenced the address with his Organisation's own computer records and his elation and surprise said it all. The victim's name and the specific address related to 'File S32'; now he had the more difficult task of tracking down that file, without it becoming obvious to his superior.

Because of the nature of the work they undertook, much of the material was data protected and generally only certain logins would access certain status levels of file. On occasion, Joe had access to these logins and passwords too, but that was usually with prior clearance, the alternative being to sign for and retrieve the hard copy from the archives. Again, not a simple task as the material contained in these files was strictly confidential. An intern, Sophie, had responsibility for the accuracy of the filing, the guarding of the logbook with signatures of those accessing the files, and the subsequent security of both operations. 'An intern, a mere trainee. If the files are so important why not someone in a more senior capacity?' thought Joe staying in the 'night job' at no small risk to himself. Still Sophie filed away and literally held the keys; keys to the banks of filing cabinets stretching across the lower ground floor of their offices. 'Working underground like some kind of more attractive female Gollum,' thought Joe forever grasping at opportunities and switching out of both 'day job' and 'night job', and into 'free time, fun time' mode. 'Yes, definitely more attractive and if my eyes had not been turned by Jessica I might be testing the water with that little minx instead. See if she knows a riddle or two?'

His opportunity came after lunch when his workload dictated the necessity to review a case requiring a hard copy file from which he could photocopy certain pages. Pages that had been altered and initialled by the original author and so would differ from the pristine computerised files locked on the digital archive back up. He paid the intern a visit in her lair and handed over his countersigned request slip, countersigned by Tess Danvers, the woman he nicknamed the dragon, again to himself, and not just because she wore lizard skin boots. In fact, whilst he had the opportunity he handed over two slips, both countersigned by Tess, although one was a forgery of his own making. 'But Sophie, with her eyes dimmed from working in the dark for so long will never notice, will she?' he thought amusingly as he waited at the allotted counter. Sophie did not notice and both files arrived with a smile, and were handed over after the prerequisite signatures were signed, with an expectation; an expectation of an invitation for a night out to wine and dine perhaps. They were received with the same smile returned and the same expectation possibly being fulfilled, that an invitation for a night out just might be on the cards. Both parties parted happily, but only one was completely satisfied.

Joe utilised the bona fide file in his 'day job', whilst purloining the other, a file on Mairie Dawson and tucked it away in his rucksack for purely his 'night job' reading. As the day dragged on he became more and more excited at the prospect that he was going to make a breakthrough. A breakthrough that might even eclipse Jessica's own abilities and success, and place him right at the top, on the pinnacle of her pedestal. 'Mm, I'd like to be on top of Jessica's pedestal,' he mused, getting a little hot under the collar.

At 4.00pm he signed out on 'flexitime' and was home by 4.25. He opened the front door, literally ran through the hall, which was looking more and more like some crazy art installation, and pulled the file out of his rucksack. After greedily reading it for a good five minutes he knew he was on the right track. He was disappointed though that no other names mentioned in the document jumped out at him but he knew that if he could find just one more name in another case file then, perhaps that would make the cast-iron link that he was desperately seeking. And then, perhaps the specifics would build and build to reveal the full picture, or at least that was his reasoning and logic.

Joe began acting like a dog with a bone. He had broken the Agency's code of ethics by secretly taking a hard copy file out of the archives without authority and forging his superior's signature in the process. To add insult to injury he had then removed the file from the premises and so breached the Data Protection Act 1998. 'All in a good cause,' he convinced himself. 'But what are the chances of me getting access to another file? How can I act on what I know? On the one hand I can tell Tess what I've found and how I found it, and we can look together through other case studies; and on the other I can speak to Jessica and possibly let her steal my thunder. But which will be most beneficial to me and cause me least problems,' he questioned? 'Well, I see Jessica as a rival, a colleague, a person with greater knowledge and experience than me, and a beautiful woman to boot. This revelation might just nudge me closer to her boudoir .... And Tess is ... well my boss and nearly old enough to be my mother,' he argued, not very unbiased, and whilst at the same time reaching for his mobile.

"Jessica. Hi, remember me. A couple of things, if you've got time to talk?" He said excitedly.

Jessica had answered the phone with enthusiasm, which soon dwindled to a more lethargic level on recognition of Joe's voice. "Hi Joe. Missing me already? How would I not be able to remember your dulcet tones? Are you checking up on me or have I left a mess behind that Tess has you cleaning up?"

"Jessica, don't be like that. I've never seen you leave a mess of any description, let alone one that Tess would notice. No, the reason for my call, apart from to hear your lovely silky voice, is that I've been doing some digging. Digging into those three murders that have just been splashed all over the papers and I've been trying to make it all add up, you know like *you* do." At this point he then went on to give Jessica a précis of how he had 'borrowed' a file from the archives and how he thought it was leading him in a positive direction. He was concerned that the 'dragon' might not see it as positively, and that he could jeopardise his job with a possible career move to the local nick, so he was turning to her for help and guidance. He did not want to reveal any names on an open phone line either as that additional breach of security may find its way back to Tess too.

Jessica's lethargy left her as quickly as an addicted gambler's profits. She replied enthusiastically, "This is sounding really quite interesting. Is it someone we both know? But, you are right to be careful; you could get into serious trouble with Tess. She can be a bitch at times, if you'll pardon my unprofessional French but you know what she's like when she gets on her 'high heels', about officialdom and bureaucracy; and 'data protection', well that's one of her pet favourites, isn't it."

"Yes, well, I am actually surprised that you didn't pick up on it yourself, as it was one of your more recent client cases. Afraid you've let your halo slip on this one. I'll have to tell you about it when we meet up but please be aware it isn't something I can bottle up for long. And I think you're right about Tess, the less she knows the better."

"Well if you're that desperate I'll come over and go through it with you this evening, if you like?"

"Well this evening would be great but I can't do it at my house. It's in such a tip, as much as I'd love to entertain," said Joe, looking round the walls and thinking, 'I can't take all this down, not yet!'.

"OK. Come round to mine. I bet that's what you've been hankering after anyway. But don't think you've got carte blanche to get up to any funny business. I'll tell you for nothing, I'm not interested in becoming wife number three."

"That sounds great Jessica and perhaps we can discuss becoming wife number three on another occasion, then? Do I need to bring anything?" He said thinking that one thing could lead to another and then you never know what might happen, so a toothbrush might be a good call.

"Just bring your files and remember, 'Mum's the word'. Don't want Tess getting wind of what you've been up to already, do we? I'll be finished here in a half hour and then I'll swing by M&S and pick up some groceries. Can you bring a bottle?" she asked rhetorically and then continued, "See you at eight. Can't wait to find out what you've dug up."

"And here's me thinking that you wanted to see me, just for being me! Going to M&S, are you? I'd better bring a decent bottle, then. OK, eight o'clock it is."

Jessica pulled her own files together and felt excited at the prospect of this meeting with Joe as she was intrigued to know if it would bring the identity of the serial killer that little bit nearer. She left her new colleagues none the wiser as she did not want them to get their hopes up but she left them all the same. As she drove towards M&S her mind was racing as to what Joe's thought process would have been and where it would have led him. She recognised that clues, which could lead to the murderer, were appearing in the public domain, and now felt that she may have possibly dropped behind the curve. Her decision reached, she mentally made plans for the next couple of hours, knowing that she would also have to be wary of Joe and his amorous advances.

She arrived home having fulfilled her intentions and treated herself to a well-earned shower but without the well-earned run that she would have dearly loved to precede it. As promised by 8.00pm she had all her culinary preparations in place except for the fact of Joe not turning up at her house.
She double checked the time and then grabbed her mobile and automatically rang his to enquire if he was running late but her call went straight through to voice mail, so she just left a message instead. 'Hi, Joe. Jessica here. Just wondering if you've been held up? You've not had a puncture on the way over, have you? Get back to me so I know when to put the sauce on the hob.' But Joe didn't get back to Jessica, so at 8.35pm she had religiously sent a text. 'Joe it's Jessica. Got a BetA offer! git n tuch. Lol J'. 'Can't do any more than that,' she thought as she carefully removed the scallops with chorizo from the oven, concentrating totally so as not to spill the lemon and sea salt butter everywhere.

All to no avail as it turned out. Joe had finally played the chivalrous knight card once too often. In pitch-black visibility between Lauder and St Boswells he had, on impulse, stopped his car to help another car in distress. A car that appeared to have inexplicably skidded off the road, leaving its two nearside wheels straddling a ditch. Joe having been flagged down by the driver and innocently stopped to offer assistance, and then with a shocked expression on his face and only a gasp in his throat, collapsed to the roadside as if paralysed by the almost non-existent prick of the auto injector. The killer reacted quickly and reversed the stranded car back onto the road, concluding with a pre-planned manoeuvre that ended with it parked up in a farmer's field, and then manhandled the prostrate body into the victim's own car. Joe was then chauffeured sombrely and with reverence to his final resting place, albeit minus the fanfare of tear jerking hymns. But at least with the solace of silent night, reflected by the eerie quietness all around him, and with just the thrum of the tyres on the metal road for accompaniment.

Lying on his side with his head positioned towards the ground only allowed Joe to direct his gaze sideways, and at best, take in part of the gradual upward gradient. Here, in his numbed and somewhat paralysed state, he studied the minute rivulets running through the creases of the luxuriant green undulating landscape. A scene, which he was still able to marvel at and find poetically comforting in its own desolate and windswept kind of way, even though it was cold, so bitterly cold. He pictured how romantic it could be to relay this vision to Jessica had they been sat close and snug by an open fire toasting each other from his bottle of Barolo; Barolo no less and at what cost but she was worth it or not as the case maybe. Now in his heart he knew that thought would never be. He imagined himself as only being mugged at the worst, with the killer having already rifled his rucksack and now searching him for specific items, in order to rob him solely of his identity but not necessarily his life.

And even in this misplaced optimism he could smile at the irony of his satisfaction at being 2 – 0 up against the police in his amateur investigation, as one: he was never more certain than now that he was going to be the fourth murdered victim and two: he knew who the actual killer was, even with the wearing of the ski mask. As he craned his neck even further, to study the killer preparing the syringe that he was convinced would take him to total oblivion, his final stream of consciousness alighted on the thought of what might have been if God had not created people to be either life givers or life takers. He knew his time was up and that he was in no position to leave any form of sign as to who was playing the reaper, as just like the other victims before him, his hands and feet were tightly bound. But his desperate last-ditched will to live meant that he would continue to struggle to free himself as he wrestled unsuccessfully with the effects of the unexpected jag from the auto injector which caused his original immobility. So it would be left to the rabbits, silfraying nearby, to memorise the tableau as it reached its final act, and possibly help to bring the ruthless murderer to justice.

On the following day, Jessica rang The Borders Agency office, worried as to whether or not Joe had turned up for work. From past experience and with Joe being a creature of habit she was convinced that he usually arrived at approximately 8.25am for an 8.30am start. So she left it until 8.45am, knowing that the receptionist would then be present and in position too. "Morning, Judy. Jessica here, Jessica Lambert. How are you today? Could you please put me through to Joe?"

"Oh. Hi, Jessica. I'm fine, and you? Joe. Joe Foster. Just a second. The line went blank and five seconds later it started ringing out, and it ended ringing out too, then re-diverted back to reception. "Sorry Jessica, no reply. He must have slept in, what with all this detective work he's been telling me about."

"What detective work's that? Has he been thinking about a change of job?" Jessica asked, as she had understood that Joe did not want to be too indiscreet in case Tess found out, so she was surprised that he had taken the receptionist of all people into his confidence.

"No. It's just that he's got a bee in his bonnet about these murders. He's been pretending to be a detective, like in one of those crime dramas. You know, the deep ones where you haven't a clue what's going on. The type of programme that shows people putting lots of pictures on walls with clues and things, then linking them together with bits of string. Whether it works or not, I've no idea?"

"And are you his assistant then?" Jessica asked jokingly.

"Oh, no. He just told me in confidence at lunch the other day. I think he fancy's me actually," she said as each word came out slower than the one before with the realisation of her error. 'Oh, well,' she thought 'in for a penny, in for a pound'. With an intake of breath she continued, "He said that he'd only just started doing it but he did seem a little excited, like he'd found something out. I told him he was nuts and should just get on with his normal job or Ms Danvers would be onto him. Anyway I've another call coming in. Shall I'll tell him you called when he comes in?"

"Yes, do that. And tell him I've sent him an email too. See you later." Jessica finished the call and flipped open her laptop, composing an email in her head whilst she waited for it to boot up. 'Sorry we didn't meet up last night. You missed a treat of a meal. I'm really interested in your news. Get back to me when you can. Hope everything's OK. J.' She reread it and pressed send. 'Nothing there to raise Tess' curiosity,' she thought. She then gathered her gear together, dropped it in the car and reversed out of the drive. Driving to work was always a constructive time. Jessica used it to plan ahead, both her days and evenings. Today, she knew that the investigation team would be buoyant with the identification of victim two and also the fact that 'Peter' was the first name of victim three. Her job now would become more pressurised, with her talent for infiltrating the killer's mind being taken to a new level. 'I must go through the car wash on the way home and I'm probably going to have to forego taekwondo class again, what with this workload on the murderer to progress,' she thought annoyingly.

*

Barnham's evening had proved both interesting and expectant too. Emma had become more vocal and had browbeaten him into allowing her to move out of the detention cell and into a safe house, despite Paula protestations against it. The only problem being that Emma's definition of a safe house and the DI's were like chalk and cheese. She wanted somewhere with more freedom and he wanted a location offering more security. Barnham knew that he should be preparing for the following day's team meeting but he also knew that now Emma had been placed in a social environment and so again within his reach, the chemistry he felt that existed between them soared to an almost uncontrollable level. Initially, in his dreams, he had been torn between the choices of three women or so he had imagined, a bit like the 'buses all coming at once' cliché. Tess with her mature but still attractive features and curves that only age could sculpt and enhance; Jessica with her beautiful captivating Mediterranean looks and lithe snakelike athletic body and; Emma with her fuller figure, sexual allure, obvious appetite, and knowledgeable experience to match.

Barnham did what he always did when confronted with choices, he took out a tipped cigarette and placed the untipped end in his mouth and proceeded to suck for all he was worth on the dry, leafy tobacco. Decisions came easier that way and tonight had been no exception. 'Yes, tonight Emma I choose you,' he thought and he meant it. Choosing between the three options had been quite easy really. Tess had come third due to age, sorry Tess. Jessica had come second due to her possible aloofness and so far self-contained lack of positive interest in him, and Emma had won outright as Barnham knew in his heart that she would be a good bet and fun to be with. And in view of her chosen career and track record he could be almost guaranteed a fulfilling night of passion.

He had always preached to his colleagues the mantra of not mixing business with pleasure but that was to his colleagues. As for himself, he had to admit that he had been hooked from the moment he had seen Emma. That same instant in which he thought he recognised her but could not be one hundred per cent certain. He almost regretted his decision of not choosing Jessica but being somewhat of a cynic and a male chauvinist, he thought, 'they are both of a similar age and if I'm being brutally honest about it, and had the chance of either between the sheets, I'd probably be confused as to which one was there!'

So he rang Emma on her mobile. Jonnie answered with a greeting, and the DI's bravado and laddishness left him in an instant. "Hi Jonnie, how are you?" the DI stammered. "There isn't a problem, is there? Everything OK? Emma OK? I didn't know that you'd been given dispensation to be with her?"

"Slow down Mr Barnham, Sir. All these questions? Yes, everything's fine here. Emma's fine. She's being well looked after and, although, I'm not really happy about this drugs thing she is still getting her medication on time. We've talked about her trying to get clean but you know...." He trailed off resignedly.

"Yes, I know Jonnie. It's not going to happen overnight."

"Anyway she was lonely by herself in this house and asked the bodyguard to enquire whether or not she could have a friend visit? And she chose me," he said with happiness in his voice.

'Mm, lucky you Jonnie. Why didn't I know this?' thought Barnham making a mental note. "That's good. And I suppose the murderer's no idea who you are or how you fit in to this? So there's no problem there. I mean you won't exactly be leading the serial killer to her door."

"Yes, that's what I thought, Sir. Anyway do you want a word with Emma? Is that what you rang for?"

"Well it is, but now that I know she's alright and being protected and no doubt, well entertained, then I'm happy. I'll ring her tomorrow, bye for now. Say goodnight for me. Oh, and just one more thing. Let her know that the drugs squad have picked up her mate in that white Mercedes, so thanks for that one." The DI put the phone to his chest feeling better that he had got one over on the competition, even if it was below the belt. 'If I can't have her then at least I'll put her in a bad enough mood to scupper Jonnie's chances,' he sighed venomously. He then sucked on his dummy and thought, 'Oh well, one down, two to go'. He rang Jessica's mobile but it went straight through to voicemail, so he quickly cancelled, as he couldn't think of a sensible message to leave on the spur of the moment. That left Tess, but by this time his libido had diminished and his ego and confidence had shrunk to match. He resorted to consoling himself with a can of lager, further sucks on his dummies and a night with his alternative mistress, TV. 'Mm, Midsummer Murders, better watch this, I might get a few tips on how to apprehend murderers!' he joked at his own expense.

*

The serial murderer's night had been far busier and it had been far more productive too. First Joe's body was dropped off at its final resting place and then the killer drove back in the victim's car, which unlike the body would never be found as it was dumped unceremoniously at the bottom of a once disused quarry that had been recently turned into a Site of Special Scientific Interest sanctuary. A welcome natural habitat for evolution to continue its work with the water based plant life, species of fish and amphibians, and insects of every variety: either living under, on or above the water, plus an array of bird life that brought twitchers from afar to this otherwise hidden ecosystem. 'Well,' thought the murderer as the car careened down the quarry side, 'sorry to intrude on your peace of heaven but it's all in a good cause'.

CHAPTER FOURTEEN

The next morning Jessica arrived at the office aggrieved with how this evening was going to pan out and Barnham arrived equally aggrieved at how his previous evening had actually panned out. She: knowing that taekwondo class would be missed, and he: knowing that an opportunity to relieve his pent up frustrations had gone begging. He mosied over to Jessica's desk to find her engrossed in pie charts, family-tree type graphs and totally surrounded by an array of reference books.

"Rang you on your mobile last night Jessica," he said casually as he picked up and leafed through one of her tomes.

"Sorry. I never got a message. Was it something to do with the cases?" replied Jessica still absorbed in her work.

"No, I never left a message. I always feel a fool and say the wrong thing or half a thing and have to start again. A bit like I'm talking now actually. And yes, it was something to do with the cases. Well no, I mean it wasn't. I had just wondered what you were up to and whether or not you'd have liked to have gone for a drink or something?"

"Well two dates in one night and both no shows. I don't know if I can keep pace with it." In order to put the DI's quizzical look out of its misery, she continued, "Joe from work, Joe Foster, he was meant to be coming over for a meal and to fill me in on his extra curricular activity." Still a look of puzzlement hung from Barnham's face. "He thought he'd found something important in our murder cases but then never showed. I rang and sent a text to see if he was working late but still no answer so I ended up eating some of the meal I'd prepared and watching a DVD instead. It was 'Skyfall' actually, and on Blu-ray, no less. I can thoroughly recommend it as an alternative to going out, but then maybe I'm biased with it being Daniel Craig as Bond, James Bond," she said playfully. "Have you ever thought of yourself as being a bit of a Bond. I mean you've never married, have you? And you're always trying to chase and charm women."

"Don't stereotype me," he said crest fallen, "It was only for a drink not full blown sex!" He blushed to a bright red as soon as he had said that. It was one of his pub chat-up lines, but not meant for the office and certainly not meant for this occasion. "Erh, sorry Jessica. Please forget I said that, I just got carried away with the moment. Team meeting in ten minutes in the incident room," he gesticulated in his business manner as he swept his hand across his brow.

The meeting had just got underway as Jessica entered, armed with papers and textbooks. She sat solo at a desk so that she could spread out her accessories in order to be ready when called upon. DI Barnham updated his colleagues as to the present status of the cases. But emphasised that more still needed to be done, as victims one and three were still unknown. He then invited Jessica to take the floor to give the audience her educated view.

Jessica stood in front of her six 'newish' colleagues and confidently started speaking. "I've spent time studying each of the three victims' deaths plus not forgetting the lucky one that got away, Emma Flynn. My instincts tell me that the killer wanted these people to suffer, for whatever reason. The first two were incapacitated by the, what was it now, by the 'epipen', an auto injector. They were then left alive to suffer lingering deaths and no one can understand how they must have suffered, nor for what period of time. My presumption is that the killer has in the past suffered at the hands of the same or, more than likely, similar abusers to the ones that these victims' profiles might emulate. We then move on to victim three. He was given the same treatment initially but then his resulting death was guaranteed to be quick or at least he would have had little knowledge of it. My take on this is that the murderer really wanted the victim to suffer, his immediate death wasn't a merciful act, but the killer became spooked and therefore concerned that he or the victim might be found before the task was completed. The fourth victim, Emma Flynn proved that point. She too was meant to die before being found but foiled the perpetrator's plans and so lives to fight another day. Although, She may find herself in possibly a very dangerous environment, as the killer may, no doubt, still want to silence her. I say 'may', because it could be that Emma just found herself in the wrong place at the wrong time. She may have been an innocent party, and because of that, fate allowed her to beat the odds. The only fact I would agree on for certain is that the murderer is one and the same person. Which is no big 'Sherlock' moment as the adhesive tape is common throughout and that hasn't been specified clearly in any media reports, so there couldn't be any copycat murders sprouting up to cloud that issue. Unfortunately, I hate to sound negative, but the proof of what I've just said will only be proven as fact if regrettably we find another body. I suggest we look after our only live asset with kid gloves, so the amount of protection given to her cannot be underestimated. I think that's all I can say at the moment."

"Well, thank you for that Jessica. Succinctly put. It gives us a good insight as to what we're dealing with, and I'm in complete agreement with your thought process. If nobody has any questions I propose more effort on Peter's surname and let's hope the public will play their part and give us some more positive leads. If we get as many positive ones as crank calls, we'll have plenty to go on. We owe it to ourselves to give this profiling lark a fighting chance. Let's get to it."

The DI, still within earshot of T/DC Murray, asked Jessica if she was free in the evening to discuss the cases further. Jessica knowing what the DI's version of 'discussing the cases further' meant said, "I'm sorry Terry ... Sir, but I've got plenty reading to keep me busy already with the murders themselves, without additional distractions."

Barnham looked disconsolate but said, "Perhaps another time. When things have quietened down and returned to normal." T/DC Murray looked disconsolate full stop. She had doted from afar on the DI and he never so much as gave her a second glance. She would have gladly given up any chance of rising up the promotional ladder for a chance with the DI.

"Yes, another time," said Jessica.

'Yes, another time,' thought T/DC Murray.

But, there was no doubt about it; Barnham was taking his eye off the ball. He considered that he was flirting with fair maidens, when in reality he was more than likely flirting with danger, danger to himself, one of his colleagues or one or more of the public at large. His eager mood had not changed from the previous night, meaning that he was still hopeful of Emma being lured by his persuasive charm. He was nothing if not persistent. The inquisitive streak, which usually enabled him to get to the truth, would never leave him even in his personal life, and so with the latest knock back from Jessica; he again, without realistic hope or concrete expectation, rang Emma.

"Hi, Emma. Just checking on my favourite inmate."

"Hi, Terry. I'm not your inmate, you moron. In fact, I'm not any kind of your mate. You let me go, remember. OK, you've got one of your henchmen barring the door here but presumably I could walk through it, any time I wanted."

"Hey, why so uppity? Are you bored with your little Sir Jonnie? Has he tarnished his armour? Not got the staying power, poor boy, to keep our Emma entertained?"

"Mm. We had a row and he stormed off in a huff back to his flat. Your snide comment about my dealer put me in a foul mood last night and so he just kept banging on about me giving all that up and going to rehab instead, and about me changing careers," she laughed into the phone. "Me changing careers, all I'm itching to do is to get back out there and further the one I've got. I've all but drained his bank account and I'm not wanting to do the same with my own little nest egg, just yet. And if I'm being honest I don't think he'll be able to keep me in the luxuries I've become accustomed to. You know what I mean? And I haven't even begun to tell him of my other bad habits."

"Can't help you there, unless you've got a bank job planned and then I'd have to bust you anyway, but that could be fun."

"That would be better than me turning into a pinny clad stereotypical housewife, who just gaily waves her pink feather duster on the doorstep whilst watching hubby drive off to work in his stereotypical family saloon."

"Now that I'd like to see," sighed Barnham.

"Men. You're all the same. Put a germ of a fantasy in your heads and your pants start itching down there."

"Talking about down there. Is Sir Gallant paying you a visit tonight or could you be persuaded to venture out under police escort?"

"Depends what the 'under' entails?"

"Well, a meal and a drink for starters and who knows where that might lead us? I know it's not the done thing to fraternise with villains and vagabonds but enough about me. I kinda think you've got a soft side too, that I'd like to get to know better."

"Yeh, I bet you would. In your dreams. You lot didn't used to be called private dicks for nothing, did you? Often wondered why though? Probably because they're always being used to do the thinking!

"Now don't be harsh. You can't judge a book etcetera"

"Well, thankfully I'm not a big reader. I used to take one to bed with me but found that I never got past the prologue, if there was one."

"Now you're talking my language. Shall we say eight o'clock?"

"Well you seem to like courting danger so go on then. You've twisted my arm. But make sure you bring your gun, fully loaded. And I don't want any of your rough stuff whilst you're interrogating me. I bruise easily you know."

The DI finished the call and thought, 'why can't I communicate with Jessica like that. Those two seem so similar in some ways but poles apart in others'. But then the thought disappeared just as quickly, as Barnham considered what to wear, where to go, and the fact that he must do something with his hair!

The evening did go well and the night even better. Terry, or Tel as Emma now called him, escorted her back to the safe house and gave the bodyguard the remainder of the night off. "Make sure you're back here by 7.30am tomorrow and no snitching. It's just between us. You're not off the hook yet for letting the boyfriend in, you know," commanded the DI. A nod came back by way of understanding. The remainder of the night and early hours of the morning took passion to a new level as far as Tel was concerned. Emma did not quite see it that way but then she had played the part so many times before no one ever knew what she was really feeling. However, she had been considerate to Tel by taking a smaller dose of her methadone than usual so as not to become too drowsy at all the wrong times. During one of their natural breaks, as Tel sipped his wine and sucked on a cigarette whilst breathing in the aroma of the one Emma was actually smoking, she cosied up and asked meekly, "Now that you've had your wicked way with me, let me see, three times is it, can you either let me out of here or score me some gear? I can't carry on with this methadone stuff. It's like cheap wine when I've been used to the taste of champagne."

"Oh, now I get it. You scratch my back. Eh. Well I can't do the latter, so I'll have to consider the former."

"Bloody hell. Talk proper English will you. What are you saying? And, for the record, I don't think it was just your back

I was scratching, do you?"

"Mm. Enough of that for the moment. I'm a man, I can't think of two things at once. I guess it'll have to be letting you out," he said resignedly.

They finished off the wine and then settled down for the remaining three hours before Tel's alarm awakened him for a much-needed shower. The bodyguard came in chirpily, as he was on his way out smiling happily but tiredly too. He had left Emma still asleep after her busy, busy night, and caught a glimpse of the additional empty bottle of McGuigans Black Label on the coffee table, accompanied by the discarded glasses. Wine he had bought on impulse and they had drunk on impulse, and now leaving the safety of the safe house his head regretted both unwise decisions. He could also not help but feel a little sadness too as he thought of her doing what they had done, but night after night, out on the streets, in cars and goodness knows where else. Her vulnerability, lack of safety and loneliness, exposed for all to see.

*

The murderer had taken a far more professional and pragmatic outlook of the evening than Barnham. There was one unresolved matter to clear up; that of Joe Foster's house. It was still covered wall to wall with possibly incriminating evidence that could not be left for the police to find and decipher. The killer visited the property under cover of darkness, using the victim's own keys to gain access. Fortunately there was no alarm to contend with, and armed only with a bin liner the task was completed within ten minutes. All rooms were closely checked but no other incriminating evidence was found apart from what had been plastered over the walls of the hall and lounge. Even the different coloured lengths of wool were tidied away so as to leave no questions asked as to their significance. The murderer then left the victim's mobile half under the sofa to give the impression of a burglar's clumsy feet having accidentally knocked it there.

*

Vinny had a confession to make. He had not taken Pop Varnish's advice and was just coming to the end of a full week at a boarding house in Musselburgh, home cooking and pleasant company being the culprits for his disobedience. As soon as he walked through the door he knew this was the next best thing to home, and on seeing the landlady he knew it could easily become the best.

I've found a great place in Musselburgh, on Eskside East overlooking the river. Reminds me of home but even better. The welcome was more than I expected but getting to know Shirley, the landlady, came as an even bigger surprise. We'd had a few chats at breakfast and that, and she'd told me a few places to visit, her thinking I was on holiday but she could see through all my bluff. She saw that I was lonely. I'd been keeping notes of Barnham meeting these various good-looking women and to be honest I've a feeling he was doing more than just meeting one of them. She looked a nice piece of totty, with everything in their right places, and lucky him appeared to be going backwards and forwards and meeting her in various places too. So I thought that I could do with a little more of what he's got; you know that charisma thing. So I gave it a try, at first we just talked, then later we started laughing and after three days, the time I should have been moving on, she said something like, "Don't go, I'm just starting to enjoy your company. Can't you stay a little longer?" And then she made these knowing eyes at me; the ones that you think are telling you that there is something more to follow but you don't necessarily know quite what. Well, I know now and that's why I'm still here.

Vinny's Pop's golden rule was in serious jeopardy. He was staying put for too long and taking his eye off his father's quest. But other than that he was enjoying himself, he had never been as happy in his life, and even considered that this murdering lark maybe overrated. What was to stop him from staying here and helping Shirley out? There was no man about the house, he had made sure of that even before flashing his best smile, and that was confirmed when she had invited him into her bed. A queen size one no less, so plenty of room in which to move around.

CHAPTER FIFTEEN

The morning saw Barnham as was, ditto Terry as was, and now Tel as is, arriving at work and spending the next three hours coasting merrily. The team update meeting was conducted through stifled yawns and a wandering mind. Lethargically speaking, he really felt like taking the day off, rather than catching a murderer. That was until 11.45am when a 999 had been received, registered and forwarded on. A male body had just been found on the lower fells running down to meet the A7 between Hawick and Langholm. A shepherd astride a quad bike rather than sporting sturdy boots and a crook had come across it as he was rounding up stray sheep. Being extremely busy at this time of year and not wanting any of his flock to meet the same fate, he had quickly penned off the immediate area, flagged it and carried on with his work. He left a mobile contact number with the 999 operative and advised that he would be available for interview once the services arrived but that, in itself would be dependent on which part of the hills or valleys he was passing through at the time as his GPS phone might or might not receive a signal. And obviously his actual location, at the time, would dictate how long it could take him to get back to the murder site location.

Hawick police, being the nearest station, were despatched to the scene but as soon as they saw the bound man and recognised the tell-tale adhesive tape, they immediately rang through to the Borders & Lothian police and asked to speak to the detective in charge of the Borders' murders.

"Hello Sir, this is PC Poole here from Hawick police. I don't know if you have been made aware yet but there has been another murder. Just off the A7, approximately midway between Hawick and Langholm. It's got all the hallmarks of your serial killer?"

A short silence ensued, followed by, "Well that's the worst news I could be given today but thank you anyway, officer. Tell me where exactly the body is located?" replied Barnham, now far more awake and alert than he had been all morning.

"It's about a mile further on from The Mosspaul Inn, heading towards Langholm, but if you get to Fiddleton you've gone too far," came the officer's reply.

"Ensure the site is held secure and we'll get the team together and set off as soon as possible? It's probably going to take us around two hours to get there, so don't be expecting us any sooner. We will notify the Pathology lab and Forensics. But if you could endeavour to use plenty of cordon tape to guide us in, that will be a great help."

"OK, Sir. Will do."

The DI's next call was to his old mate, Jamie Scott. "Hi Jamie, it's Barmy here. How's it going at your end? Still plenty of work in the cutting up bodies' business?"

"Yes, Barmy. Thought I was going to get a week without hearing from you; and in answer to your question, we're stacked out. Don't say you've got more work for us to do?"

"Afraid so. There's been another murder but this time it's down on the south side of Hawick. Is it too far for your team to travel? Do you want to liaise with Carlisle instead?"

"No, I may as well be hung for a sheep as a lamb. What have you got?"

"Yes, very good. There will be plenty of those about. It's another male, and again with the same characteristic adhesive tape binding the hands and feet. So we're fairly confident it's going to be our killer."

"What time was he found?"

"11.45 this morning; and why might I inquire do you ask?

Has that really got anything to do with the murderer's modus operandi?"

"Well actually, you've answered your own question. It means that the local paper can still call the murderer 'the breakfast serial killer'. I was beginning to worry that it might have been afternoon; that was all," joked Jamie.

"Jamie! A serious word of advice. Get out more and stop talking to dead cadavers; they are not your friends. They're never going to tell you how sick, you or your jokes are! Oh, and by the way that's a cheap pun by anybody's standards," Barnham half-joked back. He then proceeded with the formal requirements and confirmed that he would forward the official documentation calling for the Path lab to attend the murder site. The call to his Forensics' contact did not take half as long, and neither was it half as amusing. But all the same, within 30 minutes the three departments had prepared their relevant vehicles and were heading south towards England.

The DI's last thought before he concentrated on the case in hand was, 'I'll have to be careful treading this precarious tightrope. I'm heading for a fall if I don't get back on top of my game.' He approached the prepared lead vehicle, then slumped down in the front passenger car seat and brooded in silence, still struggling to completely shake off his lethargy. 'Now a fourth victim, and just after we'd managed to cross one of them off the list. How long is it going to take to catch this killer?' His quiet sullen mood persisted until they were within a mile of the murder scene and as they drove down the deserted road with the rugged terrain rising up on both sides of the valley, he thought, 'beautiful, bleak and ball breaking, not dissimilar to Jessica really'. Now relinquishing the vow of silence he addressed his colleagues with his usual professional pep talk to make sure everyone knew exactly what would be expected of them once on site.

They spent a half hour shivering as they huddled together against the wind and cold, clutching cups of once steaming coffee that they had previously prepared in thermos flasks, whilst awaiting on the arrival of both the Path lab and Forensics units. The local police had managed to track down the shepherd and he was kicking his heels impatiently but nevertheless snugly being as he was dressed in far more sensible attire, fully in keeping with his flock's own overcoats. The DI approached the shepherd, Logan Douglas, and asked him when he had last journeyed over this part of his boundary? Logan replied that it generally took two days in total to cover every acre of his land, which he did religiously, weekends and bank holidays included. So he reckoned the body must have been dumped there within the last forty-eight hours at the outside. He was thanked for this information and his time, and then continued on his own quest in searching for stray or injured sheep. Barnham had allowed his colleagues to walk around the perimeter of the penned and cordoned off areas, which to all intents and purposes were one and the same. The Hawick police's impression being that the shepherd had done such a good job that they had just wound their tape around his sheep-pen framework. The only actual discovery, by way of evidence, that the team unearthed whilst awaiting the arrival of the Forensics' team, was that this body too had been dragged, rather than carried, from the road to its place of rest. And they marked the slight gouges and indentations in the undergrowth to support this view.

Jamie and his Pathology team turned up at the same time as Forensics, and all quickly reviewed the area and carried out their respective functions, both inside and outside the pen, without disturbing or disrupting any already located possible clues. Jamie looked at the body, which had already been picked clean. No car keys, no house keys, no wallet and no mobile, this body was certainly not for identifying, yet. The victim himself was lying on his side but with his face pointing earthwards. He still wore a resigned look as if to say 'well what could I do?'

Jamie studied the body more closely and took some

temperature readings both on the surrounding objects and on the victim's body itself. He then looked into the victim's eyes, his mouth, his nose and then under his fingernails. The only item of note he found was in the latter, dirt under the nails, which was at a guess his last scratching of the earth as he tried to escape the inevitable. His clothing had not been tampered with except to remove items of identification, so Jamie surmised that no foul play of any other nature had occurred, but death was bad enough anyway he had thought. The body was still stiff which led him to believe the victim was probably in the early stages of rigor mortis but even then Jamie was confused with his own assumption. He thought aloud, "Although it's nearly the last weekend in March the ground underfoot is still hard from last night's hoarfrost, and with the body laying in the lee of the valley side there hadn't been a chance for the sun to warm it up. So I'm struggling to put an exact time of death on the victim. At present the signs are telling me 12 hours or thereabouts but I think the weather conditions are throwing me. I'll know more accurately when he's back at the lab and warmed up to body temperature. That way I can put a thermometer in the right place and do some more-accurate calculations, which will enable me to pinpoint a more exact timeframe. But I'm afraid it'll be first thing tomorrow before I can get you an initial report Barmy. What with the existing workload and all this travelling time to boot. Hope that's OK?"

"That's fine, Jamie. I know you always do your best for me. Tomorrow morning is good. But don't be any later than that, if you can help it. I've a feeling the Chief Inspector's going to be jumping on my back again, pretty soon. See you later. Thanks guys for all your trouble. When can I expect your report Derek?" This latter comment was addressed to the senior Forensics officer.

"Tomorrow am should be OK for me too. Although looking at what we've ascertained I think it will make pretty thin reading."

"Thanks anyway. I'm sure if there's anything to find you'll have found it. Bye for now."

The team then packed up, took down the cordon tape and returned the scene to the elements. It immediately reverted back to a rural stage of a sheep pen, instantly conjuring up the hard life of cold and wet conditions with very limited rewards.

The drive north was sombre and when they re-entered the station, Jessica's bemused look showed that she had no idea what was going on. "Picked the right day for an early lunch, Jessica," said T/DC Murray with venom.

"Why, where's everyone been?" asked Jessica, somewhat shell-shocked.

"We've been freezing our tits off on the lower slopes of a very windy valley that probably never sees the sun from one day to the next. That's where we've been," replied Murray still shivering from the thought of the ordeal and its end result.

"You know I'd have come if I'd been here. I don't really like dead bodies but seeing the scene at first hand might have helped me get more of an insight," replied Jessica defensively.
"Don't worry about it Jessica. We had a full car anyway. T/DC Murray always takes any death too personally. You just happen to be in the firing line today. The only thing I will say though is that whoever the murderer is he certainly likes spreading the bodies about." Barnham gave this opinion as a closure signal to the bickering in the hope that everyone would then concentrate on their work, and not on what they had seen or the ensuing friction that had arisen subsequently. As the end of the day brought in no new leads the DI gave all the operatives who had been to the murder scene an early finish. He was desperate for one himself too but felt that whilst the remaining officers and Jessica were still working hard in following up any possible clues to aid identification of the outstanding victims then he should stay as a gesture of moral support.

Jamie's report arrived before the milk. He had prepared the bulk of it in the late afternoon and the majority of the evening and finalised it at 6am for a 6.15am email to Terry's address. Unfortunately, the DI did not open it until 8.15am as, although he'd known Jamie for some years, he had little comprehension as to his workaholic schedule and therefore no intention of arriving in the office and sitting at his desk, twiddling his thumbs, whilst waiting for bad news. Even on the drive into work he had questioned his choice of career path. He was constantly engaging with thieves, junkies, and thugs, both alcohol-charged and otherwise, and even murderers. This, as opposed to say a life as a holiday courier, assisting the blue rinse brigade who could just as easily be alcohol-charged thugs with their constant inane questions about inane subjects. And then realism set in and he knew his career had been much more of a vocation, a boyhood dream of fighting good against evil. Just like all the comic heroes he had read about and watched in the days of black & white TV, when its more sedate sepia action showed significantly less gratuitous violence, and all at a fraction of the speed it is today.

His mental argument over for the morning, he pulled into the police car park surprised to see that only three spots were still available. From that observation even he could deduce that everyone was either studiously at work or they were all having their own crises about continually working with, and being subjected to, dead bodies. And no technology could contribute in any way in helping make those nightmares easier to bear or hide from. As he switched on his pc and clicked the email icon, Jamie's report rose to the top just like the release of a helium balloon but in this case the information contained within was definitely no laughing matter. He was still glancing at the alabaster-faced pictures of the dead man when he noticed he had no accompaniment. Absentmindedly, his hand dabbed around his desk searching, "Coffee, please," he shouted ten seconds too soon; as within that ten seconds Jessica, who had seen his car dithering in the car park now

196

placed a steaming mug at his very fingertips. She peered over his shoulder at the screen and said, "Joe" in a shocked voice.

"No, it's Terry actually. But thank you anyway."

"No. Joe. Joe Foster. That's who is staring out of your monitor. He's the guy I was meant to be cooking a meal for the other night but he never turned up. Didn't I tell you about him? He wanted to see me regarding something he'd unearthed about the murders. He was pretending to be some kind of sleuth hound, finding clues and tracking down villains." She said this whilst all the colour drained from her face and an outstretched arm grasped tightly onto his chair back, taking the weight of her body, and so preventing it from crumpling and collapsing in a heap. WPC Whitely rushed over to Jessica's aid and helped her back to her own seat, where she just sat motionless and silent.

Barnham had sat motionless too as he continued to stare into the screen, oblivious to the drama unfolding behind him, as if willing his new victim, Joe, to impart some of his now useless knowledge. Joe stared back with his last teardrops still part frozen to his lashes and cheeks, mimicking a religious icon with alleged supernatural powers, only in his case revealing no life rejuvenating potential. The monitor blinked and reverted to screen save mode, which in turn brought Barnham back out of his reverie. "T/DC Murray. I want you to get down to The Borders Agency where Joe worked and interview anybody who has been liaising with him over the last few days. We need to know whether he was just messing about with this amateur detective lark or whether he actually had a concrete lead. The fact that he's shown up dead must indicate that he knew something. Take Jessica along, if you like. Would you be up for that Jessica, in view of the shock you've just had?" He turned and looked at Jessica sympathetically before continuing to address the trainee detective, "At least, she'd be able to introduce you to the department boss, Tess Danvers, I seem to remember. She's been quite helpful so far," barked the DI, now in full swing.

'She could be even more helpful in the future,' he thought as he noticed stirrings in his groin area. "This experience will be a good pointer for your full detective constable aspirations too and look good on the CV," he enthused.

T/DC Murray stared at Barnham and glared at Jessica. She was annoyed that he had even thought of the suggestion of taking Jessica along; and even more so at Jessica, well just for being Jessica. 'I'm not taking that 'bloke stealer' anywhere with me. I'll do it myself,' she thought huffily.

"Oh, and while you're there can you get hold of the deceased's address. They must have it on record, so you can swing by his house afterwards. If it's not too far away, that is," Barnham concluded not noticing the hostile atmosphere of 'flying daggers' that he, the love interest, had innocently instigated. "Listen up, the rest of you. I'll be calling a meeting at 10.00am. I just need to digest, no that's not the right word, absorb the information from the Path lab report, and by then with any luck we should also have the Forensics report too. So clear your desks, ready for action." The DI returned his attention to the screen and thought, 'God, I am a man of clichés. I'd be lost without them but it certainly seems to gee this lot up'. The recipients of the cliché, henceforth called the 'clichéd', certainly appeared to respond by moving quickly around their desks, picking up phones and crashing dementedly on keyboards.

Sometime later, T/DC Murray showed her identity to Judy the receptionist. She asked to speak to Tess Danvers regarding a matter of some importance. Fortunately for the investigation's progress, Tess had the majority of the morning free and once she was informed that the police wished to see her she came out with a huge smile on her face expecting to see Terry but quickly removed it. Disappointed that she was face to face with a female officer, and one with a rather masculine and robust physique at that, she said rather abruptly, "Good morning, I'm Tess Danvers, how may I help?"

"Yes, good morning. I'm T/DC Murray," came the reply, again with a flourish of her ID card. "Could we go somewhere private? DI Barnham, whom I understand you already know, has sent me to discuss a matter of grave importance with you."

"Yes, of course. Follow me. Judy, could you organise a coffee, for our visitor?" came the tart reply.

Once in Tess' private office, T/DC Murray began.

"Yesterday at 11.45am we received a 999 call regarding a dead male body which had just been discovered. I'm sorry to tell you but we now know that the body is a member of your staff, Joe Foster." At the mention of his name Tess' hand instinctively flew to her mouth in a failed attempt to try and catch a gasp before it escaped. Her cheeks became noticeably white even under her sophisticated blusher as she sat rigid in her chair, digesting the information. "I know it's a shock but it's important that we move quickly. Jessica Lambert was in the office this morning when photographs of the deceased arrived. She identified the victim as Joe and said that she was meant to be having dinner with him, let me see," she opened her notebook and said, "Two nights ago. But he never showed up. She feels he wanted to meet to discuss a possible clue that he had unearthed on his last day at work. My job is to interview you and anybody else that may have been consciously or otherwise made aware of this clue, in anyway whatsoever. Could I start with you? Are you composed enough after the shock?"

Tess struggled to suppress the guilty feeling she now felt at her rudeness to this officer and bearer of such shocking news, but managed to say, "Yes, I am OK. I'm very saddened at the death and a little shaken but I understand the need to move on quickly with the investigation. The only saving grace, if there is such a thing, is that even though he'd had two marriages there are no children to consider." This was said as her mind struggled to come to terms with the news and so raced off at somewhat of a tangent.

"OK. Could you inform me of any unusual activity or

requests that Mr Foster may have made leading up to his last day at work? Was his manner any different to the norm? His temperament? For instance, had he been suffering from mood swings recently?"

Tess looked thoughtful and replied, "Let me just check in my in-tray and computer for you". As she manually carried out the tasks aforementioned she continued thoughtfully with, "His manner may have changed now that you mention it. Although, I don't think he had any problems or specific work issues, apart from a little additional workload with us being understaffed. Perhaps he may have been a bit more furtive and dare I say enigmatic. I did find that strange, as I've always tried to run an open and relaxed department. Ah, here it is," she said holding a slip of paper, "I knew he'd made a request for an archive file. Let me just check with Sophie as to whether it's been returned." She picked up the handset and made an internal call and received the answer. "Sophie says the file has been returned. I'll arrange for her to re-retrieve it so you can see it down in archives if you need to. The only other thing I can put my finger on is that he'd become a little pushier around the office since Jessica was seconded to the murders' enquiry but I put that down to testosterone."

"Well, thanks for your help. The DI was not too sure as to whether you'd be able to shed any light on his movements. Could you now introduce me to the staff that he usually had day-to-day contact with."

"Yes certainly. What about mentioning his …. death?" She even stumbled to say the word. "I'm thinking it might be difficult talking to them if they know of that. They are so much younger than me and may have had leanings towards him and who knows perhaps aspirations too."

"Yes I see what you mean. Perhaps we'll leave death out of it for the moment, at least until the interviews are over. I know that maybe perceived as a bit morbid but we've both got our jobs to do, have we not? Perhaps counselling might be a good option?" replied T/DC Murray resourcefully.

That being decided, T/DC Murray was offered the privacy of a meeting room to further conduct her inquiries. Once settled she called upon Judy to be her first interviewee, and began by saying, "Hi, Judy. As you're probably aware Joe is not with us today but I'm very interested in any observations you may have of his movements over the last 48 to 72 hours, whether in or out of the office."

"Is he OK? What's this all about? The only thing I know is as I told Jessica when she rang yesterday. He didn't come in then and he's not here today. Are you sure that he's OK?"

"Could you please just answer the question," asked T/DC Murray with due consideration.

"Well Joe had been playing a bit of an amateur detective role and he had got excited that he might have found out something but was trying to keep it contained, so that it wasn't too obvious."

"Found out something? Did he explain any further?"

"No, that was about it. I thought nothing more until Jessica rang, the day after I'd spoken to him, and she asked if he was in the office. And he wasn't and I haven't seen or heard from him since, which makes me really worried. And here you are now asking questions about him. Are you sure everything's alright?" she asked becoming a little distressed and tearful.

"I'm sorry, Judy. I can't honestly say anything for definite at the moment. I've just been briefed to interview his colleagues. If there is nothing further that you can add could you telephone for Sophie, the intern, that's right isn't it? The one who works in archives? Ask her if she'd come to the meeting room." Judy said that she would and she did.

"Sophie. Hi. As you're probably aware Joe is not with us today but I'm very interested in any observations you may have of his movements over the last 48 to 72 hours, whether in or out of the office. I'm particularly interested in a file that he asked you to retrieve. Ms Danvers gave me this request slip."

"Is Joe alright? He has been acting a bit strange these last few days. The slip. Yes, I remember. It was after lunch the other day. In fact, the last time I saw him really," she said becoming more worried with every sentence. "He is OK, isn't he? Anyway, he took out the file and I made him sign for it in the old ledger, you know, a bit like Scrooge made that Bob Cratchit chap do in the Christmas Carol film. Just a minute though. There were two files, not one. I'll have to go back to the archives and check the ledger again to see what the other file was. Didn't Tess, Ms Danvers, give you a second slip?"

"No, just the one, this one. Can you find the other slip or a reference for it and let me know if that file's been returned too? I'll be on this extension."

T/DC Murray was now a little excited. She could understand why Terry, she thought of him as Terry when no one else was about, why Terry got such a buzz from the job. It did tend to give an adrenalin rush as the penny dropped further and further, thus enabling the pieces to begin fitting together. Sophie rang back with S32 as the file number but was sorry to say that the hard copy file had not yet been returned. T/DC Murray then had another word with Tess, who informed her that she would email the computerised file over to Terry at the office once she had been given clearance to do so. T/DC Murray questioned this action with, "Bugger clearance, you've got a dead colleague and you're worried about protocol." As she said it she realised who she was talking to and looked quickly behind her to ensure no one else had heard the outburst at her disrespect for a fellow government employee, and more importantly to ensure no one had heard mention of Joe's death. "Sorry about that. I understand your position but we really do need that file as soon as possible. I'll let DI Barnham know of the situation and see if he can pull any strings at his end. Thank you for your time and assistance in this delicate matter," she continued sheepishly.

Tess nodded curtly before escorting the officer out of the building. 'Funny,' thought Murray, 'It's usually the other way round. I'm normally the one doing the escorting!' Once in the patrol car she rang the DI and explained what had gone on, only referring to her notes once. She also reminded him of her long-standing booking of a week's holiday starting at close of play on Good Friday, and her hope of clearing up this part of the investigation by then with the filing of her report. The DI said, "You did right. Put the fear of God up them. I'll shake some trees at this end. You've still time to get to Joe's house, I presume? I'll also brief Jessica on this, as she might be able to play the game just that little bit more stealthily. You'll get that promotion yet, Murray. And yes, I do look at the holiday roster sometimes so I am aware of your impending leave but as you know events can tend to supersede it."

"Thanks, Sir," she said, elated at the praise and heartbroken that Terry was going to speak to Jessica, no matter in what capacity and on what subject. Even though she was only a seconded colleague, she was still perceived as the enemy. And at the moment T/DC Murray felt that Jessica had more claws in her man than she had.

Barnham had another look over the two reports he had received referring to Joe's murder. Jamie's document was, as usual, very comprehensive, but to save time Barnham skipped the introduction, which referenced his height and weight etcetera. 'It's pointless reading all this now that Jessica has already identified him,' he thought. Instead he moved on to the section of how Joe died. Again, a minute auto injector type puncture mark was evident in the thigh area. More noticeable this time as the body's temperature had been kept so low with the cold weather, and as Jamie had assumed, an accurate time of death could not be calculated until it had been brought back up to room temperature in the Path lab. Once there, Jamie reckoned probably around 39-40 hours prior to the time he had been found; but as he had said he would only stake his house on it if he were a gambling man, which surprisingly he was. The toxicology report showed the same 'speedball' concoction as in victim three but other than that the victim had not even had a chance to partake of any alcohol or a last meal. There were also signs that a few animals had investigated the body, presumably during the night, but no serious chunks were missing. Other than that the dirt under the nails was native to the soil surrounding him and as per previous, there were no fingerprints on the adhesive tape binding the hands and feet. He had speculated that the epipen type jag would have incapacitated him but then the quantity of 'speedball' should have killed him quickly after that. Although as the weather suddenly turned cold the chances are that it would have slowed that process down and he may just as likely have succumbed to hypothermia first.

The DI then moved on to re-read the Forensics report. Nothing much to say there either, except that the assailant struggled to manhandle the victim to the spot where he was eventually found. The weather must have been slightly milder when he was placed there, indicated by the drag marks, gouges in the soil and broken foliage. So in conclusion, the killer was considered to be just strong enough for the deed and light on his feet as neither foot imprints nor other noticeable clues were evident at the crime scene. All identification had been removed from the victim; but the murderer could not remove the fact that a shepherd checked the area at least once every 48 hours, so obviously it had not been reccied prior to the actual killing, meaning that the body could have been found earlier than the perpetrator expected or wanted. The DI put the hard copy to one side and thought, 'Let's hope that T/DC Murray is having better luck at his house.' He dejectedly walked over to Jessica's desk and said sympathetically, "I know he was a former colleague but are you up to talking about his death?"

Her nod and weak smile was enough for him to continue, "So what's your take on the timing of the new body find? Do you think it was sooner than the killer might have wanted?"

Jessica thought and then answered; "To be honest I don't really see Joe as being part of the original killing plan. This serial killer seems to be killing more now to cover up tracks than for any other reason. I'd say there was some kind of vendetta going on at first and the victims were specifically chosen but now, if you include Emma Flynn, we're clocking up nearly as many innocent type victims as ones that could be classed in the perpetrator's mind as guilty. That's my view anyway. It seems that as we get nearer to solving one murder then the killer strikes again to neutralise our efforts. It's almost as if they're a fly on the wall, watching our every move. You don't think it could be linked to that press leak of two or three weeks ago?" Jessica grasped for a timescale but her mind went blank and she could not recollect how long she'd been on the case. "But without being a full blown detective I agree with you and reckon there could be something in the fact that this body's been found too soon. You don't think the murderer needed more time to cover up his tracks elsewhere, do you?"

"Claire!" exclaimed Barnham, recognising it was the first time he had ever used T/DC Murray's first name. "I've sent her by herself to Joe's house. You could be right! The killer might have needed time to tidy up loose ends. Try her radio or mobile we've got to warn her, just in case." PC Gough tried the radio whilst WPC Whitely rang her mobile. The instant it started ringing out another mobile in the corridor rang too.

WPC Whitely cracked out laughing as she heard, 'You're the one that I want,' by Olivia Newton John merrily playing not more than ten yards away. The sound emanating from Claire's mobile was closely followed by T/DC Murray as she entered the incident room, struggling with and fumbling over her mobile before the music ended. She failed miserably and asked, "What's the joke?"

"Nothing really, more relief actually!" replied WPC Whitely, who had a Christian name too, Sandra. "We just had an awful thought that the Gov might have sent you into the lion's den. But you're here to prove him wrong."

"OK, Sand. You're freaking me out now but you can tell me about it later. Gov, I've been to Joe's house. Funnily enough the front door was locked but the back door open." She paused to catch her breath and recollect her thoughts,

"That's the only funny bit really. Some furniture had been turned on its side, drawers left open with stuff hanging out and a pregnant space on a unit with dust marks indicating where he probably had a TV and DVD player. Couldn't see much else having been stolen, so I'm thinking it's a cover up for something else. The only thing the 'bungler' missed was a mobile phone, which had been half kicked under the three-seat settee. So that must have been too big and heavy to tip up."

As he heard the sound of his own phone, Barnham moved off towards his office but by the time he picked it up the caller had hung up too. "T/DC Murray, Jessica can you both just come in for a second. That's good work, Murray. We'll hand over the mobile to Forensics and also send them over to the victim's house to see if they can pick up on anything else. What are you making of all this, Jessica?"

"I think Claire could be onto something. The killer might have got there before her, probably was looking for that incriminating file, S32 wasn't it, and then rigged it to look like a bungled burglary. And I've been thinking about that file, there is a quicker way to get it, if Tess is going to go all-bureaucratic on us, but it will have to happen on Sunday morning. That's when there'll definitely be nobody working. Several people do go in on a Saturday to put in a few extra hours but Sunday's usually a 'no-no' after a Saturday night. Are you free on Sunday, Claire?"

"Yes, I can do that. Although, I've got to be away by around 8.45am as I'm taking the week off, remember Gov? So I'll be driving down to Carlisle straight after and then taking the Carlisle-Settle train with a connection there to take me on to Leeds. I've got family there that I promised to visit for Easter. So can you make it about 8.00am, Jessica?" replied T/DC Murray with double venom at the fact that Jessica was now calling her Claire too. Her sole desire in life had been to join the police force and she had been petrified that her weight would be the stumbling block in preventing her achieving that ambition, so when she became WPC Murray she had been ecstatic, and ever since the initial passing-out day she had insisted on colleagues and the public using that name at all times during her working hours. And her view had not changed when she started her CID training; so even now not many colleagues were used to calling her Claire, and there were probably still as many who did not even know it was her Christian name. And now here was her archrival, archrival in love, although Jessica was unaware of this fact, calling her Claire, and after having only known her for a few days too!

"Right, that's settled. Claire will accompany Jessica to The Borders Agency offices on Sunday morning at what time did you say? 8.00am, is that it, Jessica?" Jessica nodded in the affirmative. "Jessica will then use her keys to get in and her logins to access the computer and relevant archive file. Will you be accessing from your own computer; won't that leave a trail? Do you want to email the results direct to me or bring the information back on a data stick drive?"

"No, I'll access from Joe's terminal. I know his password as he couldn't keep a secret to save his life." Her sudden bright red hue confirmed the prickly warm feeling across her face and neck as she realised the gaff she had made. "You know what I mean. I'll then use my logins to get through to archives and utilise a data stick to bring out the S32 file. That way if a search is carried out in future it will look like Joe has been breaking the Data Protection Act and not me. And you can't prosecute the dead, can you? Sorry," she cringed.

"And you're happy Claire, running with this? Just you two. You and Jessica. You don't want any other back up."

"Yes, I'm fine with just us two. It shouldn't take an army and at least this way, there's less chance of leaving any telltale clues behind," she said. 'And I'm more than happy for you to call me Claire,' she thought.

"OK, let's wrap it up for now and go home and chill as best we can," said Barnham, surprisingly thinking that even with another death on their hands things were looking quite positive. He wanted to make them even more positive by asking Tess out for the evening; but then thought better of it as, in time, she might smell a rat with the Sunday heist coming up and he definitely did not want to jeopardise that little sortie. So he plumped for Emma, hoping that she had earned herself enough cash and would be thinking of having the night off from her taxing work schedule. He rang her as soon as he got to the car.

"Hi, Emma. What are you up to?"

"Hello, Tel. Long time, no speak?" she said jokingly. But the reality was that they had not spoken much on the night he had taken her for a meal and other things. "I bet I can guess why you're ringing."

"So now I've got to add fortune telling to your other talents?" Emma grunted, and he continued, "Are you free tonight? I mean no prior engagements?"

"Damn. The only engagement I had tonight was with 2g of heroin. Whoops, your phone's not bugged is it? But I could take a smaller dose if you make it worth my while. That will still allow me to walk and talk if that's what you're bargaining for. Although, if it's a repeat of the other night, I might take the lot!" she joked.

"Well, I'm thinking we'll start with dinner, and I'll look into your eyes and see what size your pinpricks are; and if they're big enough we'll go from there. You buying? Is it your treat?"

"No, it is bloody well not! How many times did we do it the other night? Even with a sliding scale rate, which I'm telling you I don't do, I should be demanding the Ritz treatment, at least!"

"Yeh, yeh. Only joking. Pick you up at 7.30pm. Is that OK?"

"Yes, OK. 7.30. But it better be a decent meal or I'll bring the 2g along with me; and we'll share it under romantic candlelight at the restaurant."

*

7.30pm was either going to be the start of a perfect evening or the end of a perfect relationship. Verification came when Vinny's mobile rang just as he was finishing his second helping of jam roly poly and custard. At the time he was in the process of evening-dreaming about the additional possible helping of roly poly to come in that queen size bed, conveniently positioned right above his head. *"Vince, glad you're there. I thought we'd lost you with not hearing for so long. Is everything OK? Have you got everything under control?"*

You can guess how I felt then. He just went on and on, and what had started as an almost romantic evening, well there was one flower stuck in a tiny vase on each table, ended up with me having indigestion. I'd had such a whale of a time with Shirley that I'd forgotten all about the real reason for being there. Then Pops rang and read me the riot act. Said he wasn't going to waste any more money without seeing a result. Said he'd been following the news up here and someone was doing a whole lot of killing even if it wasn't me. He even had the temerity, is that a word, to say that it looked like he had backed the wrong horse, and that I could come home without killing anybody if the job was too much for me. As if I'd dare to show my face in Newcastle again, well I'd never live it down. But at least I had the last laugh as whilst I was on the phone and then writing up my notes Shirley finished tidying up the dining room and made sure the other residents had sufficient tea and coffee in the lounge. That meant we could spend the rest of the evening and night together. So do I broach the subject of my dwindling funds with Shirl or leave that for another day? Have I got the guts to cross Pops and not do his bidding? Oh fuck it, I suppose I'll have to go out tomorrow and kill Barnham, and see where that leads me.

Shirley never noticed any change in Vinny, and to be honest there had not been much to notice. He was a man after all and more than happy with the here and now rather than dwelling on what the future held. They spent a pleasant evening cuddled up watching TV, on the same sofa and in the same way she and her husband had, before he ran off with the twenty something waitress from Eastern Europe. And Shirley knew from the night before that her Vinny did not need much encouragement about joining her upstairs at whatever 'Ad break' she chose.

And on that Friday morning, not just any Friday morning but Good Friday morning, for that split second, she enjoyed the surprise and luxury of waking up and seeing a young man next to her. Then jumped out of bed, took a quick shower, dried off and put on her work uniform before coming face to face with ten bacon rashers in a pan!

CHAPTER SIXTEEN

Friday brought calm to the team. In any other circumstances it could have been defined as 'the lull before the storm', only in this case it would be more accurate to say 'after the storm'. The reports from the Path lab and Forensics had been digested, and Barnham's people were hard at it, concentrating on the identities of victims one and three. On this morning after, the DI thought about the night before, and kept telling himself that on the occasions they had met, he was subliminally interviewing and interrogating Emma. When in actual fact, both had a perfect understanding of the reason for their rendezvous, in the plural, and it had nothing to do with the minimalist questioning from either party. The evening had ended no differently to the previous encounter, and was now instrumental in causing Barnham's fatigue and lethargy to spread through the whole office like a flu virus at play.

Forensics came back with minor findings from Joe's house: the back door was unlocked, presumably by the use of the victim's own keys, which had then been discarded behind the toaster on the work surface; the unturned furniture was a rouse as suspected by T/DC Murray as nothing of worth had been taken other than the TV and DVD player; fingerprints were everywhere but from Forensics' own experience they were certain that a professional burglar would have worn gloves. They felt that it would prove costly and time consuming to track every person, male and female, who had innocently left their stray prints, especially when it was a bachelor's home. And the odds were high that the prints could have been around for a considerable period of time, dependent on the thoroughness of the cleaner and his methods. As for the mobile, that too had been dusted and only one set of clear prints, were evident. It would be up to the DI himself to ascertain if the call register should be thoroughly checked for any calls made or received which could be argued to be out of sync with Joe's usual pattern.

"PC Blackwell you're into your fancy phones, aren't you? Take a look at this and let me know what's on it," said Barnham in his pre-industrial revolution mode. His own mobile was five years old at least but he could still ring out and receive calls with it, end of story. After handing it over, he headed to the kitchen, made another brew and then walked back to his own office. Before he could even sit down the PC was at his back.

"Right Sir, I think I'm sorted," he said excitedly. "It's the new iPhone 5 with a slightly larger display, a faster chip, ultra-fast wireless technology, an iSight camera and just look how thin and light it is."

"Enough, already Blackwell. It's not Tomorrow's World, you know. Bloody boys with toys!"

"Yes, sorry Sir. As well as admiring it, I've also been into the call register. Joe had already programmed names in so that makes life easier when cross-referring the numbers. His last 'call sent' was to 'Jess' and his last 'call in' of any length was the day prior, so I'd suggest that this new phone hadn't brought him many new friends. There is a missed call with a message and one text, from the period in question, which he'd not opened and they're both from Jessica too." PC Blackwell played Jessica's recorded message and then translated the text speak by saying, "Joe, it's Jessica. Got a better offer! Get in touch. J. Then it says 'lol', which can mean one of a variety of things. That's it and it was sent at 8.35pm with the recorded message about 30 minutes earlier."

"That ties in with what Jessica's already told us. She'd

been trying to track him down that particular evening, as he was due at hers for a meal. A meal to discuss something he'd found at work. Let's hope she can find out what that was, on Sunday. Yes, and I can concur on the 'lol', its usage and translation can be a bit misleading."

*

No new leads turned up during the rest of the day but no dead bodies either, so the DI felt he had a result and that it was a vindication of allowing him to look forward to the weekend. And now the evenings were getting lighter he also felt that his body was due a spring clean; and so contemplated the dreaded gym as an outlet. He could already see the results advertised by Jessica, as she smoothly and effortlessly moved about the office with such grace and élan; and he jealously thought if only he could have a little of that. That movement not 'that body', although he had to admit that he had been attracted to that too from the first time they had met over a year ago at the conference. Was it that long; and even though Emma was good company in certain areas, in fact very good company in a lot of areas, and even reminded him of Jessica in some ways, he could not imagine her ever competing with Jessica's intellectual prowess. Yes, Jessica, the perfect package, and possibly dare he think it, marriage material? Anyway, back to the gym, seemed like a good idea. The ringing phone shook him back to the present and surprisingly he was still sat at his desk and not teleported to and trapped in his permanent dream world.

"DI Barnham? It's Chief Inspector Brogan."

"Hello, Sir. Are you ringing for an update on the case?" asked the DI, as his happy smile immediately transformed itself into sad face.

"Well, more an update on when you're going to conclude the case. You're now into your fourth week, aren't you? And I wanted this bottomed and packed away before we became Police Scotland. As then we won't be able to take all the kudos once this murderer's been caught but we don't look to be going in the right direction for that, do we? What, with yet another body and that ghastly local paper bringing out that reference again, 'breakfast serial killer'. Can't we even put a stop to that? Anyway, I think I'm within my rights and the public's expectations in questioning, when are you going to catch him? And how's our new profiling girl? Isn't she pulling up any trees yet?"

"Sir, I can understand your impatience but as soon as we go one step forward we tend to go two back. The profiler, Jessica, is working out really well. She seems to have a good handle on getting into the killer's mind and her view is that the murderer is no longer killing out of some kind of morbid vengeance but more to cover his tracks."

"Is that your view too?"

"Yes, Sir. If I'm being honest I believe it is. There's a slim chance that someone is leaking out information and so fuelling the fire, so we've got to put a stop to that too."

"Betrayals! Can't have them on the inside. Can't stand Judas's. But what about the public, what are you doing for them? The holiday season will be upon us in no time and I'm already being berated over the poor show of bookings for the Easter break. Sooner rather than later, Barnham."

"Yes Sir, sorry Sir. I fully understand the pressure you are under and I can tell you that we are doing everything possible to catch this murderer. Our intention now is to get officers extracting and analysing information. In fact, this ...," he suddenly stopped and thought of what he was about to say. The Chief might agree with his methods but even he could not condone theft of data protected material, no matter what the reason, "...afternoon, from files found at the latest victim's home."

"Well, keep me posted. I need some kind of closure by this time next week. Understood?"

"Yes Sir. Good day, Sir," said Barnham drifting off again into his fantasy world so as to hide from the pressure of the job that he had coveted from being a young boy. 'Why's it always him with his badgering whine? Why don't I get phone calls from the likes of Jessica or even a text?' he thought with not a little bitterness, only softened by a comforting suck on one of his cigarette dummies.

*

No one could ever have said Vinny was religious but they could have said he was lazy, and some had. One or two at school acquired a black eye for that very observation but as he became older so his temper became calmer, and more likely than not he weighed up the odds of his success, in beating the shit out of the accuser or vice versa, before wading in. I only tell you this, as Vinny, on this day of all days, was happy to play on both virtues. One, it being Good Friday, chronologically followed by the Christian, and more importantly recreational, Easter weekend, and two, Vinny being a lazy son-of-a-bitch.

Good Friday, today. If my memory serves me right it's a bank holiday and most folk will be enjoying the break rather than working. That presumably includes Barnham and his merry men too. I know I gave Pops a positive understanding that my mark would be extinguished and by my hand, and within the next few days. But, and it's a big BUT, I've absolutely no idea where Barnham is at present. He could quite easily have jetted off for a few days or just be putting his feet up and resting. Whatever the case I am not getting behind that Punto wheel until Tuesday. I've been away from home for over three weeks now and feel I deserve a little good food, good company and social interaction. That being said I'll take up the chase on Tuesday, track down Barnham and gain back the face, which he has stolen from my family, and in particular my younger sister. But for the present I am more than happy to relax for one or two more days and perhaps take a trip to Edinburgh with Shirley if she can spare the time.

Vinny made his decisions and Shirley agreed with the one

involving her. She instructed Karolina, the other Eastern European waitress still in her employ, on what needed undertaking in her absence, and took her leave. Unbeknownst to Vinny, his lack of physical exercise and too-regular cooked breakfasts were coalescing into an accident waiting to happen. But then again becoming too comfortable with life's luxuries can often have that effect.

*

Saturday proved a fine Spring day, the kind of day to put a spring in your step and hope in your heart. The snowdrops and crocuses made way for the daffodils and the chill in the air allowed the sky to remain clear blue without a smudge of black cloud to be seen; that was until the earth revolved enough to bring on the monochrome night. Barnham's team felt very much the same way; clues were blossoming that had once been cold, and now there was hope that with Joe's amateur detective discovery new ones would be unearthed with the turn of a new day. The DI, or Terry on weekends, deliberated whether to go and collect another batch of newspapers but then thought better of it and saved his money instead. Claire busied herself with packing the few items she needed for her week in Leeds. She was not a big shopper and had certainly never been fashion conscious and so would not be taking an array of clothes; another reason for her choosing a job with a built-in uniform; but she knew that mindset would have to change if she achieved her ambition and won promotion to full detective. Jessica caught up on her various sporting activities and prepared herself for the Sunday morning heist. And Emma, well Emma caught up on her sleep after spending several active nights, either with Tel or earning much needed cash elsewhere. Whilst Vinny, yes you've guessed it, Vinny was on his way to Edinburgh with his lady friend.

Claire rose even earlier than planned on Easter Sunday. She had final preparations to make and check, plus she did not want to be late for the 8.00am meeting at The Borders Agency. The weekend so far had given her an opportunity to re-examine Joe's death, which she seemed to be constantly recollecting and picturing in graphic detail, plus the interviews at his workplace and particularly Jessica's take on how the murderer always stayed at least one step ahead of the game. She threw these thoughts in, jumbled them up and put the timer on for 30 minutes, but still they came out the same. Still slightly tarnished with no offering of definite clear-cut answers. And at the point of leaving home, impulse persuaded her to ring the DI. She wanted to take him up on the offer of another officer being present but considered that it most probably would have to be him at such short notice. She felt buoyant at that thought; what could possibly go wrong when you have the DI in tow, watching your back. She had not made the call earlier, as she did not want to disrupt, what she presumed would be, his lie in. With whom she had no idea.

But contrary to her obsession with thoroughness it had then slipped her mind, as she concentrated instead on ensuring that all her bags, presents and Easter eggs were placed by the door, ready for packing into the car. Finally, she did remember and rang. No answer. The answer phone activated. She listened to his pre-recorded voice. She shivered with goosebumps. The beep. No message. '7.32, plenty of time to get to the Agency. With any luck Jessica will be early too, so then I won't be in too much of a rush driving down to Carlisle,' she calculated.

Jessica living further away left at 7.15am even though Sunday traffic was always light so early in the morning, and especially on a weekend. She too had prepared for the meeting and she too was thinking and planning ahead in order to cover all eventualities. Even the Easter traffic or lack of it was kind to her, so she arrived first. She unlocked the front door, deactivated the burglar alarm and flicked a switch disguised as an emergency fire alarm on the wall. She then busied herself with turning on computers and arranging in order what materials she had brought in her bag. Claire arrived five minutes later; her packing having taken longer than expected with the small car refusing to expand sufficiently to make accommodation for the delicate Easter eggs not being broken. Several attempts had to be made to rectify the fragile situation.

But now she stood outside the entrance door not knowing whether to enter. She was concerned that in doing so, it would set alarms off, and was equally concerned too that the CCTV camera would be merrily recording her confused state, and documenting her presence. Jessica saw her, opened the door and seeing her aggravated glance towards the camera said, "Don't worry about that, I've deactivated it and run the tape back so that neither of us were ever here". This somehow did not feel very reassuring to Claire. But Jessica confidently marshalled her through to an open-planned, impressively decorated and modern office with furniture to match. Claire's tense demeanour relaxed as reflected by her immediate reaction in diving onto the nearest office chair and spinning round. "Wow. Aren't these, what they call 'ergonomic' chairs?" she enquired, slowing down as dizziness took hold. "We could do with a few of these at work. It might curb some of my colleagues being off all the time with bad backs," she prescribed.

"Yes. It is nice, isn't it?" replied Jessica sitting herself down at a desk and throwing a quick glance around the room. "You get used to it after a while though and it literally becomes, just background wallpaper," she continued in a matter of fact tone, as she made room adjacent to her so Claire could park up and see the screen. "OK. I've got the computer up and running. Let's see what that file number's got to tell us? What is it again?" Claire settled down, flipped through her notebook, read out S32, and Jessica input it. A further password box popped up, which Jessica quickly filled with four stars. "Right, this is it."

Jessica plugged in the data stick and instructed the

software to download the complete files with the prefix S32. As it was downloading Claire spotted on the scrolling screen that Jessica's name appeared as 'file caseworker' and that it was an actual live file on 'Mairie Dawson'. The snippets she gleaned, as it moved through the various pages, left her in no doubt that Jessica was the author of these documents.

"You knew this woman? Had you forgotten her name or what? I mean look at the date; the last one is quite recent. Must have been just before Barnham invited you to join the team!" exclaimed Claire furiously. Jessica had prepared for this moment.

Both women went for their bags at the same time but Jessica's movement was a bluff. As Claire's head was momentarily turned away Jessica's left hand rose and fell, and Claire gave a gasp as a small sharp pain registered in her thigh. She immediately sat up and turned to Jessica with accusing eyes, both for turning out to be the 'bad apple' and for stealing her Terry's feelings away from her too. She opened the hand that had reached into her own bag and dropped her mobile onto the floor, following it herself within seconds.

Jessica had to work quickly as she had no idea whether anyone else would in fact decide to work today. She knew the remaining incriminating file numbers of the other victims, which now needed removing from both the electronic archives and hard copy archives. She was thankful at having spent time in her early days overseeing these two functions as it allowed for a speedier operation. At the same time she mentally noted the necessity of tearing the latest page from the old ledger in the archives themselves, whether Bob Cratchit liked it or not. The only other person who had notification of the files in question was Tess but her own rules would now be her undoing. She had always specified 'no names, no pack drill,' and now those words would never allow her to recall, neither the files nor their subject matter, let alone the subjects' names.

Logistically speaking Claire was more of a problem than the previous victims. Jessica had meticulously planned the attack but even so Claire's weight was working against her. She was also regaining consciousness due to her body mass absorbing and neutralising the drug that much quicker. 'I'll have to bear that in mind with heavier built people,' thought Jessica somewhat methodically as she managed to shoehorn her victim back onto the chair. Fancy, one of the chairs that Claire had so enthused about was now being used as a prop in her very own downfall as it transported her to the fire exit, close by. Jessica bound her hand and foot to ensure there would be no nasty surprises and as it was daytime she taped her mouth too. Again, this was all part of the preconceived plan; as was the fact that she had not really worked from her own desk, not even Joe's but a desk that had a spare terminal with a generic password.

Having moved her own car to the fire exit door at the back of the building, she wheeled Claire out on the chair and manoeuvred her into the front seat. She then brought Claire's car round too, transferred a couple of items to it from her boot and vice versa from Claire's already packed car, and parked it up well out of sight. Once they were both strapped securely in Jessica's car they set off on a journey.

A journey, which would eventually take in some wonderful scenery that Claire may or may not enjoy, but the destination of which would forever remain a mystery to her as more than likely, before journey's end, she would be dead. 'Quite ironic really, with today being the day worshippers believed that Christ rose from the dead,' thought Jessica dryly. Eventually, Claire did come around and began fighting against the seatbelt restraint. But Jessica, calculating how strong she would be, had ensured that her hands were bound securely behind her back so that she had no chance of releasing them or making any effort at using them in a club-like weapon effect. Claire began mumbling, grunting and then panicking, as she understood the seriousness of her situation, and recognised what a dangerous, manipulative person was sitting next to her.

Without warning, Jessica reached across and released the

tape covering Claire's mouth. And not allowing any time for even a wince, she said, "I don't usually do this, you know. I'm not into last confessions and the entire God thing. But you've intrigued me somewhat. You've always seemed antagonistic towards me and I couldn't understand why, and I've never had the opportunity to ask? At least, not until now anyway. So tell me, what have I done to upset you?"

"You'll never get away with this. Terry, the DI, I mean, he knows exactly what's going on, I spoke to him this morning and we agreed on a plan to trap you," she said with confidence in her voice.

"Oh, I see now. It's all about Terry, the DI. You've got a crush on him, haven't you? Probably had it since working with him in Newcastle, but unfortunately for you, it looks like his eyes and dick, have always been elsewhere. Well, I can put your mind at rest for what it's worth. He's tried it on a couple of times with asking me on nights out and so forth, and although I could have been tempted at one point, I know from experience that you don't let men get too close. And anyway I've been far too busy. I can understand that a one night stand here and there might be good for the soul and keep you in the swing, but when they get familiar and start to rule your life, and take you for granted that's when they can become very dangerous and vindictive. Take Grannie's second husband, for example. Eventually, he didn't seem totally satisfied with her and so came after me as well. But when Grannie found out she put a stop to it. We never spoke about it again, so I don't exactly know whether it was as much, because he'd spurned Grannie, or more because of what he'd done to me. They're both dead now so it doesn't matter to them but with me being here and so much younger too, I've still got to live with it, a continual itch to scratch, if you know what I mean. And anyway if you had spoken to Terry like you say, why didn't he come 'a running' this morning? Plan backfired did it or has he got other fish to fry?"

"He said he'd be watching my back, so he will, you just

221

watch. Anyway, are you saying that you never fancied him at all? Your mind was always on other things?" Claire asked playing for a little more time.

"Oh, come on. Some watching! And for your information, yes, with the planning and execution involved in murders on this scale, my mind is always focused on the specifics. I can't afford to spend much time thinking about girly nights out and hooking up with blokes. I blow hot and cold in that department anyway, and I've sure as damn it not met Mr Right yet and who's to say that if I did, he wouldn't be saying one thing and thinking another? No I get my endorphins' rush through my sports, particularly the running. I do all my serious thinking and planning then but even I'll be the first to admit that this caper has now got a little out of hand."

"What planning? There's not much planning required when you're wearing two hats and one of those belongs to the actual murderer, and the other fits the profiler," she scoffed. "The profiler who, what do you know, has the capacity to accurately predict every move in the jigsaw. How convenient. What a surprise. Let's give a round of applause to the cheapskate magician. Killing to cover her own back rather than for the reason that she first intended, for vengeance, I presume. You were right though, in your professional profile analysis, but you would be, wouldn't you. It is your personal vendetta. Against people you've come across who treat others similar to how you were treated by your Grannie's fella. Well it can stop now, Jessica. You don't have to kill me. Give yourself up, and you'll get good care and help in a psychiatric hospital. I don't think you will ever see prison. They'll keep you in a room by yourself and you'll have a garden view. It'll be almost like a hotel," babbled on Claire, negotiating her life away.

"I don't think so, somehow. Anyway I've still got one or two more jobs to do, and then I think the whole murder hunt will collapse like a pack of cards. So I'll stop then. Although I do feel somewhat satiated already. Perhaps I will try and find myself a fella too, just like Grannie. And, by the way, don't keep calling me Jessica. I've noticed how you've always used it with venom; so stop pretending we're friends. And as far as your plea to hand myself in goes, I can't really see myself being drugged up to the eyeballs, flat on my back and staring blankly out of a window watching flowers grow, can you?"

"Who are the other one or two? You mentioned one or two more jobs? You may as well tell me, if I'm dead anyway. It's not Terry is it? And who else, your boss at work?" asked Claire quite concerned about the others earmarked for the same fate and yet unable to warn them.

"One right and one wrong. Yes, your man Terry, who I've got to admit you've shown so much love and devotion to, is one. And really I ought to kill him just for that reason alone. For the fact that he's never noticed how much you love him. But at least you'll have the satisfaction of being together in death. We both know that he is bright enough to eventually put two and two together and then link the trail back to me, so before he gets his abacus out, he'll have to go. And the other surprisingly is Emma Flynn. Did you know that Terry boy was having more than a tête-à-tête with her? He has had his arm around her equally as passionately as he has had protectively. So the chances are that see knows too much too.

"And I'll let you into a secret. She's already seen me on the job, when I murdered that Peter bloke. She saw me do it. I'm sure she recognised me when she was in the station that time but for whatever reason she's never said anything and I keep wondering about that. It bothers me. In a good way I might add. She intrigues me. So the jury's out on that one. She's keeping Terry happy and whilst he's happy, his mind's probably not on top of his job. Wouldn't you agree? Anyway we're here now so we'll have to stop this little chat. Have a good journey?" Jessica's final words sunk into Claire's brain as she gave another gasp from the jag of the auto injector sinking into her thigh. However, this one had been prepared with the 'speedball' concoction, and so would take no time at all to see her on her way.

The car was parked in a secluded spot, one that Jessica had visited several times before. There were no obvious signs of footpaths passing close by or tyre tracks to indicate that it had become a lovers' hideaway or was used as a secluded picnic area. And if anyone should happen by, Claire was positioned as if asleep rather than anything more sinister. Jessica knew that there would be an element of risk involved but hoped to be away for only an hour at the most. Feeling confident with the location and giving the area a final check for any stray prying eyes she quickly changed into her sports gear, checked she had all her keys, locked the car and ran off in the direction of The Borders Agency. To all intents and purposes she was now an athlete out for a Sunday run or to the uninitiated, a jogger.

She reached the offices, applied her surgical gloves, collected Claire's car and moved it off the premises. Then ran back to the office front doors, opened up and switched the CCTV back on. 'Now the tricky bit,' she thought. 'If my calculations are correct I can cut across to the rhododendron bushes, crawl through those, and then nip over the low wall by the roadside. I won't know if I've been successful until the police pay me a visit or not as the case maybe,' she surmised as she limbo'd and crouched to avoid the CCTV's prying eyes. She then drove the car to Claire's house, opened its back doors and boot, took out all of Claire's belongings and conveyed them back into the house. She came back for the TV and DVD player, which she again transferred into the house. Her idea being to confuse and obscure, a 'smoke and mirrors' kind of effect. Anybody watching would think, 'well it can't be a burglary as the possessions are going in the wrong direction!'
She then drove the vehicle into the garage where she set about thoroughly vacuuming the driver's seat and floor well. She inserted a new cleaner bag, replaced the vacuum in its usual spot, locked the car, the garage and the house. She then

continued on her run without a care in the world, just glad to be free and enjoying doing something she loved so much. She arrived back at the, would be 'lovers' hideaway' that still wasn't, having disposed of the incriminating cleaner bag en route. Took the towel and rubbed herself down, had a refreshing drink and snack, replaced everything in her holdall, and started the final stage of Claire's journey knowing she had plenty of time to kill before nightfall. It took her eastwards on the A168 towards the coast and North Berwick, her destination of Tantallon Castle becoming ever closer. She passed through the village of Gullane and took a left turn just after Dirleton. Here, she had what she considered to be a well-earned rest in Linkhouse Wood.

Always prepared, she had various drinks and healthy snacks to see her through the remainder of the day. She'd even brought enough for Claire too but with hindsight that was now an unnecessary luxury. At 11.30pm she recommenced her journey, passing through North Berwick itself and finally arriving at Tantallon Castle at 12.10am. By this time she was ready to shed her dearly departed hitchhiker and she knew exactly the place: just before the castle road proper, another road branched off to the left leading towards the cliff tops. Jessica turned here and stopped immediately before the edge to consider her options.

Firstly, she carefully executed a three-point turn, ensuring that she was never dangerously close to the sheer drop. Then it only remained the small matter of manhandling Claire out of the car, cutting the tape that bound her hands and feet and almost reverentially rolling her over the edge, where she would be welcomed by the jagged rocks and sea beneath. It took all her strength to undertake the task and she was relieved to see Claire's few personal possessions following her as they too, soon became indistinguishable from the white cap waves that came up to meet their fall. Jessica's last task was to vacuum the polythene cover which had been taped to the passenger seat and floor well. She then threw both the portable vacuum cleaner and plastic sheeting over the cliff edge, watching the latter glide down gracefully, to all intents and purposes, looking not dissimilar to a translucent albatross.

The journey home proved both tiring and saddening. Yet another person had been needlessly murdered at her hands and all due to her childhood abuse, which hung heavily around her neck like a millstone, preventing her from either forgiving or forgetting. Her Grannie's remedy had been to remove the problem but that was not sitting as comfortably in her own head as there was more than one in the way. She drove carefully and within the speed limits in order not to attract attention from any quarter. Arriving home at just after 1.15am, she immediately stripped and placed both her running gear and the clothes she had originally worn to The Borders Agency in the washing machine. And placed herself in the shower thinking that her trainers were the last items she needed to clean plus the well and pedals of her car. Fifteen minutes later she collapsed into bed expecting guilt-ridden nightmares to keep her tossing and turning but she immediately dropped off and slept the sleep of the dead instead.

CHAPTER SEVENTEEN

Barnham planned on taking a leaf out of Jessica's book by going to the gym on Sunday. He had gone to bed the night before, well early that Sunday morning to be exact, having willed himself to stay awake and watch the end of 'Argo'. As he pressed 'off' on the relevant remotes he made the cataclysmic decision to embrace a more active lifestyle where 'couch potato' was not identified as an active ingredient. Even he could recognise that his present habits were never going to be a panacea for a healthy old age. He had been laying on the sofa massaging his stomach as a prelude to his heightened expectations but still it remained soft and flabby with very little muscle tone found hidden behind multiple creases. This recognition led him to contemplate amusingly, 'not a six pack in sight, but plenty of its contents tucked away inside!' So, a new regime it was to be, three months late, as far as New Year resolutions go but a new regime anyway, and then pigs would fly!

He awoke to the alarm, set for 8.00am, and soberly and sedately pottered about in Sunday morning mode before his brain caught up reminding him of his promise. Originally he had intended journeying to his own local gym in Newcastle, perhaps combining it with a visit to the family for Easter, but the drive south would bore him he knew, and the dead bodies meant that he needed to remain close to the action he argued. So instead he moved up a gear from pottering to searching and then collecting his kit together with a view to going locally. As he did so, he noticed the flashing light on the phone, an indication of a missed call. He checked for a message and then punched in 1471 to reveal the caller's number. Racking his brains for comprehension he eventually arrived at T/DC Murray's mobile. Teasing his brain further he encouraged it to ask why she would be ringing and the reply came, 'Claire is going with Jessica to The Borders Agency at 8.00am today. You asked her if she wanted more back up and she said 'no', but perhaps now she's changed her mind'. He dialled her mobile but it just rang out. He checked his watch, which indicated 8.20am. 'Must have been quicker than I imagined they would be,' his brain said. He then flicked on the TV to catch up on the latest news and felt really stupid. 'How old are you? Now multiply that by two; take off say the first 32 if you're being generous, and that leaves you with the total number of times in your life that the clocks have either gone forwards or backwards. For your information at 2.00am this morning they went forward one hour. So you've lost an hour of your life without even realising it,' his brain said with annoyance. 'And that's why I missed Claire's call and that's why she's not now answering the phone. She'll be driving down to Carlisle already,' he thought. 'Correct, numpty. Now turn over that belated new leaf and get to that gym,' said his brain or was it his conscience, tussling with his lazy 'laddish' alter ego.

Disappointingly, on the following day Jessica did not quite reciprocate with Barnham's leaf taking. In fact, she had never had any aspirations to be like Terry Barnham, and particularly not now. The reality being that she was the exact opposite, and she would have been mortified at the thought of feeling her washboard stomach and thinking, 'God, I could do with more beer in here.' Surprisingly for her though, after Sunday's exertions, she was at odds with Barnham's newfound ambition. She had no desire to run, visit the gym or undertake any other exercise whatsoever. Her energies had been totally concentrated and spent on the previous 24 hours, 23 if you allow for the clocks going forward, and on mentally planning what she was sure would become her final hurdles. But being confident that she had adequately covered her tracks by deleting the incriminating files she took the opportunity of relaxing a little and catching up with household chores, particularly that of cleaning the car inside and out, and her other love, reading, whilst still leaving enough time and energy to formulate her final murder plans. She also guiltily rang in sick, even though she had put her name forward as part of the skeleton staff for Bank holiday Monday. But the exertion and excitement of the weekend had taken its toll, and so left her no choice. WPC Whitely took the call and sympathised lamely, hoping that she would feel better soon.

The new Barnham, well as far as one day at the gym would allow him to carry that badge, called the reduced bank holiday team together, totalling four in all, WPC Whitely, PC Blackwell, PC Gough and himself; PC Tranter having booked the day off, previously too. He chivvied his limited audience, "OK, you three. We're definitely moving in the right direction. But today we're much depleted, what with T/DC Murray on a week's leave and now Jessica ringing in sick, so you'll have to double your efforts. But let's be optimistic, as the saying goes, 'less is more.' Let's uncover the names of victims one and three; we already know Peter is the first name of victim three; let's get back on the phones, wear out some more shoe leather and get results," he exclaimed as if geeing up his last three warriors before they charged in to battle, likening himself to a today's version of William Wallace. His mind cleared and questions came to the fore, as he spit out encouragingly, "Still no news on dental records? No sobbing would-be widows ringing in about their missing hubbies? Chances are that some will probably be glad their good for nothing men have gone missing. And what about victim one, you owe it to him after his shockingly cold and lonely death? Get to it before the Chief has us all back filing, if that's still a job in the police force?" 'And to cap it all with Jessica off sick I'll have to wait her return to see what's on that data stick,' he thought miserably.

Barnham's depleted team, still in 'dragging their feet Bank Holiday Monday mode suddenly perked up when a call came through from an oilrig in the North Sea off Aberdeen. PC Blackwell took the call and noted down the information. And with a "No, thank you very much," he replaced the handset and shouted, "Sir, I think I've got something here. That was an engineering overseer, a Mr Snowden, from an oilrig off Aberdeen. He, and a few of his workmates, had been looking in the paper at the pictures of the murdered victims and thought that they recognised one of them. But with the eyes closed and all that, Mr Snowden thought it best to wait until the guy was due back on the rig, or not, as the case may be. Well, today's the day and he's not shown up. Mr Snowden says that it's most unusual as he is always desperate for cash and had never blobbed in the past. Could be the guy we're looking for, and his name is Peter too. Peter Faulk."

"That is good news. Did they give an address?"

"Yes Sir. Got that too. Lives right here in Edinburgh."

DI Barnham and PC Blackwell shook lethargy aside and called at the address given. The smell of stale urine attacked their nostrils as soon as they entered the stairwell to the tower block. Four floors up; having waded through discarded takeaway boxes, soiled nappies, dog and human excrement and innumerable syringes, they arrived at the door of '417'. The wailing of at least two children could be heard behind it, accompanied by a barking dog. As PC Blackwell knocked all three sounds stopped momentarily, left a pregnant pause hanging, and then restarted as if from the instructive motion of a conductor's baton. A weary looking woman answered the door and both officers glanced at each other as if to say, I think we've got the wrong flat here, as she appeared to be from a much older generation than their photograph of Peter, even in his dead repose.

"Hello, we're police officers. We're looking for Mrs Faulk?" Her obvious shock and then slight nod of affirmation led the DI to continue, "I'm DI Barnham and my colleague here is PC Blackwell. May we come in?" Both presented their warrant cards by way of entrance fee. Mrs Faulk's nodding became more pronounced as she moved to one side to allow her unwanted visitors access through the door. "We're here to talk about your husband, Peter."

Her fleeting eye contact said it all. "It was him in the papers then? Well, good riddance. Couldn't have happened to a nicer bloke, I don't think. He treated me and my girls like shit and now he's gone and paid the price."

"Well before we get into details, could you please take a look at these photographs and confirm that this is your husband?" asked the DI using a sympathetic tone.

"Yes, that's definitely him. But I don't want none of your sympathy sounding voice. Only thing he was good for was the money. But saying that, half the time he nicked our benefits and blew those as well as what he earned. So, I'm glad to be shot of him. I'd have never rung you, you know. I thought if I rang, then he'd probably turn up again or it would affect my benefits. But I'm glad now that it's all over and we can get back to how we are when he was out in the North Sea."

"I'm afraid we'll need you to identify the body. Can you do that for us? Will you be able to get someone to look after the kids?" the DI asked, peering around the woman at the two young heads peeping from behind her back."

"Yes. I'd be OK for about an hour. The lady across will come and babysit. My oldest girl is out doing her shopping at the moment, so we have a tit for tat arrangement. But any longer than that and I might be struggling."

"OK. We'll sort things out at our end and let you know when. Do you have a contact number?" She looked nonplussed at this so Barnham continued, "A phone or mobile number?"

"No. I don't. We usually have Peter's phone when he goes to the rig but he left the flat weeks ago and took it with him on that occasion." The two officers thanked Mrs Faulk for her time, and again gave their sympathies even though she was not in the market to receive them. The also informed her that they would organise an officer to call round and inform her about the identification time, and that it probably would happen within the next 36 to 48 hours. As they descended the stairs, slaloming around the detritus just like Olympic downhill skiers, Barnham could not help but feel elated and saddened at the same time. Elated, that three out of the four victims had now been identified and saddened that people had to live like this. People struggling to get by, who put up with all manner of trials, and then had whatever luck had been allotted, pulled right from under them. 'There but for the grace of God,' he mused. "Remind me to ring Jamie about arranging for Mrs Faulk to make an official ID of her husband, will you, Blackwell," said the DI, "the sooner the better, I'm thinking."

*

Vinny woke up to the wonderful aroma of bacon frying, and he was convinced it would be just that little bit burnt, just the way he liked it with the streaky edge of fat, crisp and crunchy.
But then muesli met the bottom of his breakfast bowl while a few extra nuts and sultanas topped it off, informing him of a set change in his blissful world. He scooped on a dollop of natural yogurt by way of solace and there it was, his healthier morning starter. Not even an egg to go to work on. Who asked for that?

Shirley was behind it, beginning by inferring that everything should be in moderation, and after their initial fling she did mean everything. She had a liking for Vinny and was now even looking out for his health. She was hopeful of his return but being a pragmatist she also presumed he may not, but if he did he would need to remain in good shape. Her livelihood was in the boarding house; whatever his was she had no idea, but the boarding house she definitely must remain, come what may. And looking in from the other side we could foresee that Vinny's life, never mind livelihood, might be snuffed out in seconds should he make just one wrong move and fall off that tightrope.

What's happened? A few days and nights of bliss and now I'm on gruel. Women, I'll never understand them. I told Shirley yesterday I had to leave on Tuesday and now she can't push me out of the door quick enough. It was a mistake telling her last night, ended up back in my room, solo, and even with me saying I'll keep in touch, even that had not appeased her. But perhaps it's for the best. Gives me the impetus I need to get the job done. Once it's under my belt, I'll nip back home and see Pops, and then come back here to carry on with a bit more of happy landlady and lodger.

Vinny packed and paid, Shirley pouted and sulked. He promised he would return and soon. She turned her back as he walked out, and headed for his car. Opening the tailgate, an arm came round his waist and a mouth searched for his. "Jeez, Shirl. You gave me a fright. I never heard a thing." Shirley continued hugging and pummeling his cheeks with kisses as Vinny's heart calmed down and sped up all at the same time. "Probably a good job I didn't have a fry up today, it might have given me a clutcher with that shock."

"Sorry luvee, sorry for being such a cow. Come back in and I'll make amends," she fawned.

"Honestly, I haven't got any time left. Pops wanted me to get on with my job on Friday and it's now Tuesday, so I'm under added pressure. But when it's done and I've been home to report I will come back. Promise. In fact, if it goes quicker than expected I'll come back even before going home. Deal."

"Whatever you say, Vinny. Take as long as is necessary but just keep your promise," she said with pleading eyes.

They hugged for a little longer and then Vinny undraped himself and climbed into the driver's seat. Shirley looked on both doe, and dewy eyed as Vinny drove off, leaving her to console herself by the side of the road.

*

Tuesday and Wednesday came and went without any significant advances. Jessica was back in on the Tuesday and disappointed the DI with the fact that her mission had failed as she could not find any files whatsoever relating to any of the initial three victims, and with her fiction, by saying "I presume that Joe must have found what he thought was dynamite and then covered his tracks so that Tess would not be any the wiser. Only thing is that it looks like he didn't cover his tracks from the killer, who constantly seems to be that one step ahead of all of us. Joe must have coughed up as to what he was up to at home and the killer then trashed both him and his house in search of the incriminating evidence. And to cap it all T/DC Murray never showed up either."

'She'd probably got her timings an hour out just like I did,' he thought dejectedly. By Wednesday evening Barnham was almost back to his old self. His desire to become the next Mr Universe had deflated quicker than the Government's fiscal policy and he was now back to chasing women with a vengeance, and wondering if it was too soon in the day to get an alcoholic drink. He contacted Emma early in the afternoon and found that even though she had agreed to see Jonnie, she was prepared to break that if he would take her somewhere romantic, with no strings; because she was sick of strings and men who wielded them, if the truth be known. More particularly, men who thought that they could have a meaningful relationship with her and try change her ways into the bargain.

Terry said, "Deal. I'll surprise you. Be ready at eight," and hung up feeling buoyant and depressed both at the same time. In reality, he was wavering between the two moods in the same way as between the two striking females, who had both surreptitiously inveigled their way into his professional and personal life with neither of them seeming to be quite genuine.

Emma on the surface appeared very open and candid but underneath she used her body to block any further intrusion, whilst Jessica was more reticent and furtive behind that perfectly sculpted mask, so inferring that she was not being totally honest and had something to hide.

Jessica was thinking the same. She had spent two days observing Barnham and could almost see the cogs going round in his head and feel his turmoil. His experience and detective skills were leading him inexorably towards the only likely conclusion, unbelievable as he thought it was. She knew that he was swayed by her physical looks and so could not bring himself to believe that she would be implicated in Joe's murder, let alone the other three but then again, the other possibilities were fading fast. She ruthlessly calculated that only a couple of days remained before her bubble would burst, where her veneer would be peeled away to reveal the ruthless killer that she had now become. A result Barnham was so desperately searching for. Though for the present, she still posed an enigma to him, even if one, which he was slowly but surely unravelling. 'Soon be time to be proactive rather than reactive,' she thought.

At last I've tracked him down. I'd been camped almost outside his door and keeping an eye on his bedsit in Grosvenor Place, thinking that the guy's got to sleep sometime. And there he was, he came out and got in a taxi. Pops has been on at me again, giving me one more week before the cash stops and I'm on my own. I can't live on my own, at my age! And as much as I think Shirley likes me I'm sure she would get fed up of keeping me after a while.

I followed the taxi and it picked up one of the young birds I've seen Barnham with before. Mind you she looks a lot more attractive tonight. Anyways, they were dropped off at a hotel in Edinburgh. I'm sat watching the entrance from a pub across the way. There's no escape this time Barnham, it's you or me fella.

CHAPTER EIGHTEEN

Barnham was true to his word. He picked Emma up at eight and they both took a taxi into the centre of Edinburgh. She gave him the up and down once over and guffawed, "Black leather trousers! I knew you came from the same city that educated Bryan Ferry at university but I didn't know you dressed like him too."

He came back playfully with, "You don't look so bad yourself, Emma. You scrub up well for a ...," and left the sentence hanging mischievously. He had forewarned her by text to bring warm clothes and an overnight bag, and as the taxi pulled up at the Bank Hotel on South Bridge, one of the junctions on The Royal Mile, she would soon understand why. A glorious box shaped building with a colonnaded facade welcomed her eyes. A façade suspended above at least one floor if not two, which would not have appeared out of place in a Greek tragedy, let alone Edinburgh. Emma soaked up the exterior greedily, bringing to mind the atmosphere of the solid and trusted banks of the Wild West, which somehow never lived up to their rugged sound and secure reputations. She was equally impressed with the interior too with its polished dark wood and spic tiled flooring. Terry signed in, was informed that Dinner would be served shortly, and then they were shown to their room. "Is it to madam's liking?" asked Terry with a wide smile on his face.

"To my liking? I love it. Do you want me to get my kit off now?"

"No, no. Slow the horses. The night is yet young and I've promised you a romantic evening with no strings, remember."

She rushed over to him and kissed him sweetly. A kiss with meaning that she never usually gave anyone, and one which even she hardly recognised. Terry gladly reciprocated but was stopped by the internal phone with a voice saying, "Dinner is now being served in the dining room, if sir and madam are quite refreshed?" Both of them giggled and crashed onto the bed as Terry choked out, "Better than the Ritz, this is Ems."

"Can I at least decide what I'm going to nick, as well as the dressing gown and shower stuff, before we go down?" she joked, as she did a complete spin around the room and carried it on out of the door.

Walking down to dine, arm in arm, she felt happier and more comfortable with this man than she had with any other for some considerable time. He had just called her 'Ems', which had unlocked memories from years ago, childhood memories of being called 'M' but by a different voice, a child's voice. She knew Huey from the waste ground called her it too but that had never awoken any positive connotation, in fact it generally had the adverse effect.

Once seated and over the next hour, they enjoyed a three-course candlelit dinner with aperitifs for starters and a bottle of Chateauneuf-du-Pape to accompany their steak 'au poivre' main courses. Emma drank more than she should have but was still in control, knowing that there was no such thing as a free dinner!

She had only allowed herself the minimum heroin before leaving the flat, and so was hopeful that her only drowsiness would come from alcohol if not, dare she hope, from an orgasm. But surprisingly for Terry, even he still had other things on his mind. After coffee and mints they retrieved their overcoats, left the hotel and hooked up for the short walk to the Tron Kirk clock tower further up The Royal Mile. Once there, they met up with a group of like-minded people who

Emma did not know from Adam, or Eve. Like-minded in that Terry had pre-booked a guided tour of the underground vaults, weaving spookily beneath this part of the Old Town, and this was the meeting point.

Once inside, he held on tightly to a still slightly tipsy, giggling Emma, to prevent her from falling on the uneven ground as they were guided by candlelight on a journey through the Blair Street Underground Vaults. The guide entertained with tales of darkest deeds, brought to life by other flickering candles hidden in tiny nooks and clefts. The faintest breeze creating eerie animated shadows to add an extra edge to the intrepid ambience. The haunting history was brought back to life in a time when ghosts and spirits still thrived in this underworld, just a few metres or yards, as they would have been then, beneath their home city. Emma clung on for dear life in her excitement and experienced shock-horror as each new fact was revealed in ever more dramatic fashion. Her giggling had long stopped and was replaced by low uncontrollable shrieks, which she tried unsuccessfully to stifle. After their allotted hour's tour they resurfaced, once again to the night's bright lights on The Royal Mile. Emma threw her arms around Terry and smothered him in kisses, "That was fantastic. No one's ever done that for me before. You're even more of a romantic than I ever expected, in a scary sort of way," she gushed.

"Ah well, just wait for my 'piece de resistance,'" he said mysteriously as they headed in a westerly destination towards Cowgate, in search of Greyfriars Kirk.

"What? Is that when we're in bed?"

"No, no, no. Get it into your little head, I said I'd be the perfect gentleman and have I not been that thus far?" asked Terry, as he continued to tease Emma with tales of yesteryear and stories of how she would have thrived in her career as a 'lady of the night' down in the vaults, until some plague or other caught up with her. Or perhaps it would be a murdering thief who got to her first, slitting her throat for her nightly takings and then leaving her there, her lifeblood draining away as she lay on her back, just as she had become accustomed to in life. As Oscar Wilde prophetically deliberated, 'life imitates art'. Walking on in their amorous state, neither really noticed anyone else nor appreciated the wonderful multi-coloured architecture towering over and corralling them from both sides of the road. Buildings loomed large and looked down at them too, through their glazed window eyes, as this journey drew them ever closer to the Kirk. Emma joyfully ran through the tunnel that supported the majestic George IV Street above, shrieking like a young girl at the imaginary spooks and ghouls chasing at her back but as yet still uncertain of what was planned and where her final destination was to be. Her only certainty was of the happiness she was experiencing in running free beside this Janus of a man with his two sided head. Her only reservation being the knowledge that it would all come crashing down on the morrow when she would need to stick that needle in just one more time. One more time, when she might not even call it her 'friend,' because in reality it chased all her true friends away and left only 'like friends', friends in the same boat. Terry too, was having fun, he knew she was bad news and that work and pleasure should never be mixed but, as he took out one of his dummies, thinking, 'Wow, that's the first nicotine rush of the evening,' he could not help envisaging a life that could possibly include this effervescent bundle of joy running with her heels clacking in unison to her squeals, mirroring the percussion of 'The Last Night of the Proms'.

*

These two are like 'jack in the boxes'. I can't keep up with them. I thought I'd blown it whilst on watch back at the hotel. I was just about to go for a pee when they came out the hotel doors all lovey dovey. But no good for me as there were too many people about. I hadn't anticipated Edinburgh being so busy at that time of the night. I needn't have been so concerned about losing them though as they only walked a few yards up the road and then joined the back of a queue. When that dispersed I went up to see what it was all about. 'Underground Vaults' it said. What, are they bank robbers now? Some kind of Scottish Bonnie & Clyde? Apparently not, it's like a series of spooky streets running beneath buildings and houses. Whilst there, at least I had the sense to check if they came back out at the same place. And the answer was no they did not. When I went to the actual exit I caught sight of them running along the road, and then I lost them.

*

Emma suddenly came to an abrupt stop. She was so out of breath that she almost bent double whilst trying to refill her lungs, her arms and hands clenching her knees to support her upper body. Still in this unladylike position she craned her neck towards Barnham and gasped, "Terry, do you really know what we're doing here?"

They had just turned into Candlemaker Row and Terry stood looking ahead and replied, "Of course I do. I've brought you to see the dog's grave." He took out a set of large keys, which he had borrowed from a friend of a friend, and opened an old iron gate that gave off more than a slight squeak and shudder. Emma straightened up but was nonplussed by this definite statement, just as she had been with the whole evening. She never had him as a fun man but how wrong she was. And now he had come out with a statement like that.

"Sorry. I never knew you had a dog?"

"I didn't, and I still don't, but I'll introduce you to him anyway." They walked along the side of Greyfriars Kirk and into the old Kirkyard. "This is Bobby's grave and monument. Bobby, a Skye terrier, died in 1872 and was buried here in this graveyard, nearby his alleged master, John Gray. You see, even though it's 140 years later I still use the term 'alleged' as the law dictates. Anyway, the story goes that Bobby had guarded his master's grave for the last fourteen years of his life and basically starved to death in the process. Fourteen years, probably far longer than the age most boys would have reached in those days, what with the hard life they led and the tasks that they were expected to undertake. He was well known then and still is today through folklore, or doglore, being passed down through the years. There's a statue commemorating the dog's selflessness over there opposite a pub called, wait for it, 'Greyfriars Bobby's Bar'. We can nip down this path and through the headstones and have a look if you like. Get a drink too, they should still be open," he said glancing at his watch.

"Right, David Attenborough. Thanks for the blurb on our four legged historical friend and specific thanks for the offer of a drink. I think I'm beginning to sober up, what with all this running around, excitement and information thing you've got going on." They walked on slowly with Emma clasping Terry's hand for dear life. Their route was in almost pitch-black darkness, except for the glow of the streetlights seeping through the leafless trees from the surrounding streets. Branches casting eerie, almost nonexistent, web-like moving shadows across the headstones. Terry said in a theatrically menacing voice, "Body snatchers used to wait for new burials and then come here at the dead of night and dig up the fresh bodies which they could then sell to medical schools for use in anatomy lectures."

"Oh, you're full of useless information tonight. I hope you're saved some energy for later. I don't want you choking on your encyclopedia, when I'm meant to be repaying my way," came back Emma, squeezing his hand even tighter.

"I don't think there's any chance of that happening. I've been taking testosterone shots intravenously, you know," he said jokingly. "Right, I think we just need to cut through this way." As he spoke they came up against a particularly large monument enclosing a cloaked figure of a man, which made Emma jump until she realised he was made of stone. "John Bayne of Pitcarlie, a 17th century Laird," he read. "Well Emma, at least we're in good company. 'A lawyer and possibly a treasurer to Cromwell' too," he continued reading.

"What are the chances of today's lawyers and treasurers being buried here in future years, I wonder?"

"Am I bothered," replied Emma thinking that the promised drink from the promised bar was fast vanishing as time moved on and the stocked mini bar at the hotel seemed a long way away.

"OK. I'm boring you now, am I? The pub's just through here." He had never felt happier than at that moment and he knew in his heart he was probably going to say something silly but after rehearsing the words a couple of times, all that came out was, "OW!" as his brain notified him that he had just been pricked in the thigh. The arm of a black dressed figure withdrew, and the figure itself waited silently for the expectant result. Terry clutched his thigh in shock and looked at the assailant in horror as his brain worked overtime. He knew instantly what he was dealing with and fought to keep himself moving in an effort to will the drug through his body at a more accelerated rate. As he began to lean at a dangerously acute angle Emma came to his assistance and tried to hold him upright. He still managed to have the strength to push her behind him, to a place of safety, thus preventing the killer from a second opportunity of taking her life. All three players were frozen in amazement at the effect of the drug taking so long. Neither Emma nor Jessica had experienced this problem before, Emma having already been on the receiving end. With what little thought Terry could still transmit through his brain cells he presumed it was because of his leather trousers, the toughness of the material had neutralised at least some of the dosage as it had probably been absorbed along the length of his thigh instead.

He sat down with a thump on one of the 'table top' type tombs and rubbed that area of his trousers, as if in slow motion, to dissipate any excess drug and prevent it entering his bloodstream, and for the first time concentrated on his attacker. A diminutive black shape with ski mask just as Emma had described in her witness statement but what she had not stated was that you could see the distinctive brown eyes through the mask. The brown eyes that Terry had seen immediately and fallen for over a year ago but that had never been his nor now ever would be.

"Jessica" he slurred, "Why?"

"Don't be asking me that now, there won't be time for me to explain and the chances of somebody happening upon this little scene could be quite high, wouldn't you deduce, being a detective? Anyway, I told Claire all about it."

As if recognising the name, Terry raised his head and tilted it inquisitively as if to indicate that he was using what little part of his brain was still active. "But, don't worry; she's not going to say anything because she's dead already. Perhaps you can ask her when you meet up." Terry's face registered shock as Jessica adopted a crouching position and continued calmly with her preparations for the speedball, which would take him to oblivion.

Emma, still frozen to the spot on the other side of the tomb, hoped that Jessica would forget she was there, not dissimilar to the reaction of a child. Jessica looked up from her preparations and smiled directly at her. It was a warm smile and just for an instant, the eyes smiled too.

Emma panicked even more, 'what sort of vindictive person is she; who can ever have given birth to her in the first place?' she thought, straining to stand up and run, yet fascinated at the same time with this killer's coolness and aloofness. She thought about double jeopardy and wondered if the same rules applied for murderers' victims too? Could they try and kill you twice? But maybe that little legality would have to be resolved later if only she forced herself to run now.

At the split second she made her mind up to stand, stretch and run, Jessica stood too. She held the syringe in the air and pointed it in the direction of what little light was polluting this part of the Kirkyard. Speedball squirted off the end of the needle, affirmation that Jessica was now armed and ready. She had to admit she had no particular grievance with Barnham, in fact she quite liked him for what he was; and her opinion of his talents as a DI was high, making that the sole reason why she was here in the first place. But it boiled down to her desire for life being greater than his.

She approached quickly but cautiously, even though her ability to bring him down was never a doubt in her mind, with agility and athleticism on her side, plus being far fitter than him any day of the week. Still Emma gave a start at the sudden movement, and just as quickly Barnham managed to catch Jessica's right wrist, the wrist attached to the hand holding his death. He had not enough strength to stand up, but neither had she enough to push him down further. They remained locked for 30 seconds with Jessica waiting out the time for the original sedative to achieve its optimum effect.

Barnham finally began to weaken and called for Emma's assistance before losing total consciousness. Emma jumped up from behind his back, adrenalin pumping and, with the trees casting a blackout shadow, she too grasped Jessica's wrist and began gingerly prying the syringe out of her hand. Once in control, and very familiar with such a delicate yet deadly instrument it took Emma only seconds to dexterously manoeuvre the syringe into position as a weapon of attack, whilst Jessica, now her prey, remained restrained and stationary with her wrist locked in Terry's vice-like grip, as if rigor mortis might have already taken hold.

Time stood still as Emma deliberated; all three looked at each other, waiting for the final move in this deadly game of chess. Who would topple whom? Emma remembered the recognition of those eyes from the episode at the skip and Jessica suddenly understood why she had such an affinity to Emma, and why she never really wanted her dead in the first place. The eye contact continued as Barnham's strength finally drained away but still he held on, for dear life, itself. Emma raised her arm into a throwing motion as if to discard the weapon and ensure it remained out of harm's way.

Jessica whispered, "M."

Emma immediately reversed her action and plunged the syringe into Barnham's chest. She looked into his pleading, accusing eyes and wept. Jessica gently took her hand away, and ensuring that it was spent, took out the syringe and replaced it in her bag. Barnham had moments left to understand what had happened and what he had lost.

"Have you never had children Terry, or even brothers and sisters? The affinity, the bond between siblings can be immensely strong. But between twins, even non-identical, it's unbreakable. And surely at some stage in your life you've heard the saying, 'blood is thicker than water?'" said Jessica gently and not without regret.

After tracking them both for much of the evening, she had seen how happy Emma could be but if she was being perfectly honest she knew it could never work; what a police officer and a prostitute, a title more likely for a 'kitchen-sink drama', she thought.

Barnham now lay horizontal and motionless, and looked at the two killers, his mind the only part of his physiology still active, played over and over, 'now that I see them both together, they are one and the same, but then again, not.' He slowly started drifting without even counting backwards from one hundred, and just about managed to raise a tiny flicker of a smile as he croaked, "What will Jamie make of this?"

The DI rested on top of a cold stone slab covering a monumental tomb and poignantly to his right, was buried John Gray, the master of Bobby. Emma, who had just about composed herself, burst into tears again and rushed towards him. She hugged and kissed him, willing this act to bring him back to life and all the while begging for forgiveness in order to ease away the guilt of her now heinous action. Jessica pulled her away and gave her a sisterly hug, a twin's hug, one that had been missing from both their lives for too long. Emma said with a sob, "Until today I was a drug addict and a prostitute amongst other things but now I'm a murderer too. Is there no end to my evil talents?"

Jessica replied, "No sis. The world is your oyster now but first we need to take a little trip to the coast with your ex boyfriend, if you're up for it? And then I think we could both do with a stiff drink."

EPILOGUE

This Barnham guy's some weird dude. I'm glad he wasn't my boyfriend. I eventually caught up with him and the girl as they entered a graveyard. I mean, who I ask you takes a girl on a date and visits a graveyard? It certainly would not be top of my dates' list. They were in there a few minutes, wandering around looking at gravestones. Anyways, I thought I was pretty sneaky at following people unobserved but there was this other person, a woman I think, and only slight, not like my Shirley. She jumped out of nowhere and started doing all this Ninja type stuff. Fair put me off my aim. Honest. I did have my gun out ready and with the safety off too. I was on the verge of pulling the trigger but knew they would all run off if I missed, and then that would have given the game away. Well eventually the three became two as Barnham ended up laying over one of them table-top type of tombstones. He then stopped moving and the two girls stooped, grabbed an arm each and started to drag him off. I just stood there dumbstruck behind a tree. 'Bugger me! They've only gone and topped him. Done my job for me,' I thought. No need for the gun now. Didn't even have to lift a finger! But I'll have to think of a good story to tell Pops. Maybe I'll give Shirl a ring first though, and see if she's still up?

Thank you for taking the time to read book one in 'The Gemini Borders Trilogy'.

I hope you enjoyed the drama. If yes, would you please be kind enough to visit Amazon and leave a review.

Book two called **'The Dizygotic Twins'**, is the second in The Gemini Borders Trilogy, and is available now.

In this book, the long-lost twins have clues to solve and places to go, in order to fulfil their parents' ambition. Parents who died, to protect their children's futures.

'The Dizygotic Twins' travel through Europe in their quest, chased closely by a Camorra clan, a form of Italian mafia, who it transpires are after the same end result.

Several loose ends from 'Blood Is Thicker' are tightened up but nothing is ever that straightforward!

Regards

Toni Parks